BASTET'S
DAUGHTERS

ALSO BY LYN McCONCHIE

BASTET'S DAUGHTERS

LYN McCONCHIE

WILDSIDE PRESS

For Lorraine,
in memory of Star Girl

If this were the ancient Egypt of our time line, the year that this story begins would be around 1365 BCE.

It isn't.

If this were the ancient Egypt of our time line it would be only a nation.

It's an Empire.

If this were the ancient Egypt of our time line it would be known by that name.

It's Napata.

And if this were the ancient Egypt of our time line then the Gods wouldn't be real. It isn't and—

They are!

I

The soldiers of the Pharaoh came at dawn. Shardis could hear the bewildered voice of Shemet, the gatekeeper, protesting the intrusion as the men thrust past him. The Lady Khepera had begun the invocation as she stood on the mica-marked square before the image of the Goddess, and beside her—as she often did—sat Anati, the matriarch of the Shrine cats. And though they came bearing the words of the great ruler, yet the soldiers had sufficient politeness to wait at the doorway until the invocation was completed.

Shardis eyed the intruders dubiously from the corner of her eye as she stood at the back of the room. At fourteen she had been a Daughter of Bastet for more than nine years and she was attuned to events within the shrine, and to the body language of those who lived there. None of the other Daughters made an obvious show of their disquiet, but the older priestesses were watching. She could tell that by the way their bodies tensed under the light, woven robes.

Only the Lady Khepera showed nothing. Shardis found her beautiful, although her nose was a beak and her lips rather thin. Her brown eyes were lustrous and, as yet, her honey-toned skin was fine and unwrinkled. Khepera was as graceful as a cat in her movements, and like all Bastet's priestesses, she wore her uncut hair falling past her hips, confined only by the worked gold circlet on her brow bearing the figures of cats. In the chill of dawn she wore a short cape over the robe that bared her right shoulder, but that was thrown back as she chanted.

Her clear voice soared up, the inner room of the shrine within the main temple constructed to pick the sound from that exact spot and cast it forth, louder, more resonant, and with the power of the Goddess. Above them on the plinth the statue of Bastet glowed in the dawn light.

> *You of the Sunrise who wake and sleep.*
> *You who lie couchant in dreams.*
> *To you appears Bastet the Great,*
> *Whose eyes see all, whose claws are death.*
> *Bright Lady who sees and strides this world by night and*
>   *day.*

Vanquish those enemies who would assail us,
Guide us forward and bring us safely home.

She bowed three times slowly to the statue before she turned and her voice rang out again. There was no emotion in the tone, only a clear knowledge of who and what she was. High priestess to Bastet, wise with the wisdom of the fifty years she had served—and elder sister to the Lord of the Lion Domain.

"You who come to the shrine in darkness, whose purpose is darker yet. Speak as it is given to you to speak and go."

The soldier's officer, a brawny, deeply tanned man of middle age, bowed low. "Lady, remember that the words are not mine, I am only the mouthpiece of another." His voice firmed to the sound of one who recites a learned piece. "Thus says Akhenaten, Lord of Napata, Lord of the lands beyond the Dark Sea, even unto the Far Isles, to the Great Sands, and East to where our Lord the Sun rises. 'Aten-Ra spoke to me two years ago saying that all the world should worship the sun and the sun alone.'" He paused for breath and Khepera spoke into the silence.

"I remember. I remember also that the Priests of Amun had something to say about that."

The officer's lips twitched slightly. The uproar that announcement had caused, particularly in the Land of the Two Rivers, had been tremendous, long-lasting, and was becoming increasingly ferocious as the Pharaoh continued to insist on having his way. Amun's shrines had combined to reject the Pharaoh's demands and, as they were backed by the temples of Thoth, and the Lords of three of the eight Domains—and those three large enough to equal four of the other Lords' holdings—thus far Pharaoh's words had been just that. Words!

The officer nodded. "Thus says the ruler. 'My words have been ignored and rejected. I shall show my people that Sun-Lord Aten-Ra is ruler in all the lands and that His power shall not be denied. In four moons the river floods, before then shall the priestess of Bastet bow before Aten, they shall pray to the Sun before all the people—or the shrine shall fall and those who support the Goddess shall be as the sands that blow. Here—and gone.'"

Shardis felt the indrawn breaths of those about her. The threat was clear, not only to the shrine but also to the Domain of the Lion. Shardis knew that tale from their history: the Lords of the other domains prayed either to Aten the Sun or to Amun. Oh, there were other Gods, and ordinary folk prayed to them. But of all the eight domains, only the rulers and nobles of the Domain of the Lion prayed to Bastet.

Kahosen, once Lord of the Lion Domain, was Khepera's great-great-grandfather and he had ascended young to his rulership during a time of strife. Leading his soldiers in battle behind the Pharaoh, he had been struck down by an enemy's spear hilt and would have died but for the appearance of a war lioness. The beast had killed the attacker and paused, standing astride the fallen Kahosen. It had lowered its great head, then, as he stared up, the brown eyes had flamed a brilliant, translucent green and into his mind had come a small purring voice:

"Kahosen, remember Me. Honor Me. Accept as brothers those who do likewise. In a time to come when all seems lost, let your blood call on Me, and there shall be made an answer."

The beast had bounded off, but to Kahosen, Lord of the Lion Domain, out of sight was not out of mind. He survived his battles, returned home and built a shrine to Bastet in her twin aspects of Cat and Lioness. More still, he had obeyed the command given and in a land that believed in the purity of its own blood, he had accepted into the domain the outland soldiers—and their families—who had once fought as conscripts beside him.

Within the Domain of the Lion lived Kalts from the Far Isles, Cymoryans from beyond the Dark Sea, and a handful of families who claimed to come from a land named Iona. The ruling family of the domain remained of the ancient pure bloodlines, but even so, the Domain of the Lion was accounted less by the Lords of the other seven domains, who scorned as inferior those who were foreigners from beyond the borders of great Napata.

The officer gave a low-voiced order to his men and after they marched out, he lingered. Khepera joined him by the door near where Shardis stood and, while their voices were very quiet, she could hear what was said if she strained to hear.

"Kahoret, is this truly the intention of Akhenaten? He plans the destruction of Bastet's shrines and of the Lion Domain if we do not bend to his God?"

"Cousin, it is so. Another officer bears the same warning to the Lord of the Lion Domain. I have managed to get myself transferred to another city. I leave—if fortune favors me—before the time of the Floods comes, so that I have a choice and need not take arms against kin at the ruler's command.

"But I know already that my own superiors have their orders. You are to be harassed from now on to make you understand that in this you and the Goddess are powerless and have no choice. The pressure on the temple will become a little more each quarter moon, as it will also be against the Lord of the Lion Domain. You will all bend to Pharaoh's will, or you shall be broken."

"But why? We are one domain, and that smaller, less than the other seven. Why would he bother when the domains of the Hawk, the Cheetah, and the River Horse worship Amun?" Her mouth opened suddenly in a gasp of understanding. "Ah, yes, of course. We are to be an example and also, we are the one domain that the others would not rush to aid in the face of Akhenaten's army. In destroying us or having our Goddess submit to Aten, he indicates that he is serious in his intentions."

"Even so. And make no mistake, cousin. He is very serious."

Khepera nodded. "I understand. Will you be at my brother's house tonight or must you remain with your men?"

His smile was wry. "I trust my men to keep silent on my comings and goings. Tell our cousin that I shall attend him after the hour of dusk." Khepera raised her brows in question. "Ah, well, I trust my own men, but other officers may be less trustworthy. However, should some officer find me gone after the guards are set there are excuses I can make that would be—understandable."

Khepera smiled back. "The women of the Street of Veils are always inviting."

"Truly, and everyone knows that I am a man who likes women." He rolled his eyes at her and his second cousin, who had grown up with him as a child, stifled a giggle inappropriate to her age and status.

"Go, before your men wonder what keeps you. I shall see you later."

"Walk in safety, cousin." There was a clear warning in his voice and Shardis drew in a startled breath. Was he suggesting that the High Priestess of Bastet, voice of the Goddess, might not be safe on the streets of her own city of Hanish?

* * * *

Khepera turned at the tiny hiss of breath and realized that the child had been listening. She made up her mind in that instant. The girl had a vocation, there was a sign of that in the girl's face, and more, the cats of the Shrine favored her. She considered Shardis briefly, the pale skin, the bright green eyes, the lithe and slender form. The child was fourteen now, four years older than Khepera had been when she joined the shrine and knew even as she walked through the entrance that here, now, and for always, was her heart and her home. She believed that it was so for this child also.

At this moment both remembered their first meeting.

* * * *

She dreamed. She was only five, so she didn't understand much of what she saw. She understood only the blood, the terror, the people who ran seeking sanctuary—and who found none. But in the dream she heard a voice, warm, like a great cat purring.

"Little kitten, strange things shall happen but you shall not fear. One will come who shall watch over you. Fight when the time comes, and go with the one I shall send for you."

She fell deeper into the dream, cringing as people died, as death fell like a blanket over those about her.

"Sleep dreamlessly, kitten, my little kitten. Remember this dream when it is time to remember, remember also that the future is not set, and in that which may come you shall play a part. When you wake you shall recall nothing of your dreaming, but you shall find a small sharp knife that you shall conceal about you, and that knife you shall remember at need."

The dream faded, she slept. When she woke at first light she remembered nothing of the dream or command, but somehow as she did her chores, work too heavy for a small slender child, but she was beaten if they were not performed, she found a knife. An old one a cousin, favored of their grandfather Taphis, had owned and misplaced. It was a small knife, the hilt of worn, scratched bone, but the blade was good metal and sharp. Something in it called to her, and she hid it in the breast of her ragged robes.

It was as well she did so.

Her grandfather came to find her later that day. "You told Ritseh that she should not go as wife with the man I chose for her. Why?"

That she could answer. "He wants her to do bad things. In the end she'll die; he'll kill her. I know, I heard." She had dreamed, but she was still young enough to mix waking and sleeping knowledge.

"One who listens, a girl child, and useless. Well, I have a remedy for your listening and the food we waste on you. You won't listen again, worthless female of a worthless dam. I'll see to that."

He led her outside, found a hide sack and, with child and sack each in one hand he walked down to the wadi's edge. It had rained all of the previous day and rained still. The wadi brimmed full behind the fallen earth that had broken away to make a brief dam. In another day the water would break through and rush down the slope, carrying with it anything it held.

He picked up a large stone and the child, dropped them one after the other into the open-mouthed sack, tied it shut, lifted it, and with a swing of sinewy, still-powerful arms, hurled it into the mud-stained water. Inside the sack the child sprawled, confused, frightened, still not understanding what had befallen her—until the water began to seep in through the tied top of the sack. Then she knew all too well. She'd seen this happen to her cousin less than a year earlier, but Tisheke had not had a knife.

Mumbling prayers to the Goddess, the child tore the knife from the bosom of her robe and slashed at the hide sack. It slit, water poured in and the child squirmed out. The water was rising but the sack had come to rest only feet from the water's edge, and she floundered towards the land. Then she reeled back. Her grandfather stood waiting, smiling, a stick in his hands. If she escaped one death another waited. She hesitated, waist deep in rising water, knowing she was about to die and unable to choose the manner of her death.

Behind the old man a horse moved and a woman's voice spoke, clear ringing tones of authority tinged with anger.

"What do you do with that child?"

Taphis didn't bother to look behind him. He was master in his village, all dozen miserable houses of it. No one had the right to question his authority.

"Mind your own business, woman, or you may join her. I drown a worthless female, an eavesdropping little bitch who has cost me good trade. She's mine and I do as I wish."

A hand was laid on his shoulder and he spun with a wordless shout of rage—to find that he faced a uniformed guard, and behind him four more, while the woman on the horse was dressed in the robes of the High Priestess of Bastet. Taphis was a bully, but not normally a coward. However, he knew that this woman wasn't only High Priestess, but also elder sister to the Lord of the Domain of the Lion—on whose land he lived. To offend her was to offend both religious and secular authority, and to do either could be deadly.

He bowed to the ground. "Lady, High One, forgive this wretch who did not know it was you who spoke."

The words were simply repeated. "What do you do with that child?"

"She is a waste of our food, Great One. She does little work, she is lazy, a liar, a maker of trouble in my household."

"So you drown her as you would an unwanted puppy?"

"We are poor people, Great One. We cannot afford to keep her." He raised his face, eyes grown cunning. "If the Great One would wish to buy her …?"

The woman held out a hand to the child who splashed towards her and Taphis hid his involuntary snarl in a whine. "Lady, Great One, if you take her without paying it is theft."

"You threw her away," the woman said coldly. "If I take garbage discarded and worthless as you have twice claimed, then it is no theft."

She lifted the filthy, soaked child, catching the eye of a guard. "But you shall be paid, Lord of this kennel. You shall be well paid."

Had the man been other than the brute he was, she would have paid in gold for the child. Bastet had sent her to find one who, in time, would be valuable for the temple—but Khepera did not approve of those who drowned children. From the look of the girl, she'd been overworked and underfed for all her years. She would be better away from here.

She urged the horse back towards the city and the child heard a sudden cry from behind them. The noise became that of a sound beating and howls of pain. She started slightly in fear, before understanding the lady's words and relaxing. Grandfather Taphis was being paid as the lady had promised, very well paid. Safe in protecting arms, she giggled silently, but she remembered why her life had been threatened. She'd be much slower in future to admit what her dreams taught her. Seated on the horse in front of Khepera, Shrine's Lady, High Priestess of Bastet in the Domain of the Lion, Shardis of the village of Taphere went to her new life very content and almost unafraid.

* * * *

Khepera dismissed the other priestesses, holding Shardis beside her with a wave of her hand. Once they were alone she turned to the altar, bowing her head. From the corner of her eye, she saw that the girl did likewise.

"Bastet, Lady of Light and Dark, the times are dark and may darken further for those who love you. You know what I would ask: not the great question, for that is for your judgment, but the lesser question. Will you share wisdom and answer?"

Power rose like the purring of a great cat, it encompassed the two who stood waiting, enfolding them. There were no clear words, only a feeling of approval. And at their ankles, her soft fur brushing against their leather-sandaled feet, Anati wove her sinuous body, trilling a greeting to the One who was Kin.

The feeling faded and Khepera laughed softly, bending to pick up the big sand-colored cat and very gently flick a finger against the gold earring the beast wore. "It seems that I am right, since the great and the small agree. Shardis, find food and drink to break your fast. Go to bed after noon and sleep. An hour before dusk I shall come for you. Tell no one of this, but be warmly dressed and waiting for me."

Shardis bowed and nodded. "To hear is to obey, Lady."

Her mind clamored with questions but she would say nothing. She had learned when she was younger that those in power do not like children who talk too much and that it can be dangerous for the child. Since then she had not dreamed, not during the years in which she learned not to fear. But these past few days she had begun to dream once more. Nothing momentous, nothing important, or even from the what-might-be's of the future. But—she *was* dreaming again and she wondered what that meant.

She ate, drank thin beer, and went to her chores—those were easy—for she cared for the cats of the shrine and that was a task she loved.

"Anati, lady in fur, sister to She who rules the night, I wonder what you think of that silly old Pharaoh? Ouch!" The feline matriarch had extended a set of claws and pricked the child's arm lightly. Shardis giggled. "Oh, I see, you don't think much of him either. But," her voice sobered and dropped to a whisper. "I think he's dangerous. I think he's like grandfather, a man who will have his way at all costs. Someone who doesn't care who is hurt, even those he says he loves, so long as his will is obeyed."

The claws struck a little harder and the girl squeaked, glaring down to meet eyes narrowed in clear warning. Looking up, Shardis fell silent at once. Anati would not warn without reason. Someone must be listening, but who could be an enemy here? This was Bastet's own shrine. She turned, making the movement a natural one as she reached for the small bone comb with which she groomed the cats.

Shemet, the gatekeeper, stood in the doorway, watching the cats and smiling his sometimes vacant smile. Shardis relaxed. Here was no true enemy, only a man whose wits were not always with him—ah, but one who could talk too long and loud to the wrong people of those secrets that he might overhear. She considered the thought. Perhaps when the Lady Khepera came for her tonight she should speak of this? The Lady had said that the times darkened. It could be that whatever plans were made, it would do the shrine no good to have them told abroad.

One of the kittens bounced over to the gatekeeper. He scooped it up, holding it lovingly in huge, powerful hands. The kitten purred, thrusting a small head insistently against Shemet's fingers until he stroked it. Shardis watched them and smiled. Shemet was a man of great size and strength. He idolized the Lady Khepera who had rescued him from the casual brutality of his family and given him a place where all were kind to him.

Shemet had not been born broken-minded. He had been strong and intelligent until he joined the army and in some accident—what happened was never known to his kin or the Shrine—he suffered injuries to his head that left him slow of wits much of the time. Sometimes he seemed to remember what he had once been, and he could still fight as a trained soldier at need, but to fight distressed him. As gatekeeper for the

Shrine of Bastet in the city that honored the Goddess, he had not had to fight in a hand of years.

In his uniform he looked almost normal, and he'd learned both what he should say in his role, and his duties. Once he had such things firmly in his mind he did not forget, but he needed the routine. He could not cope with anything new. He was still distressed by the way the soldiers had brushed him aside, not allowing him to perform his proper role as keeper of the gate.

She spoke reassuringly. "Shemet, don't worry about those men. It wasn't your fault."

"The Lady will be angry."

She was unsure if he meant the High Priestess or the Goddess, but she knew both would understand. "No, no, Shemet, they know you always do your best. That is all any man can do, and they are not angry with one who does his best."

"The men were bad," the gatekeeper said solemnly, as if pronouncing a verdict. "They pushed past me. I asked them who they were and what they wanted and they said nothing. That is not right. I am the gatekeeper; they should answer me."

"Yes, it was bad, and wrong too. But they had a very important message for the Lady."

"I heard." His mouth turned down at the corners in anger and distress. "Pharaoh says that we must worship the Sun-Lord now. That is wrong."

She was unsure how much he really understood, but he seemed to have grasped the main point.

Shemet stroked the kitten and put it down before he spoke again in tones that might have belonged to immovable stone, had stone a voice. "I love Bastet and the cats and all the kittens. The sun is good, it is warm and bright, but it does not sleep with me at night. It does not purr and love me." He turned and tramped away, as if he'd said all that needed to be said on the subject. Looking after him Shardis wondered if perhaps he had.

She worked the remainder of the day, retiring after an early afternoon meal to sleep in her tiny cubicle. With her went Trah, Anati's very large, muscular son, who lay on the pallet in the curve of the child's knees and purred her to sleep.

Shardis woke an hour short of dusk and ate a little bread washed down with beer. She dressed carefully. It looked as if Khepera was taking her to the meeting with the Lion Lord. If that was so, she must look her best to uphold the Shrine's reputation. Soon temperatures would fall as night closed in, so she added a warm wool cape to her ankle-length robe. She would be walking some distance perhaps, so she donned her other pair of sandals, whose soles were less worn. She was sitting cross-legged, waiting quietly on her pallet when Khepera entered.

"Good girl. Say nothing and follow me." The High Priestess walked through the shrine, Shardis behind her, one pace to her left. They walked together in the ordered silence. Oddly, all the Shrine's other residents were elsewhere, even the cats. All save Trah, who paced to Khepera's right with the air of one who knows where he is going and plans on going there—no matter what is said.

Shardis grinned to herself. She'd like to see anyone prevent Trah doing what he willed, or going anywhere he wished either. But it was a measure of the day's strangeness that the cat would leave the Shrine. If he actually planned to come with them, it would be the first time that Shardis had ever seen a cat from the Shrine set foot outside the walls. Of course, she'd only been there nine years. Perhaps the cats did go out rarely, or perhaps she had missed seeing one depart.

They passed the gate, and to her surprise Shemet was also absent. Shardis however had a good brain, some understanding of intrigue, and a natural shrewdness. At this hour on a normal evening there should still be priestesses about. If everyone in the Shrine was somewhere else, it was by design.

They walked through the streets quietly, Trah padding along with them, sometimes ahead, sometimes behind. It was as if he was on guard, Shardis thought and would have said so, but remembering the order she said nothing, only watched as the big cat seemed to sink closer to the ground, becoming more and more alert. Ahead, as they neared the edge of the Lion Lord's compound, she could hear voices. They sounded as if the owners were drunk and quarrelsome, and fear slid though Shardis. Surely no one would dare attack a High Priestess?

They came from dusk into the torch-lit larger road. With a sinking heart Shardis saw she could be wrong. Soldiers watched as they emerged from the side-street. They did not wear the same armbands as those who'd come to the Shrine, but she feared that made the situation worse.

With the soldiers was a war leopard: not a small cub under train-ing, but an almost adult beast. A leopard did not answer to Bastet or her daughters as did cats and lions, and both women recognized the danger. Small as leopards went, the beast must have come from the deserts of Kush. It was a formidable beast nonetheless—and a soldier whose ac-tions could always be disclaimed. Nor could the beast answer questions from a superior as to why it had acted as it had.

Khepera's voice rang out loud and clear, so that all within earshot should know who—and what—moved against her.

"Soldiers of the Ruler, why does your war beast stand ready to attack a High Priestess of the Goddess?"

All along the street men halted to listen and stare, some frowning. This was the Lion's Domain and they revered Bastet.

"A High Priestess?" came the answer. "Why, I do not believe that there is a Shrine of Aten within this place. Nor does the Lord of the Sun have priestesses. We must face an imposter." The voice was exaggeratedly drunken, the voice of a man who plays a part, and an edged, underlying insolence colored it.

"I am the Lady Khepera, sister to the Lord of the Domain of the Lion, High Priestess in the Shrine of Bastet. In the year of the Surrender of the Cymoryans, my great-great-grandfather received the Gold of Valor from the hand of Pharaoh himself. The Lord of the Domain holds his lands reaffirmed and recorded from that day."

The titles rolled out, heard clearly by all in the still air of evening. These men would not be able to say thereafter that whatever they did had been done in ignorance. Nor would they be able to claim that they had not known her for who—and what—she was. Slowly Khepera reached a hand behind her and swept Shardis back into the shelter of a doorway.

"A lady? Why then we must all bow." The officer turned to the leopard. "Do you hear, spotted one? The Lady Priestess bids you bow before her."

As if by accident he released the leash. No one would hear the soft hiss with which he signaled the leopard to attack. No one would see his mouth shape any word. But the leopard was war-trained, and the hiss was all that was required. That and the hand apparently raised to catch the leash, but instead pointed out the enemy. The leopard obeyed, and it had almost reached Khepera as it bounded forward eagerly—before it faced a smaller but no less deadly champion.

Bastet's cats were larger than the usual street cat by a half. Trah was larger again by the same. Still outweighed by the leopard that was easily twice his size, another factor aided him.

For behind him Khepera was chanting under her breath. Shardis caught a few words and recognized the invocation, which could also be a curse.

"… be near me and avenge …"

Standing before the woman and child protectively, Trah seemed to swell in size and strength. The moon was rising and Her power could aid his fight. The leopard hesitated, for this was not a human that he faced, nor another beast of war of a kind he recognized. Obedient to his master's command, however, he tried to reach the human enemy. Trah's head had sunk between his shoulders and his singing cry scaled up into a harsh, wild battle scream as the leopard struck.

The animals stood breast to breast for a fraction of a second. Then they became a whirling, tearing, tangle of fur. Over and over they rolled and thrashed as the leopard tried to reach the true enemy, but always the cat was before him. Smaller, faster, just as savage, fighting for the humans he loved.

Trah held his own in the battle, while in the street people cried out in awe and horror. Shardis peered from behind Khepera, tears streaming down her face. Trah fought as champion of the Goddess, but he was out-classed, out-weighed, and he could not fight forever. Yet she knew he would fight so long as there was life within his form; there would be no retreat and she knew the only possible ending to such a battle.

Spotted fur showed patches of blood now, black in the growing dusk, while sand-colored fur was bitten and slashed, the blood of both beasts streaming from their wounds. Still Trah held. Khepera gasped in fear for him; she loved the cats of the Shrine, but Anati's son had been her favorite since he was born—a single, fat, squalling kitten—four years ago. Exhausted, rent with a score of wounds, blood trickling from flanks and neck, Trah fought on. He slowed, but like the wolf, he would die with his teeth sunk deep in the enemy.

Shardis could bear it no longer. From behind Khepera's arms she looked upwards and cried out, knowing what she offered. "Bastet, aid him! My blood in sacrifice at Your desire!"

The beasts halted briefly at the raw pain of her cry before springing at each other again, yet she believed the Goddess heard. Trah seemed to gain weight and strength. The animals crashed together, the leopard forgetting training, forgetting everything but that he must kill this demon that ripped and tore with a wicked understanding of the weaknesses of kin. Driven mad with pain and battle fury it rolled, turned about in the fight. It now faced men as it regained its footing on the street. Not men it knew, but strangers smelling of terror; these too must be the enemy.

It sprang and a townsman went down, screaming in pain and terror. Out of the dark an arrow flew and the squalling, blood-mad beast died with a final convulsive kick. Trah dragged himself to his Lady and laid his head on her sandaled foot. Khepera wept openly as she stooped to gather him up.

A voice rang out, not loud but with clear authority. "What happens here?"

The Ruler of the Domain of the Lion, Lord Pahotep strode into the torchlight, bow in hand, his personal guard about him. "Sister, you bleed."

Khepera straightened with Trah in her arms. "Not I, my brother, but this, my guardian. He, a cat, fought a war leopard to save me, and by the Goddess he held it back. See, the beast is no less wounded." She pointed to where the leopard lay.

Pahotep, who loved cats, lightly touched the cat's bloodied fur. The ripped head lifted a little. Trah purred softly, his tongue came out in a rough caress across Khepera's hand, his flanks heaved once—and were forever still. There was no more need to fight, to remain in a wracked and torn body, for he had won and saved the ones he loved. Now he could go home to She who had created him.

Nearby, a devout woman raised the traditional lament for a fallen soldier, honoring the cat as she would have honored a warrior hero. The officer who had loosed the leopard scowled, slipping away into the dark with his men. Who could know that a miserable cat could fight like that? A warrior himself, he reluctantly acknowledged that the lament was justified, that the Sun-cursed beast had been a true fighter.

But his superiors would not be pleased. They hadn't necessarily expected to kill the High Priestess, but Isara, her Second-in-Power, was weak, a woman who could be persuaded to save the Shrine by publicly bowing to the Sun. And once she'd done that, the shrine could be quietly disbanded at leisure, as soon as the lesson of its example had sunk in to those of this Domain.

All that was required was that Khepera be too ill or injured to rule the shrine and that Isara take charge for just long enough. That would not happen now, and he would have to explain his failure. He cursed as he returned to his tent. Apart from anything else, he'd spent a full year training the leopard, and now he'd have to find another one.

2

Brother and sister walked amidst his guards, Shardis between them. Khepera carried Trah's limp body and tears rolled silently down her cheeks as she walked. The girl was sobbing, Khepera noticed, and then there was the child's oath. Bastet could be capricious, and Shardis *had* offered a sacrifice of blood to strengthen Trah. Khepera had little doubt that the Goddess had granted the prayer and would expect her due in return even if, like all cats, she were in no great hurry.

Once back in the shrine she'd talk to the Lady of the Moon and discover her wishes in the matter—and in a number of others, if Bastet would favor her with information. The recent events made it very clear that the idiot currently on the throne meant every word of his threats. The High Priestess hadn't ruled her shrine for thirty of her fifty years there, without being aware that words could conceal as well as reveal.

The Lord of the Two Rivers could say that Shrine and Domain would be destroyed—if they did not bow to Aten. There was no promise that if they did, they would not still be destroyed. It would be to Akhenaten's advantage if it were so. Her brother, Lord of the Lion Domain, was no fool, and would be as aware of that as she. They would take council together over the body of one foully murdered. The child who offered blood would attend, and before them would lie the dead champion of an outraged Goddess. She was not one to be ignored.

"Sister, give the body to me," Pahotep said gently as they reached the inner courtyard. "I shall give it to those who will mummify it with all honor." He clapped his hands and spoke a quiet order to a man who nodded obedience and left to summon a priest.

Khepera gave Trah into his hands, allowing herself one last caress of her friend as she did so. "Very well. We must talk, for the matter becomes more urgent."

"And more dangerous for us all," Pahotep added, laying Trah's body down gently. "That a Child of the Goddess lies murdered, slain by what I believe were Pharaoh's orders, makes it clear to me that Akhenaten is serious in this talk of one God only."

Khepera shook her head. "Serious, yes, but not guilty of intending Trah's murder." She answered the questioning look. "No, my brother. I was the intended victim." His lips tightened, and she explained further.

"I don't think that I was necessarily supposed to die. But Isara would speak as High Priestess in the Shrine if I were, for some reason, unable to do my duties. She is a good-hearted woman, kind, devout, and sensible, but she is also easily talked into changing her mind. I might give orders before I became unable to rule, but if Pharaoh's agents threatened the shrine and all within, then she would agree to their demands in the belief that she was saving us. I have never named her officially as my heir, but in truth she functions as such."

Pahotep nodded thoughtfully. He recalled the woman, built like a pregnant mare, brawny of arm but, he thought, fairly thick of brain as well. "So all that may have been intended was to injure you sufficiently to give Isara control. She could be convinced to obey Akhenaten before you recovered enough to countermand her decision."

"Exactly."

"Yet once pointed at prey, a leopard may not be called off easily. They may not have intended your certain death, but they had no care if it should happen," Pahotep said, iron in his voice. "Nor are you least beloved of those in my city. Had you died it would have been war. I would not hold back. My honor, the honor of my House would demand it."

They stood, each thinking deeply, Shardis standing silently to one side. She, too, was thinking; in her case, that many of the people in this city of Hanish were devout worshippers of Bastet. The tale of how one of Her cats had been slaughtered by a war leopard belonging to out-city soldiers would travel through the city with the speed of lightning. Harassment could go both ways—and that would not sit well with either the Ruler or his officers in the city.

Khepera looked about. "Where is our cousin? It was he who came to the shrine to bring Pharaoh's words. He said he would join us as soon as he was free of his men and the officers of Pharaoh who watch him. Is he waiting?"

Her brother frowned. "I've seen no sign of him. Perhaps he could not escape the watchers."

The scuff of sandals sounded at the door as a priest entered. Pahotep turned to smile. "Sharmere, one here requires your skill. I have no time to tell you the tale now, but take Trah and see that he receives the rites suitable to a warrior who died with great valor, doing his duty."

Kahoret looked surprised. "Not as a child of the Goddess?"

"As a child of the Goddess, yes, but also as a warrior. He receives no less than a man of my guard, had he died earning the Gold of Valor, and with the eternal gratitude of his Lord."

The priest bowed low as he accepted the small, bloodstained form. "Lord of the Lion, it shall be so. All the prayers shall be said, all reverence given. The proper amulets shall be placed within the wrappings. He is to return to the shrine once all is done?"

It was Khepera who answered that. "He is, and with a formal guard suitable to a noble warrior who goes to his rest."

Sharmere bowed himself out, Trah's body cradled in his arms.

Pahotep looked after him, then turned to his sister. "You fear that the soldiers might try to take the body?"

"It would be another way of harassing the shrine and showing disrespect for Bastet. I believe they would hesitate before making an open attack on an honor guard of the Lion Domain. That is too open an attack on you, and they are likely to save such a thing for the last days of the moons granted us."

Pahotep snorted. "Yes, and of that—and of what we may plan to do, and what could come from such plans, we need to talk. Food and drink will be supplied in a moment. Come to my room; I will set a guard at the door." He turned to lead the way and noticed Shardis. "Who is this?"

"This is Shardis. I have spoken of her. She is a true and faithful Daughter of Bastet, and she is favored by Anati."

"Ah," was all her brother said, but their gazes met in wordless understanding.

Shardis said nothing, but watched her Lady and the lady's brother. They were of the pure blood but each in his or her own way. Khepera was fine-boned, with small hands and narrow feet. Her hair flowed silver-streaked black, framing a long oval face with a delicately formed mouth. Her brother was almost twenty years younger, heavy in the shoulders and upper arms, his face blunter, framed in hair that fell, cut square across the brow, to just above his shoulders. In the style of the older families, neither wore a wig.

Once in the large, airy room, Khepera sat on one of the divans, signaling Shardis to sit at her feet. Pahotep too took a seat after calling orders. Plates and goblets appeared and an old man joined them. Shardis stared, and then lowered her eyes hastily. She had never seen a man so old. He was shriveled by time, his face a myriad of wrinkles, his wig doubtless hiding a bald head, but his eyes had the alertness of a man who is still in full possession of his senses.

He wore well-crafted, scarlet-dyed sandals, a very finely woven full-length robe with a light woolen cloak over it—a man of such age always felt the chill. The cloak was thrown back a little to show the great pectoral collar of beads and precious metal about his neck and shoulders.

The collar was magnificent. The beads were not cheap faience or clay, but were made of amber, amethyst, citrines, topaz, jet, and other stones she did not recognize, carved and smoothed into long ovals. The fine-drawn wire on which they were strung was electrum, that mixture of gold and silver so highly valued in Napata. The collar extended from the points of his shoulder to the center of his back, and to the lower breastbone in the front. No one would see such a pectoral and not know that this man was to be given honor.

She saw the figure shaped and outlined by the bead colors and the amulet on the lower fringe then and understood: Thoth, the Ibis-headed Lord of Wisdom. Here was one of those scholars who spent his whole life studying, delving ever deeper into strange and arcane realms. Such men were often found in great households, revered for their wisdom, honored for their learning—and useful for the advice they could give to the Lord of a Domain. The Shrines of Thoth tended to be neutral in any quarrel save one that touched on their own rights.

She wondered if this man would feel that way. Thoth was an old God, one not so much actually worshiped by the nobles in Napata as deeply respected for what his priests brought to the land. Yet the Pharaoh had made it clear that all would worship Aten of the Sun. How did that leave Thoth and his priests? Two years ago they had stood with Amun against Pharaoh's decree. It could be that they, being so wise, had a path to suggest.

Khepera, too, considered that. She had known Remekh all her life; while Thoth and learning were his Gods, still he loved the Lion Domain and its people, and he regarded Pahotep as a son. He had been a friend of her grandfather, and once he had come to live here, somehow he had never chosen to leave again. He had free use of the Domain's records, too, and might be able to suggest something from precedent.

She nibbled the pastries a servant brought and drank the watered wine, seeing that Shardis had something to sustain her. Alabaster lamps had been lit in the room, and she could hear the light sounds of the guards' steps as they patrolled the corridor.

Pahotep was silent as he ate and drank, while Remekh waited, smiling at all three of them until a scratching at the door signaled another's approach. His voice was thin with age, but there was a note of command.

"Bring the scrolls in and place a table before me where they may be unrolled. Have you the weights, the ink and quills? Good. Place everything for me, then depart."

The servant obeyed while those in the room sat mute. Once he was gone and the door curtain pulled across, Remekh unrolled a scroll.

"This is the wisdom of Thoth as given to his servant, Meremrebet, in the year that the Hittites last rose against our ruler." He saw Pahotep tense and nodded. "Yes, that is also the war in which your great-great-grandfather Kahosen achieved renown. The two things may be linked."

Khepera looked interested. "How so, wise one?"

"All things have their own time and place. To all things there is a turning of the seasons. Winter comes to lie quiet upon us, then with spring come the floods heralding the summer's rich fertility, and the dying of the year brings time to prepare for winter again. The Gods know what comes before we do, and sometimes they give warning."

Pahotep stirred. "And you think the words of Meremrebet may be such a warning?"

"I do. Harken to his words." He read from the scroll. "'And it was revealed to me thus, that a ruler shall grow proud in his folly, deeming himself great above many Gods. He shall oppress the people, saying that his chosen is above all, and that all shall bow. Then let the portal be opened, let the people flee injustice. Let them go forth to a place that is like to their own and let them flourish there.

"'Yet shall it be made known to them that there is no return from that place they have chosen, nor shall any know what passes in times to come in the place that was theirs. They must go, knowing not the road they take, but trusting in the Gods who shall surely spread their wings over their people.'"

He allowed the scroll to curl back while brother and sister stared at each other.

"It fits events," Pahotep said slowly. "But I can think of other times in our history when it would have fitted as well. And others may occur in the future. What is to say that it means our Pharaoh, our Domain, and this time and place?"

Remekh smiled, showing toothless gums. "Well questioned." He unrolled a second, smaller scroll. This one had gilded lion-heads at the ends of the ivory winder, indicating that it belonged to the Domain of the Lion.

"This was in your own archives, son of the Lion. I think that none read it since it was placed there in the third year after Kahosen returned from the war to take up his rulership. It, too, was written by a Priest of Thoth, and is a partial copy of the words of Meremrebet. It repeats the warning, but it continues." He read from the scroll as he unrolled it.

"'This I dreamed after I copied the scroll of Meremrebet for the archives of the Domain of the Lion, not once only did I dream but thrice—and as all know—a dream that comes three times is a true-dreaming and is from the Gods. This I dreamed, the voice said to me, "like to like." The scroll I read then recalled itself to me, repeating the words of the Great One, these being Her words and in, as I believe, Her own voice.

""Kahosen, remember Me. Honor Me. Accept as brothers those who do likewise. In a time to come when all seems lost, let your blood call on Me, and there shall be made an answer.""

He looked up at them. "Meremrebet's words may be general; they might fit what happens here and now, or be intended for another time to come. But this scroll is explicit. And there is this. Kahosen obeyed in true and generous measure. He had his men build the shrine to Bastet, nor did he stint in size or quality of the building. Always since his generation, one of the women of the Lion has served in that shrine, not by demand from without, but by her own devout desire.

"Kahosen opened residence in the city and in some of the smaller estates of this domain to the ownership of those who had been conscripted to serve in the war. Five generations have some dwelled here. And, Lord of the Lion, they love and are loyal to the House that gave them a place. Should you rise up, they will rise with you, should you depart, they will follow at your call."

Khepera had studied in her time, had read many of the scrolls of teaching and quietly listened to the arguments of the priests when others of Thoth visited Remekh. She spoke now.

"'Like to like,' he wrote. Could he have been thinking of the theory of Amatsunake?"

Remekh looked at her approvingly. "So I think."

On the floor Shardis stirred, and the old man dropped his chin to peer at her. "Ah, child, you wish to know of that theory, perhaps?"

"If it pleases the wise one to explain," Shardis whispered. Here was important information, she knew it. Knowledge that might save those she loved.

"Then hear what Amatsunake thought. He believed that our world and all in it are like earthenware platters that are stacked one atop the other. All of the same material, all of the same size, yet all different, each in their own way. In dreams he penetrated to other lands that were like ours. In one world, the great tremors of the earth that destroyed Ur of the Chaldees and sent those who survived running to Napata for shelter did not occur. We did not receive the wealth of those who fled, nor their wisdom. Instead, their people grew great and in time warred with us, and we were the lesser.

"In another dream he saw that those Hyksos who came against us many generations ago and were flung back in a single battle, instead won that battle and many others. They prevailed and ruled Napata for many years. We arose and flung them out at length, but again, we were the weaker for it. In both dreams, Napata was not the great land that it now is, for we ruled only the inner lands. Those places to the Dark Sea, to the Far Isles, to the great Sands, and sun-wards, none of them bowed to Napata. We were far less than we are and will be."

Shardis's restless fingers touched Trah's blood, still on her sleeve. A small, high, singing rang in her head, and her mouth opened without conscious thought as she quoted: "'In a time to come when all seems lost, let your blood call on Me and there shall be made an answer.'"

"Just so, child. Your High Priestess asks if perhaps Amatsunake was right? If Pharaoh is determined to wipe out the Domain of the Lion and Bastet's worship, then perhaps a way of escape for all, a portal, could be opened to such a place and you could escape?"

"But if others live there, would they be pleased to see us? Wouldn't their Pharaoh be the same? Would the Goddess rule there too, or would there be other Gods who expect us to worship them?"

"They have different histories, or so Amatsunake wrote. But ponder this, child. If such places are very many and all different, could not one be found that has room for us? One where Bastet rules?"

Khepera nodded, speaking soberly. "So I think. We are the daughters of Bastet. She would not send us to a land where we would be slain. What sense is there in saving us if we still die?"

Pahotep gazed at them. "But there is this: Amatsunake dreamed. Not all dreams are true, no matter what one might believe. Even he did not present it as Truth, only as a true dreaming, and we cannot be sure that it was the case. Nor can we be certain that the Lady can, or will, open a portal to other lands, or that we would survive in such places. No, I think we learn all we can of the possibilities while we wait, we watch, and see how the Pharaoh acts and what he does against us. If it is clear that the threat is against all our lives, then may we take counsel again and further speak of Amatsunake's theory." He stood.

"I will send guards with you, my sister, and the child. Fare well and safely. Your warrior will return to you in the time appointed."

Khepera rose and lifted Shardis gently to her feet. The girl's legs had cramped.

"I thank you, brother." She turned to Remekh. "And you, wise one. I shall think on all said tonight." Her expression hardened with anger, "I shall also remember Trah and those who killed him. That is not over."

"Walk carefully there too, sister," Pahotep advised quietly. "They are soldiers of Pharaoh and not of the Lion. To act directly against them is to act against Akhenaten, and to stir up the common people against them, too, may not be wise. Be like the cat, patient for long and long—until the prey runs into its jaws."

His sister nodded reluctantly. Khepera could see the sense in that, but her heart grieved and she yearned to see someone pay. Of course, not everything done must be known to all, or enacted in broad daylight.

Pahotep, who knew his sister, could follow her thoughts as well. "And do not arrange for the man to suffer some strange fate, either—even if you can find him where he has fled. He may die in a genuine accident, but Akhenaten will assume the man was murdered and he'll make inquiries. And a ruler asking what common people know will not be gentle." He looked at her meaningfully and she winced.

No, their Pharaoh had shown himself ready to torture and kill. Her vengeance might have to wait or be given up. She sighed. If it must be, then that was the will of the Gods. But if Bastet demanded payment for the life of one who'd been Hers, then Her High Priestess would be very willing to comply.

She pushed Shardis gently before her as they left, with Pahotep's guards around them. The child was almost asleep on her feet. It had been a long night—and for the High Priestess, it would be longer still.

She saw the girl to her bed, but Shardis clung to her sleeve briefly.

"Lady, I dreamed a greater danger is coming. Beware loud voices and those who seem not to look at you."

Khepera smiled down. "I heed your words."

She knew that the child true-dreamed now and again, never apparently at her own wish, but nonetheless it could be a hugely valuable gift. It was, she believed, the reason she'd found the child before her vicious old grandfather drowned her like an unwanted puppy.

She dismissed the guards, and went to the inner shrine where she bowed before the statue of the Goddess. She spoke of what had occurred and how Trah had died. Then she began the threefold rite. The chant was formal; she spoke it twice before hesitating.

> *Pasht, Lady of the Moon,*
> *Of Light and Dark.*
> *Defender's Shield.*
> *Avenger's Sword.*
> *Who sees the slayer,*
> *Thief of Light and Life.*

Be near me and avenge,
Trah's death and bring,
Thy curse upon that head.

She dropped to her knees and wept then. Wept for the beast she had loved, for the days that were gone—perhaps forever—when a ruler honored all the Gods, great and small. For the danger in which stood everything she had known, and again for Trah, whom she would miss with all her heart.

He had fought a greater foe, his wounds draining his strength, yet still he had remained between her and the leopard. At the last, he had crawled to her feet, purred for her as she held him, licked her, and died with the salt-taste of her sweat in his mouth.

Blazing with sudden fury she hurled herself to her feet again. Bowing almost to the ground she chanted the third time, softly, but with an intensity that awoke small echoes in the room. It was not any of the formal prayers, but one made personally, from Khepera to one she loved and served, and it was laden with grief, fury, and the formless fear of what might be coming.

Pasht whose claws bring down the Moon,
Who rules the Dark when the moon is lost.
Sword of vengeance, shield against evil.
One of thine is slain, unjustly—
Even as he fought for she who also lies in thy hands.
Thy curse upon the man who sent the slayer forth,
Thy curse upon his waking and sleeping,
Upon his life and his Ka.
Thy claws on the scales of Judgment.
Weighing it down to his damnation.
Let him know that thy claws may be hidden,
Yet are they always there!

She ended with an almost feline hiss on the last word.

"Lady Khepera."

Furious at the interruption of her prayers, Khepera whirled. Isara stood before her.

Oblivious to Khepera's anger, Isara continued. "A soldier has come to speak with you. I said that it is far from dawn and you should not be woken, but he insisted. He says that he brings a message from kin that you would wish to hear."

"I shall see him. Bring him to the petition room." This had to be word from Kahoret, she thought. She stopped to tighten a loose sandal strap before hurrying to meet the messenger.

He was a short man in his late twenties, with almost blond hair, hazel eyes, and sun-reddened skin. Had he been with her cousin when he brought the Pharaoh's words earlier? She drew herself up, nodded to the man, and waited for him to speak. To receive yet another shock.

"Lady Khepera of the Noble House of the Domain of the Lion?"

"Yes." Stop wasting time and speak, her eyes said.

"Lady, I am Neshang, soldier-servant to Kahoret, officer of the Pharaoh—may He be forever blessed by the Gods." That last was said in such a way that made it clear that, so far as Neshang was concerned, every God in the Pantheon would curse the Pharaoh instead, if he had his way.

"I have ill news. My master Kahoret lies gravely injured. By thieves in the city—so it is said." The rich disgust in his tone made clear his opinion of that. "An officer of the Pharaoh found my master lying in the street, having dragged himself from the alley where he was stabbed. He is alive, and while he was conscious he bade me come tell you this and see you summoned to his side to invoke the aid of your Lady, for his life is in danger."

Khepera brushed aside the whisper of panic. Kahoret lived. Within her own shrine there were priestesses who looked to the Lion aspect of Bastet and had healing abilities. Kahoret knew that, and he was asking for their help. He was warning her, too, that this had been no mere attempt at theft. Well, she would come, and if she was too late, at least she was warned.

She summoned two of the healers, and at her query, Neshang told her that he had brought a dozen of Kahoret's own men with him as guard for the healers. They set off for the place where her cousin had been taken—to live or die according to the will of the Gods. Her chief healer carried a long staff with the insignia of a Lioness atop it, and any who saw that would clear the way for a healer to pass.

As they hurried through the streets, Khepera glanced at the man who had brought her the news. By his looks he was no man of Napata, and he seemed surprisingly loyal to one who was. She met his gaze.

"Neshang? Of what people are you? How did you come to serve my cousin?"

"I was a slave," Neshang said briefly. "I am Ionian, taken in battle when I was fifteen by another tribe and eventually sold on the slave block in Thebes. Kahoret purchased me, and then freed me. He said no man could serve loyally if he was owned, and in war, he did not wish to have a servant he could not trust. Lady, I would serve him with my life. He is a good man, a true noble."

Khepera considered this as they walked. "What do you know of recent events?"

Neshang's look was bland. "All that my master knows I know, noble Lady."

"And what do you think of these events?"

"I am a servant, Lady, it is not my place to think. Yet, if I were commanded to do so, I would think that even the highest stoops to folly. The rat runs, the cat pounces, and the rat is no more. The fish swims, the ibis strikes, and there is fish on the table. In other places there may be other people, but always there will be those to strike and those who fall."

His mouth shut in a quick, hard line and he moved more swiftly along the narrow, dusty street. Khepera asked nothing more. He had couched his reply in riddles, but she understood. He thought their ruler acted unwisely and Bastet and Thoth would bring him down. He probably had no idea how that should be accomplished, but he seemed confident enough that it would happen. And—his comments also suggested that he told the truth. If he knew of Remekh and that other place sought, then it was true he was deep in Kahoret's confidence. He was trustworthy, because her cousin was a good judge of men.

3

Kahoret still lived when they arrived, although he was weak from loss of blood. His men took up unobtrusive posts while the merchant family who had taken him in, on being told that he was kin to their Lord, stood anxiously by. The chief healer laid her staff against the wall and waited on the decisions of Shrine's Lady.

Khepera swept in, thanked the family fervently, persuading them to leave the room. She stationed further guards at the door and in the corridor to ensure that the family overheard nothing, and motioned her healers to attend her cousin, all apparently in one movement, or so it seemed to Neshang. He hid a grin; his master had chosen well, it appeared. This noble might be female and a High Priestess, but she was no pampered fool to stand about wailing while a kinsman needed her commonsense.

The healers sprang to her command. Khepera waited, seated on a stool that Neshang brought for her. Kahoret was stripped of his torn, filthy, bloodied clothing and bathed carefully before Healer Merem and her assistant Temmah began to assess the damage. After a period of concentrated activity Merem reported.

"His skull is not cracked, Shrine's Lady, but he suffers from a disturbance of the brain often found in cases where the victim has suffered a blow or blows to the head."

Khepera looked at her. "So I thought likely, but what of my cousin's wounds? His servant says that Kahoret was stabbed several times."

Merem's reply was a wide grin and the shake of her head. "There is nothing to worry about *there*, Shrine's Lady."

Khepera stared until light dawned. "I see: the wounds are superficial and not really serious. So all we need to worry about is the disturbance to the brain?"

Merem nodded. "Your cousin seems to have anticipated an attack, Shrine's Lady." Her grin widened a little further. "I have never seen such a thing before—but beneath his robe and cloak he was wearing a leather tunic. It fits well, so that under loose clothing and with only the light from torches in the streets, an attacker would not notice it. It is sleeveless and covers his back down to slightly below his waist, as well as his entire chest. In this he would move normally but have considerable protection."

She moved to the pallet and lifted the object under discussion. "See, it is made from boiled leather and has been shaped to fit your kinsman, most probably while the leather was still heated and malleable. His attacker stabbed him five times and most probably believed that each strike went home. They did not. The point penetrated only very slightly each time, just enough to draw blood."

Temmah joined in. "The head wound, too, would bleed as they do. Your kinsman, Lady, would have been an awful sight: blood covering his face, blood showing on his robe. From the blows to the head and the grunts of pain he would have uttered at each strike, it is little wonder his attacker believed him slain."

Merem summed up their diagnosis "The stab wounds are superficial and of little importance so long as they have been thoroughly cleansed, and that we have done. I will see to it that they remain clean so that there is no infection. I do not believe that the head injury is such that your cousin may not be removed from this house—if this is done under my supervision and very carefully. He must not be jolted. Would you prefer he be taken to the Shrine, or elsewhere?"

Khepera thought, conferred quietly with Neshang, then made her decision. "We shall move him in a few hours, at dawn. When it is light enough to see what we do, but it is still cool. Neshang, you and two of my cousin's men go to my brother and tell him what happened. Say that of his kindness a room should be prepared for Kahoret. The healers of my Shrine shall attend him if this does not cause too great a disruption. Return with his answer as soon as you can."

She was dozing, leaning back against the wall when Neshang returned, barely short of the dawn. Kahoret had not yet regained consciousness, but both healers were satisfied with his condition.

"Lady Khepera, Pahotep, Lord of the Domain of the Lion, says: 'Come with all speed. Everything will be ready, and my own men shall stand guard with those of our cousin. Your healers shall have beds beside their patient and all they ask for shall be provided.'"

Khepera dragged herself wearily to her feet. "We'll need something for Kahoret to lie on so that we can move him without jostling him."

Neshang looked triumphant. "Lady, so I thought. We brought a light wooden pallet with us, and I have detailed those who will carry him. They are strong, steady men who will not let their officer fall. And," he added significantly, "others of his men will spread around us as we walk. Should any man attempt to cause the carriers to stumble, they will not succeed."

Khepera looked at him. "That was very well thought of. I am glad, too, that his men are loyal. Let us prepare." She turned to the healers. "Merem, what should we do?"

Both healers were busy for a while before they stepped back. Kahoret was secured to the light pallet. He had been bathed again, dressed in a clean robe, and the back and sides of his head were padded to prevent any impact. They had managed to get a little cool water down his throat, and soaked cloths covered his forehead.

"We are ready, Shrine's Lady."

The soldiers lifted the pallet with their officer and, in careful step, marched from the house. Wearily, Khepera followed. She wasn't as young as she'd been and the physical activity, the stress, the worry, and a night without sleep were taking toll of her ability to anticipate what to do next.

As the small procession neared the domain compound there came the sound of running feet. A boy fled past and two men followed some distance behind him, shouting threats. Neshang noticed, as did the guards, that neither man seemed to be looking at them directly; however, as they closed with the procession they edged sideways until they were running directly at the carriers. Khepera recalled Shardis's words and screamed a warning.

Neshang seized the staff from Merem's hand, leaping forward to meet them. As they came level, he spun to one side, flinging the staff out at knee height, even as the carriers stopped, managing to stay in step. The other soldiers closed around Kahoret, swords ready. They were unnecessary. The men had no time to avoid the obstacle and tripped over the staff, sprawling in the dust.

Despite her exhaustion, Khepera's mind worked with unexpected speed. She stepped forward, eyed the men and, in a loud, clear voice, announced: "These men attempted to attack the High Priestess of the Shrine. Let them be bound and handed over to the Lord of the Lion Domain whose sister I am. He shall deal justice." The last words had a significant emphasis.

One man began babbling hastily. "Nay, Lady, it was not you! I revere the Gods, and I swear oath to Aten we meant you no harm. It was ..."

His companion rolled against him and, with an odd cough, the first man fell silent. One of the soldiers sprang forward, but quickly as he moved he was too late. Even as he snatched at the second man a blade flickered, and the second would-be assassin too would never reveal anything. The soldier rolled the man back to reveal in his hand a knife with a long, narrow blade. He held it up.

"Such a knife could have made the wounds our officer suffered."

Merem reclaimed her staff, and studied the blade. "That is true. Such being so, and if these men were those who tried to kill your kinsman, Shrine's Lady, best we go very carefully. Twice they tried, twice they failed, and then, so that they could not be questioned harshly and perhaps reveal their paymaster, one slew the other and himself." Her gaze met that of her superior. "No man dies for nothing, Lady."

The procession moved on, passing the gates of the compound. Pahotep met them, leading them to the rooms prepared and once Kahoret was settled, taking his sister aside.

"All right, let me hear the full tale now. I've sent for Remekh to attend us."

Khepera sat down and sighed. "Let wine be brought. Brother, I swear I am too old to have such nights."

Wine arrived and Remekh immediately after it. He sat silently, waiting as the Shrine's Lady drank, gathered her thoughts, and began.

"Neshang, once a slave, was purchased by our cousin Kahoret and freed. He is a man of great sense and loyalty, who serves our cousin as his soldier-servant. He came to the shrine after Kahoret was wounded and this is what he said."

She described the events of the night. "And one final thought, my brother, wise one. We had the would-be assassins in our hands. I said that they would be taken to you for justice. They could have bargained with you, told all they knew and gained at the least a clean death, without torture. At the most, if their knowledge had been of great value, they could have gone free with coin in their hands. Taken ship to another place. Yet the older slew the younger and then himself when it was clear the other would talk. Merem the healer said that no man dies for nothing."

Remekh looked at her. "Which says to us all, that one of them knew two things. He knew if they talked they would certainly be killed—probably in very unpleasant and prolonged ways—by those who sent them." His voiced deepened. "And that from those who sent them, there could be no escape—even with the aid of a powerful Lord. Who is greater than the Lord of a Domain?"

The question fell into silence. No one needed to answer.

Pahotep resumed the discussion. "Let us think about events thus far. Soldiers released a war leopard that was intended to injure or kill you, my sister. All they succeeded in doing was killing a cat." He glanced at Khepera. "I mean no reflection on Trah. He fought and died as a warrior of valor."

He returned to his theme. "The leopard ran mad and I shot the creature after it began savaging one of my people, something for which no law in this land would take me to task—and I have set very public inquiries about that event in train. This attack on you was followed by an attempt to murder our cousin. Far from killing him, he survived, and could almost certainly name or at least describe his attackers. So they made a second attempt, hoping to throw him from the pallet so his injuries would prove fatal."

He shook his head. "What we have to date is an endless procession of incompetence."

Remekh chuckled. "Yes, and we can guess the leader of the parade. What we must do now is strike a balance between being ready for trouble—and asking for it."

Khepera smiled for the first time that day. "One person's curious and tenacious is another person's nosy and stubborn," she said. "I suggest we stay within the law, but within those bounds we make, and continue to make, a lot of very public noise. Let other Shrines see what happens to one innocent of any wrongdoing, guilty of mere existence. After all, a valiant and noble officer of Pharaoh has been struck down. Should not Pharaoh's judges examine this event?"

Pahotep nodded. "You were attacked in the street, first by a war leopard in the company of soldiers apparently unable to control a supposedly trained animal. And by what right did they have to bring an untrained beast into the city, where it attacked my people? Then two men attempted to assault you, one of whom—when apprehended—committed murder and suicide to escape just punishment."

Remekh cleared his throat. "I agree; all of this should be brought to the attention of the courts. I should be the one to do it, for obvious reasons."

Both of his ex-students nodded. Remekh had considerable power and respect within the hierarchy of the temples of Thoth. He was a renowned scholar despite his long-time residence in an obscure province of lower Napata. No judge or court would ignore his complaint. And an attempt to silence him would bring the power of the temple of Thoth in Thebes on their side.

"And if someone tries to silence you completely?" Khepera asked. "Dead, you can't ask awkward questions of anyone."

The old man snorted. "Akhenaten has the social conscience of a hen. But he isn't that much of a fool. Alive I may be talking, but Thoth's temples aren't necessarily listening. If I'm murdered they will assume, rightly or wrongly, that Pharaoh knows more than he should about my death, and they'll throw all that they are and have onto the scales on Bastet's side.

"Worse still from Akhenaten's point of view, if that happens the Priests of Amun may do likewise, seeing the chance to win by unifying all the other shrines and temples of the Gods against Aten-Ra. That's the last thing that Pharaoh wants. No, any further attempts will be subtler—and probably more dangerous. But now we three should each find beds and sleep. It may be some time before Kahoret wakens properly. The healers are with him, soldiers watch over his bed, and if we are rested we will act with more sense when adversity comes."

Khepera nodded. "Send word to the Shrine that I remain here, brother. I'll use my old room, if that is well."

They retired, each to sleep for several hours but no longer, since all were worried about Kahoret and recent events.

* * * *

In the dark of the night, a thief worked. Nehuche was skilled and worked alone, so none could betray him. He slipped through the window of a merchant, the linen sack about his neck filled with fine jewelry. He grinned as he dropped lightly to the ground and replaced the iron window-guard. This haul would keep him in comfort for moons.

A city guard, late on his route, walking very carefully because of an acute hangover, padded silently around a far corner. He saw the figure leaving a window and yelled—before subsiding against the wall, clutching his head. He gave chase, cursing the thief who had caused him pain and whose apprehension would take him beyond his shift.

Nehuche wasted no time. He sped down the nearest alleyway, swerved around an old, dry well, dropping the sack down the shaft and pausing long enough to spill loose stones and dust over it. He fled as the swearing guard gave chase. Taken by another guard more by misfortune than ill-management, to the embarrassment of the first guard nothing was found on the prisoner. Still, he was tossed into a holding cell to be taken before the chief judge in the morning.

* * * *

It was an hour past midday when The Lord of the Lion Domain, his sister, and other interested parties gathered again to eat, drink, and begin once more the discussion of what could be done about the attack on Khepera, and Pharaoh's possible intentions and plans.

As they ended the meal, a guard coughed from the doorway. "Noble ones, the Lord Kahoret wakes. The healers ask that you attend them."

Khepera was first through the door, her brother and the priest right on her heels. Stools were brought and they sat. Kahoret was lying on the bed. His head was lightly bound to a headrest, his eyes were open, and Temmah finished giving him a little watered wine. His eyes went to his kin as they entered and Merem was quick to speak.

"Kahoret, be silent as yet. Save your strength."

She sat on the stool beside him and turned to the Shrine's Lady, the Lion Lord, and Remekh—whose quality she recognized at once.

"The Lord Kahoret woke a short time ago. He is coherent, and I have given him something for the pain in his head but he must remain still for several days, not sitting up or moving his head. Temmah will stay to care for him. Above all, he must not be agitated or upset. Now, he gave a description of the two men who attacked him and it matches those who died as we carried him here. This means …"

Pahotep cut in. "This means that while we don't have to worry about further attacks by that pair, we now don't know what other assassins may appear, and we have no way of recognizing them."

"That is so, but the Lord Kahoret reports that the younger man spoke as he stabbed. "He said 'a gift from the Pharaoh, and gold for us. Let your kin remain rebellious, and we'll soon be rich men.'"

Remekh nodded. "Explaining why the two were so desperate to kill Kahoret, and when foiled, why they died rather than be taken alive. The younger one talked when he—as he believed—slew his victim, and when they fell to Neshang's staff, the younger talked again. Even evil men have families. It may be that it was not only an agonizing death that they feared, but that death for those they loved as well."

Pahotep grunted. "If Akhenaten schemes against the Gods and the Lords of the Greater Domains, he'll make certain no one is able to accuse him." He stood "Lie on your pallet, cousin. Grow well. We have need of you, but it will not benefit the Domain of the Lion if you move too early and become worse. Besides, your injuries may help us. Lie still and leave us to see what can be done."

Kahoret's voice was weak but clear. "I hear and obey, Lord of the Lion. Let my superiors know what has befallen me so that I am not marked as missing or deserted."

Khepera patted his shoulder before she left the room. "Be well, cousin. I shall see that the army and your superiors are told."

Pahotep took her arm once they were in the corridor. "Yes, we shall both do that. I'll call my own guards and we shall go now. Remekh, do you come with us? I may need your wisdom. Thanks be to Bastet that we obeyed your word and slept. I foresee a long day as yet."

The old priest walked with them as guards were summoned.

For once Khepera accepted the use of a donkey-litter. She pulled the curtains closed until only a small gap remained, allowing her to talk to the men who walked on either side, but preventing most passers-by from seeing who was within. They proceeded in silence for the most part, exchanging only a quiet question and answer now and again.

At the court, Pahotep called for judges and magistrates to hear a complaint. Men came running and the three were ushered into a large airy room, slaves wielding fans took their places, and wine was offered. The chief judge entered, a short, stout man in his thirties, with hard eyes and a bland expression. He had been appointed by Pharaoh and did not answer to the local nobility. Consciousness of that was obvious in his stance: he had authority and knew it. But for all his pomposity, he genuinely revered the law and upheld it ferociously.

One of his scribes attended, unrolling a new scroll and setting out ink and quills to take down the complaint. Any further findings and any conviction would be added as they came to hand, and once the case was closed the scroll would be filed in the law court's library. Behind the judge's chair a servant stood to take his orders. Once they were settled, a guard spoke in formal tones.

"The Judge Atepmut hears those who come for judgment. Let you state your complaint before him."

Remekh understood ceremony and how a man of this kind desired public respect. He bowed, his pectoral swinging forward showing the outline of his God in the colors of the beads and again in the amulet depending from the collar.

"Lord who gives the Law, who is above Gold, whose only love is Order, and who sets his face against Chaos: hear us. We petition thee for Justice, for only one who has thy power may grant us a true and considered judgment."

A very faint tinge of color showed in Atepmut's cheeks. This domain was far from the major cities of inner Napata. There he had been junior to more important men. He had agreed to this post hoping that here, without superiors, he would be granted the stature and respect he craved. This was his opportunity.

Atepmut steepled his fingers together. "Let you speak; I, Atepmut, Judge under the laws of Napata, hear."

Pahotep began. He detailed how a war leopard in the street had attacked his sister and how a cat from the Shrine defended her. Atepmut, also a cat-lover, was genuinely angered by the tale.

"This leopard was supposed to be trained? Soldiers had it leashed? The cat from your Shrine died?"

Khepera stood and bowed. "That is so, wise one. Trah crawled to me and died in my arms. When I looked about for these men who had failed to do their duty, they had fled." She gave a *very* clear description of the soldier who had released the leopard, describing minutely his uniform and badges of rank and regiment.

"Before it could be slain the beast also mauled a tradesman in the street. My brother tells me that the man is gravely ill from his wounds, which may well go septic. If you find that the beast was uncontrolled, then there should also be a judgment against these soldiers—or their regiment—for the injured one's family."

Atepmut spoke to his servant. "Send out men to ask questions. I want to know who these soldiers were, if this animal was a trained war-leopard, and if so, how it was that it ran uncontrolled to attack citizens of Napata. The law is clear that the great war-cats must be leashed and muzzled in the streets." He turned to Remekh. "Is this all the complaint?"

"No, wise one. There is more, and it is strange and ominous. I fear there may be some conspiracy against the Domain of the Lion. And a conspiracy against nobles may also be a threat against the ruler—may He live forever—under whom we all serve."

Atepmut kept his face expressionless but inside he was rejoicing. If there was a conspiracy against the Pharaoh himself and Atepmut rooted it out, then he'd be greatly rewarded. Furthermore, he would have served the Law—a twofold blessing.

He signaled Pahotep to continue and heard the remainder of the tale. How a kinsman of the Lion Lord—and soldier of Pharaoh—had been attacked and, still more suspicious, how, when Kahoret had survived the attack, there had been a further attempt to murder him. And, to add to that, how when prevented and surrounded, one of the killers had immediately slain his companion and himself rather than be taken alive.

Atepmut was horrified to the depths of his law-giving soul. It was all extremely suspicious, not to say highly irregular. Soldiers walking the streets with an uncontrolled war leopard? Men who fled when the unleashed beast attacked a High Priestess, then savaged an honest citizen? They must be found and brought to account.

As for the two killers who had twice made attacks on a soldier of the Pharaoh, they were dead. There was little he could do about that, but it was unlikely they acted alone. They should be identified and their associates questioned rigorously. No, there was some sort of a dangerous conspiracy here and he'd root it out.

While Khepera, Pahotep, and Remekh sat in polite silence, Atepmut gave instructions; he sent men running in many directions, each with orders to discover the truth and return with the information. Once all were dispatched he sat straighter in his chair.

"I thank you for bringing this to my attention. You may be assured that I shall get to the bottom of this and justice shall be done."

Pahotep rose and bowed. "I would expect no less from a judge sent to us by our ruler. We are fortunate in this far domain that He graced us with one who is a man of Law, wise and honorable."

Pahotep swept his companions ahead of him from the building, installed his sister in the donkey-litter again, and started back to the compound.

In his court, Judge Atepmut, still flushed from the compliment, commanded the next case brought. He eyed Nehuche with disgust when the man was marched in, shackles loading him down. He was left to stand alone before the judge, who snorted.

"You again?" He turned to the arresting guard. "With what is this man charged?"

The city guard winced. He told his story and Atepmut regarded him with a scathing glare. "So, you saw a man climbing out of a window. You could not identify him from that distance. You challenged the man and he ran. You gave chase, losing sight of him a number of times in various streets. Eventually you caught up with a man who was running. You recognized the runner as a person believed to be a thief and arrested him on suspicion. Did you find anything on him that could have been stolen?"

"No, Lord Judge Atepmut."

"Can you be certain that this man is the one whom you saw climbing from the window?"

"No, Lord Judge Atepmut."

"Can you even be sure that this is the same man who climbed out of the window and who you pursued?"

The guard could see where this was going. "No, Lord Judge Atepmut."

"Then it would seem that you have wasted the court's time. Do you see any reason why this citizen should not be freed?"

The reply was glum. "No, Lord Judge Atepmut."

Atepmut eyed the prisoner severely and leaned forward until only Nehuche could hear him. "I know very well that you were thieving, and so do you. But the law is the law. Without plain evidence I will have no man convicted. You have been lucky before my court before, but be very wary, Nehuche. One day you will be taken with proof of your wrongdoing, and on that day the full power of the law will fall upon you."

Nehuche bowed silently and departed as soon as his shackles were removed. Outside he grinned to himself. Atepmut wasn't a bad man for a judge, at least he was honest. Now he'd check that no one was following him and retrieve his ill-gotten gains. In consideration of his fortunate escape he'd attend Bastet's temple at the earliest opportunity and donate a small something. He had another reason for his visit, but that remained in his heart, for to think of it too openly could call down misfortune. The Gods did not like those who presumed on their luck.

* * * *

For the first half of the journey all in Pahotep's group were silent, until they were out of earshot of anyone who might be following or listening. Then Pahotep smiled in satisfaction.

"That should start something interesting. The noble Atepmut is clever, but no one's told him of Akhenaten's plans. He has no idea that recent events are an attempt to put pressure on Bastet's Shrine and the Lion Domain. He'll stir everything up, ask questions that will have everyone talking, and if by a miracle he does find that soldier and makes him talk, I'm not sure who'll be more embarrassed."

Remekh chortled. "If the soldier talks and names a superior officer who ordered him to endanger the life of a High Priestess of Bastet, all of the temples will complain. If the superior officer admits that Pharaoh ordered him to arrange the event, the screams of every High Priest and Priestess will assail the Gods. And if a judge brings open scandal to the Cobra throne, then the judge will be the most grievously embarrassed— probably to death!"

Passers-by may have wondered what was amusing their nobles, but no one asked. Which was as well; it was not a joke that could be easily explained.

4

Over the next ten days, all was quiet—well, moderately so. Word had, as anticipated, spread through the city that soldiers had endangered the High Priestess of Bastet and that a citizen had been hurt instead. The army was still refusing to pay compensation, claiming that the leopard had been in the city because of an illegal act by a specific soldier, and that compensation should be sought from the soldier's family. Since Renzai had apparently left the city and had no known family, that suggestion was not well received either.

The common people reacted as expected. Soldiers found themselves in more fights than usual in taverns. Whores all suddenly raised their prices. Small children flung rude words and dung and vanished amongst crowds who obstructed passage and seemed to have all been struck blind simultaneously.

In the Shrine of Bastet, Khepera led the prayers as usual, while Shardis cared for the cats and tallied offerings received. She noticed one in particular, a pouch of silver bits dropped into the bowl before Bastet's statue. The man, apparently devout and seen in the temple before, smiled at the girl. Uncertainly she smiled back. There was no lechery in that look, rather a gentleness, an approval. It unsettled her, and she did not know why.

Kahoret improved daily, tended by Temmah. Remekh read a long list of dusty scrolls, many of which had not been untied for decades or even generations. Pahotep went hunting now and again and, as patient as any cat, waited to see what the judge, Atepmut, would discover from his questionings—and if he discovered anything, what he would do about it.

The only thing out of the ordinary was Anati. The big feline grieved for her son. She searched for him, crying sadly, hunting and sniffing in all the Shrine corners. Her lament when he was not found became a piercing wail that unnerved many of the lesser priestesses. Shardis went to Shrine's Lady with the tale.

"She hunts for him, she cries, and I cannot comfort her. Lady, please, is there no way we can explain to her what happened?"

Khepera felt like weeping herself. The cats of Bastet were not ordinary cats. They had intelligence—true, it was feline and not human—but they felt emotions, and they could communicate surprisingly well with any human they liked and trusted. Khepera had been deficient in not making Anati understand why her favorite son had not returned. She went in search of the cat and once she had found her, picked her up gently and brought her to the statue of Bastet. There she placed Anati on the floor and bowed to her Goddess.

"Lady who rules the Night and Day, I cried to you for justice and a curse on the man who slew one of Your own. But I have been remiss. I did not think that his mother might also grieve, not knowing where the one she loved had gone. Please, my blood to pay for her knowing, in token that I accept my wrongdoing."

She stooped, offering her wrist to Anati who placed a claw delicately on the vein and flexed her paw. A single drop of blood stood out on the honey-colored skin. Anati sat and cocked her head abruptly, as if a voice had spoken. She looked up at the statue, eyes gleaming, and uttered a small chirping sound.

A question?

She sat motionless, ears cupped forward, listening to a long reply.

Anati chirped another question.

Answer was made. Then she looked up at the Shrine's Lady, chirped politely, and trotted away.

Khepera smiled after the furred form. Anati knew that Trah had died, that he had died as a warrior, and not alone but in the arms of his Lady. He would be honored, returned to their home and, if possible, he would be avenged. More content, she returned to her duties—and Shardis reported that Anati cried and hunted no more.

At the end of ten days the peace was abruptly broken. Both Shrine and Domain compound received a message from the judge that they should attend him. They'd been conscious that he had been diligent in his inquiries. There'd been gossip, not the least of it that he'd gone in person to the soldiers' barracks and demanded a list of all war leopards within the city of Hanish. He'd received one, found and inspected every beast and discovered that—officially—none were missing.

So far as Atepmut was concerned, this meant one of three things, none of which he approved. That the beast had not been a war leopard—in which case what was it doing with soldiers in the city? Or that it had been, in which case either it had been immediately and improperly deleted from the rolls, or—far worse—that officers were lying to him. He set out to discover which and found a trail.

Pahotep, Remekh, and Khepera, with Shardis in tow, attended the court. Held in custody was a man Khepera recognized, even if his broad smirk was no longer in evidence. Atepmut called her forward politely and indicated the man.

"Lady Khepera, in your complaint you said you would recognize the man who released his war leopard to your endangerment. Is this man, known as Renzai of the Theban Regiment, the man you saw?"

Khepera walked forward to examine the prisoner slowly before turning to bow to the judge. "He is the man, Wise One. Nor am I the only person who saw him. You may not accept the testimony of a child, but Shardis, junior priestess in my Shrine, was with me at the time. She too saw the man clearly."

"How old is she?"

Khepera signaled Shardis to stand forward and indicated her. "She has seen the great river flood fourteen times, wise one."

Atepmut considered that, then studied the girl. She looked sensible and intelligent and she neither posed nor cringed. "Let her speak."

Shardis copied her leader's bow and address. "Wise One, Shrine's Lady thrust me behind her when the beast advanced. Yet past her I had a clear view of the man who held the leopard. He wore the uniform and badges of the Theban regiment, and he smiled when he let the beast go free. I remember him well." She raised her hand and pointed to Renzai. "That is the man."

Her reward was a look from the prisoner that should have dropped her in a small heap of cinders onto the court's marble floor.

"Lord Judge, both of the women lie. I had no war leopard. I was not in the city when these events occurred. My officers told you I was on guard duty at the barracks at the time and not in the city."

Atepmut nodded. "Renzai of the Taueret Regiment, you have told me that, as have your officers. Let us now hear from them—and others who shall witness."

Two officers marched in and swore that Renzai had been on guard duty at the time discussed.

Atepmut smiled at them. "But how can you be certain of this? Yes, the record scrolls show that he *should* have been there. But was he? It is not unknown for a soldier to have another do guard duty in his place for a fee or favor. What witnesses have you that this man really was walking his post?"

Both officers had a nasty feeling about this probing. They had seen the line of ordinary people, shop keepers and traders, waiting in the anteroom where witnesses were held. It was likely that, apart from the priestesses, someone else, or even quite a number of someones, had seen that fool Renzai—and that they would swear to it. Better to toss him to the wolves than be caught out in lies they dare not explain. If it came to it, they had a remedy they could apply to a single soldier.

"Lord Judge, you are right. We cannot swear that this man stood his post as recorded. We think that he did, but in the end, we cannot be completely certain."

Atepmut noticed the quick looks exchanged between the officers. They knew something of the events but had no intention of being involved. Very interesting; he'd take this a step further.

"And the war leopard? It was said that none were missing yet there are a number of witnesses to say that this man had a beast, a leopard, with him."

"Ah, that is a misunderstanding, Lord Judge. We have consulted the scrolls; Renzai was training a young beast. It was not yet on the records as fully trained."

Pahotep stepped forward. "Wise One, under the laws of Pharaoh it is utterly forbidden to bring an untrained war beast into the city, let alone one unleashed and unmuzzled. This was not only done, but the beast was freed, my sister's life was threatened, a man of the city was badly injured, and compensation was refused his family since it was claimed that the beast was not an official war-leopard.

"Now his officers admit that their soldier did have such a beast, so this man lied to you openly. Moreover, compensation *is* therefore due and must be paid by the regiment. I ask also, how is it that this Renzai was able to bring his beast from the barracks and past the guard who was on duty at the gates—*to prevent just such abuses?*"

Atepmut was quietly enjoying himself. He wasn't sure what was involved here but there was little doubt in his mind that there was some sort of conspiracy—and a substantial flouting of the laws. Atepmut was a hard and ambitious man; he'd risen from quite humble beginnings as judges went, and he was determined to rise higher. The law was in many ways his true God, and if these men did not respect it, they were the enemy.

He leaned forward in his seat. "I, too, wish to have an answer to that."

The senior officer shrugged. "Lord Judge, soldiers are soldiers. The beast may have been smuggled out, or the guard bribed. We shall make an inquiry. But that is for us to do. The soldiers of Pharaoh do not fall under your judgment save that the offences occur against civilians and within certain limits."

Atepmut felt a flash of fury. They were right—in some ways, but only in some. And this Renzai *did* fall under his authority.

"As you say, officers. Then let you conduct your inquiries as I shall conduct mine. It is clear to me that this soldier's crimes fall under my authority. He broke army regulations when he either smuggled or bribed his beast past the barracks guard, but he broke Pharaoh's law when he brought an untrained beast into the city. Pharaoh's law was further broken when the beast was sufficiently uncontrolled to attack civilians, and when this man lied to me. Nor am I satisfied that your own actions are beyond reproach. I shall speak to your superiors on that, but as for this man, he shall be questioned further as soon as I have completed my day's work here."

The officers briefly crossed looks. That would not be good for them or for Renzai. Questioning did not mean wine, cakes, and polite conversation, in the course of which a few questions were asked in a civil fashion. It meant pointed questions asked, answers encouraged with pointed objects. And Renzai would talk; he had no reason not to. Fear of what was at hand would be far more potent and effective than a vague threat of their displeasure in the future.

"Lord Judge, we must consult our superiors, as we are uncertain of the legality of your intentions."

Atepmut wasn't. "Do so. But I have stated my intentions. They are legal and they shall be carried out."

The officers departed at speed to consult, not so much their superiors, but their co-conspirators. Atepmut turned back to the prisoner and the case.

"Let us hear the other witnesses."

They did. A long parade of people who lived and worked in Hanish and who could testify that Renzai had been in the city that day. Yes, he'd had a war leopard with him. Yes, he had purchased various items—soap, wine, a towel, a small faience amulet of Aten—in their booths or shops and they had seen him closely enough to recognize him. Yes—from two of the trader witnesses—they knew the man, he was a regular customer. Yes—from a trader and his assistant in the amulet booth—they could identify two of his companions as well.

Atepmut sent a runner after the officers at once, requesting that the two solders be presented at his court that day. Right now in fact, just as soon as they were found.

(His face turned an unusual shade of red when, in reply—shortly before the court ended—he was informed that the soldiers in question had been transferred the day before. To a delta area several hundreds of miles away, and that it would take five or six moons to locate and return them—if at all. He was convinced that until the moment that they had been named they hadn't been going anywhere.)

He ploughed on with the witnesses and the case. "Soldier Renzai, your officers have testified that you were indeed in possession of a war leopard. They said it was young and untrained as yet. How old was the beast?"

Renzai wasn't sure what was going on. All he knew was that he'd been told to take his leopard into Hanish, where a woman would be pointed out. He was to release the leopard, apparently by accident, wait until it had done some damage and then call it off and apologize profusely. He had the vague impression that she was a heretic, that he'd be promoted quietly in the near future if he did as he was told. It was never a bad thing to please your officers—as they'd be the first to tell you.

Instead his leopard had been killed, the wrong civilian injured, and the woman turned out to be not only elder sister to the Lord of the Lion Domain, but also Shrine's Lady to Bastet—one of the more revered of the minor Gods. Worse still, those who asked him to do all this now denied that they'd ever told him anything. He was branded a liar, a breaker of a whole list of army regulations, and worst yet, an incompetent who couldn't train or control his own beast. He broke earlier than his superiors anticipated.

"The beast was almost three, Lord Judge. An' I only did as I was told. They said she was a heretic, an' that she was supposed to be got out'a the way for a while. I didn't smuggle the leopard past no one, nor bribe no guard. I was let go by those officers."

Atepmut sucked in a deep and triumphant breath. "The two who were in my court? How did they let you go?"

"They just walked me out the back entrance. M' mates joined me once I was down the road. They didn't know nothing." They really hadn't—although they probably guessed there was something planned, but he wasn't getting them into trouble. "I was told a man would come up to me an' say where I could find the lady."

Atepmut was onto that. "A man. What man? Describe him?"

Renzai did his best but he hadn't really looked at the man, hadn't known he'd need to. "Just average, Lord Judge."

Further questioning elicited only that the man had sounded like a man of Napata, looked like a man of Napata, wore the clothing of a man of Napata, and could have been anywhere from late youth to late middle-age. That eliminated women, children, the very old, and most obvious foreigners, leaving about a fifth of the population of the city—even supposing that the man was an inhabitant.

Atepmut sighed in exasperation. "Go on. This leopard of yours, what about it?"

"He was near three, Lord Judge, an' he *was* trained. Trained him myself all this past year or more, *an'* he's on the regiment rolls. Dunno why they said he isn't."

There were a lot more questions—which elicited very little information, save that this soldier was an idiot, and in trusting him to carry out his orders, his officers were scarcely brighter. Atepmut ordered Renzai removed to the cells, adjourned the court, and waved for the complainants to join him.

"Lord Pahotep, High Priestess, I fear you are right and there is a conspiracy against you. I am uncertain if it is against the Domain of the Lion and you, Lady, as sister to the Lord, or if the conspiracy is against both Domain and Shrine together. What is clear is that the army, locally at least, is heavily involved. I plan to approach the temple of Aten send urgent word to the Pharaoh. It cannot be his wish that those in his army conspire to injure or murder his nobles."

No one disagreed with that assessment—although they all could have. There were honest, decent priests in Aten's temple as there were in those of the other Gods. It would be interesting to see how those priests reacted once they discovered what was going on in Hanish. And how the officers would react to being called back to court to explain Renzai's very public accusations.

The first reaction occurred in a small, hot cell under the courts of law. Renzai was taken down at the close of the session and left there. In a cell corner, hidden from the door, he found a pitcher of wine. It was good quality wine, unwatered and potent. A lot more potent than he realized until some time after he'd drunk the last of it—but by then it was too late.

Word reached the judge who said a number of things before asking questions. Most unusually no one knew anything, no one had seen anything, and there was no proof of anything. Atepmut fumed. The law he revered was being flouted over and over. A man had been murdered and while he knew how and could make a good guess at why, he had no idea of who had performed the actual deed. He summoned the jailer.

"The cell the prisoner was placed within. Was it the same cell he had been in before he was brought up to court?"

"Yes, Lord Judge."

There went another possibility. Someone just placed the pitcher in the same cell.

"Were any strangers seen about the cells or corridors?"

"No, Lord Judge."

That was distressing. There was a good possibility the killer was one of his own staff. Just how far did this conspiracy spread? What was it all about? Atepmut dismissed the jailer and pondered. He didn't like the feel of this. There were ramifications of which he was unaware, and he needed to know more. How could he act effectively if he remained in the dark? He called guards and quietly set out for the tiny temple of Amun in Hanish. He had a friend there.

Asosi proved to have some enlightening—if upsetting—information and even more distressing gossip. The priest observed his friend. Atepmut had always respected the law. For him it was the foundation of his life and all that he was. Yes, he was ambitious, but in a way it was more for the law than for himself. If he reached the position of senior judge the law would be better served, and he was probably right. Asosi decided to tell his friend everything he knew—and much of what the temple of Amun in Hanish guessed.

Atepmut was staggered and a little incredulous once he heard everything. "So you are saying that Pharaoh intends to bring down every God but Aten? That to do this he plans to begin with the Shrine of Bastet here, and that as part of this plan Shrine's Lady would be murdered or badly injured, her brother's kin—an officer—would be murdered, and the army here are acting as assassins?"

"In a word, yes."

"But—but—why?"

Asosi settled himself more comfortably. "Bastet is one of the minor Gods, although it is true she is greatly respected for the healing abilities of her priestesses and their ability to interpret dreams. Her actual worship, however, is really only important here in Hanish and in the lands of the Lion Domain. And there are eight domains."

"I know that. What has that to do with anything?"

Asosi elaborated. "Amun's shrines have combined to reject the Pharaoh's demands thus far. The Lords of three of the eight Domains back us, and those three are large enough to equal four of the other Lords' holdings. Only the Lion Domain stands out. In the other seven either Amun or Aten is the main God—with Thoth greatly respected and his priests acting often as advisers to the Domain Lords. In the Lion Domain most of the population worship Bastet. This domain is smaller in population and the lands are less fertile. It is separate from most other areas since it is south and west of the more fertile and civilized lands."

Atepmut began to see. "So if attacked, few would even know what was happening, let alone come to its aid?"

"Exactly, my friend. But if Shrine's Lady appears before Pharaoh's throne and publicly bows to Aten it is a strong example. He can point to her as the first of the shrines of minor Gods to accept Aten as ruler over all the others. With that he can quietly pressure other shrines to do likewise. We think he wants them to believe that so long as they do this, they will then be left alone."

"But you don't believe that?"

Asosi spoke carefully. "I do not, and my superiors think it unlikely. Look at war. An enemy can raid our boundaries, nibbling our flanks, taking small bites of our lands and people. Each time they seem to be satisfied for a while, each time they return. No bite is enough to rouse us to attack—until at last they have everything and we are dispossessed."

Atepmut understood, "So if a ruler persuaded all the minor Gods, the Gods of the ordinary people, to bow to Aten, then he has reduced the war to two Gods: Aten and Amun, with Thoth on the sidelines. It is to the apparent benefit of the minor Gods to stand aside from the war—or to aid Aten, since they have bowed to him. And if the Lion Domain has been destroyed, then that too is an example to the other Domains. It could sway one of the rebellious three and that would be sufficient to win without a battle."

"Possibly." Asosi smiled unpleasantly. "I would lay down no coin on such a bet. The Domains are not so easily cowed, but yes, it is possible. The ruler thinks so, and if He is wrong, well then, the Lion Domain is still gone and cannot stand with the rebellious three against him."

Atepmut desired specific information. "Gone? You mean he would kill everyone?"

"Of that we cannot be certain. But my superiors believe so. At least everyone of the House of the Lion, and all those in Bastet's Shrine. If the rest of the people lay in the dust and beg for mercy, bow to Aten, and perhaps pay heavy fines, they might be permitted to live." He looked at his friend and spoke slowly.

"Consider this however, Atepmut. A ruler needs lands and wealth with which to reward the loyal. To do that it is necessary not to have claimants for that land or property. And—many of those of wealth in this Domain are those whose ancestors were not men of Napata. Why should a ruler allow foreigners who may not be loyal to him to benefit over those loyal members of his own people?"

"Those *foreigners* have lived here for five generations," Atepmut said angrily.

"And our own people have worked this land for a hundred times that many generations. No, they are foreigners, so says the ruler."

Atepmut returned home with a lot to think about. He'd stepped into stinking offal dumped in the streets by another, but if it remained on his sandals and he trod it elsewhere he would be blamed. But—his heart and his respect for the law insisted—none of this was *legal*.

The Gods were the Gods; some were greater but that made no difference, they should all be revered. A ruler plotted to destroy an entire Domain and its nobles, not for anything it had done, not to punish any great crime or treason, but as an example to terrorize others and so that the possessions of the people could be used to buy loyalty elsewhere. A temple was to be overthrown and its people murdered. The army, acting under the ruler's orders, sent out assassins, war leopards, and arrant liars—even into his own court.

The Temples of Amun were quietly resisting. The ruler had decided that if He could sway the minor temples to the side of Aten and destroy one Domain to overawe the others, then His God would prevail. He might be wrong in that belief, but it would make no difference to those already slaughtered.

If the ruler won this battle, then any High Priest with half a brain could see that their temples and God would be of no further use. Akhenaten was determined, from what Asosi said, not just to have Aten as *the* God, but as the *only* God. Once Aten was preeminent and the Domains all bowed to the ruler, then at his leisure he could destroy the minor Gods before Amun too fell, and no one would remain to protest.

Atepmut was judge under the ruler, yes, but was the ruler, semi-divine or not, above the law? No, not to Atepmut's way of thinking.

In the following days he considered cases that came before him—and which involved soldiers' complaints against citizens of the Lion Domain—more carefully. He neither broke nor even bent the law, but he could and did find more loopholes on the citizens' behalf.

In the Lion Compound, Kahoret improved daily while Pahotep and Khepera visited him regularly. Pharaoh opened reports of events in Hanish, fumed and consulted priests in the temples of Aten. Remekh wrote letters to various priests of Thoth in a number of cities—receiving considered, and occasionally very odd, replies. Shardis worried, for as a junior priestess old enough to be trusted she often did the shopping, and she heard things. The healers Merem and Temmah were extremely busy and had no time for anything else. Bastet brooded in silence over Her Shrine, waiting in cat-like patience for what would happen.

And in an inner lane of Hanish late one evening, three soldiers set out to show a whore named Ankhemah what happened to those who were ungenerous to the army.

5

It might have passed over. Soldiers do get rough, whores do get beaten. But Ankhemah was a pretty, laughing girl, popular with local men, and even many of the women did not dislike her. When she reeled out of her rented room covered in blood and weeping, a number of people were ready to help. And they all heard what she said when the first of them asked what had happened. Her first sentences were coherent; as shock and loss of blood set in she fainted, but by then her words were heard by too many for the matter to be kept quiet.

"Soldiers. They said I should give them what they wanted for free— as everyone in the city would be doing once the army took over. We'd all be slaves; they'd own us and they'd be rich once Bastet was gone and they looted her temple."

It is the nature of things that soldiers do get rough, that whores are beaten. It is not acceptable for an army to take over an entire city inno- cently minding its own business, enslave the population, loot the shrine of the most revered Goddess there, and commit the Gods only knew what other excesses and atrocities. In an hour everyone in the city had heard what the soldiers said to Ankhemah and what their neighbors thought.

By the same time the next day there had been a number of incidents. They were no longer the mostly casual acts that they had been previ- ously. A soldier who was rude to a shopkeeper was later found dead in a ditch. Another who idly flung a small stone at a passing cat—and missed—had much larger stones flung at him—which did not miss. He took shelter in a shop and would have been peremptorily evicted by the owner had he not spent all of his money on items he didn't want. It was worth it for the temporary shelter—but the now-penniless soldier, nonetheless, resented it.

He returned to barracks, reported his treatment, and he and several friends returned to the shop. There they overturned furniture, struck the shop owner and, when his daughter protested, she was threatened and one of the soldiers laid hands on her. What might have happened after that no one knew since Pahotep's guards arrived and arrested all who appeared involved.

They arrived in Atepmut's courtroom and he had the whole story quickly. To him, as to the people of Hanish, the main question was the truth of the story told to Ankhemah, not the foolish acts that followed. He began by questioning the sequence of events, however.

"You are Kanake, soldier of the Theban Regiment?"

The soldier stood to attention. "I am, Lord Judge."

"You are charged with having entered the shop of a man of this city together with two other members of your regiment, where you overturned items in the shop, struck the owner when he protested, and laid hands on his daughter, threatening her. I will hear why you did this."

Kanake hesitated, unsure if that was a genuine offer.

Atepmut frowned. "I am serious. I wish to hear why you, a solider, should behave in this way towards civilians in a Napatan city."

Kanake looked down at his feet. His actions did not sound well when the Lord Judge put it that way. As if he were guilty of unprofessional conduct. That wasn't so—not really. He looked up to find Atepmut looking back with the air of a man who waits patiently for a reply.

"It started by accident, Lord Judge. I was sitting outside a place where I bought food. I was eating bread and meat when a cat came up to beg for a share. I gave the animal a bite of meat but it would not go away after that. I meant no harm, but I tossed a small stone. I did not hit it! I would never do so intentionally, but the beast ran. The next thing I knew people were shouting and flinging stones at me. One cut my face and I was afraid, so I ran.

"They chased me into a shop and crowded outside in the street. If I left the shop I would be set upon again so I stayed. The shop owner began to sell me things I did not want. He insisted I buy or leave. I spent all my money on a heap of rubbish. By the time the crowd was gone I lost all my wages and I was angry."

"So you returned to the barracks and told your friends?" Atepmut concluded. "Then you all went back to the shop to return the shopkeeper his goods and demand your money in return?"

Kanake dug his toe into the floor. "Sort of, Lord Judge. I wanted my money back, I didn't return his goods. He deserved to lose them for cheating me."

"And the girl?"

"That was an accident, Lord Judge. She came at me, pulling my tunic and screaming. I pushed her away and she fell. She flew at me and scratched my arm. All I said was that girls who attacked soldiers could get attacked in return. I meant that she could be smacked, Lord Judge. Not that we'd rape her." His voice was indignant. "I am a soldier of Napata. I don't rape Napatan girls, and she is only a child anyway. I wouldn't hurt a child, not on purpose."

Atepmut took that with a grain of salt. If the girl had actually hurt the man she'd be hurt in return. Not rape, perhaps, but a beating most likely. And with the girl crying, clothing being torn, it was all too possible rape would have occurred, no matter the original intent.

The whole business began because this idiot threw a stone at a cat in a city where cats were sacred. A thought occurred to Atepmut.

"What God do you worship, Kanake?"

"Well, Aten officially, Lord Judge. He's a soldiers' God, says Pharaoh. But at home my family worship Min, the God of those who travel the desert. My family organizes caravans that trade across the sands."

"So you come from Coptus?" Kanake nodded. "And what would your family do, Kanake, if a stranger came to your city and flung stones at Min's statue?"

Kanake scowled, his voice quick and angry. "We'd fling stones back, Lord Judge, and if he survived we'd have him before the court for a judgment." He paused.

"Yes," Atepmut said quietly. "But you might also take from the man all he had instead, to teach him not to outrage a God. And wouldn't he deserve such punishment?"

"Yes." Kanake agreed, suddenly understanding. "I did wrong. I did not think and I did wrong. But the city has changed towards us, Lord Judge. We were always welcome here, then we were not and we don't know why. It made us all angry."

Atepmut leaned forward in his seat. "I will tell you why, Kanake." He held up a hand. "Listen and understand." He told how soldiers had beaten Ankhemah. "And as they beat her they said that she should give them what they wanted for free—as everyone in the city would do once the army took over. That everyone in the city would be slaves, the soldiers would own us and they'd be rich once Bastet was gone and they could loot her temple."

He studied the expression on Kanake's face. "Do you understand now? It would be as if your regiment came to Coptus and said such a thing. Would your family, your friends, be happy to hear they were all to become slaves, and that the temple of Min was to be looted and torn down?"

Kanake shook his head.

"The soldiers who beat this woman were of your regiment. Why would they say such a thing? Why would they threaten the city of Hanish, her people and her Goddess?"

"I don't know, Lord Judge. It's true that there are strange rumors. Servants attend officers and hear talk. You know how it is. Talk gets passed around and someone adds to it, someone else wonders, and that tags on to the story and so it goes."

Atepmut nodded. "Indeed I know. Listen, the descriptions of the men who beat Ankhemah are thus." He described them and Kanake nodded.

"I know who at least one of them is, Lord Judge. His name is Rebetsu. He's been disciplined a number of times for causing trouble with civilians. He'd have been discharged but he's a good man in a fight."

Atepmut decided that the information was more useful than harshly punishing this idiot.

"Very well, let the complainants come forward and hear judgment." He looked at Kanake. "You insulted the Goddess when you flung a stone at Her child. For the period of one moon you shall attend the Shrine of Bastet to do hard labor, as Shrine's Lady shall direct you. I shall obtain your on-duty schedule from your officer and all of your free time, save for work, meals, and sleep, shall be so spent."

Kanake bowed, feeling that he'd got off lightly. If he'd insulted a God in some cities, they'd have had him flogged to death.

Atepmut eyed the shopkeeper and his family. "On the most serious of your complaints, the soldier says he did not intend his words to your daughter to be a threat to her honor. I find the words used were sufficiently ambiguous that his explanation is believable. He did not handle her in a way that suggests otherwise. He merely pushed her from him. However, it is an insult to the Goddess that you thought only of making a profit from this soldier's attack on one of Her children. You should have called the Hanish guard when this man fled into your shop. For this, you shall return the soldier's wages to him, nor shall you be compensated for the blows he struck. He shall return to you the items that you sold him. This is my judgment. Let it be so recorded."

His scribe scratched diligently at the papyrus as the complainants departed. The shopkeeper didn't look pleased, but then he shouldn't swindle soldiers. It could lead to all sorts of trouble—and in other places in the past, it had. Atepmut didn't want to see that sort of thing here. Kanake, relieved, bowed low and marched out as the judge considered the man's information.

A name, Atepmut thought, that was worth a lot. Now all they had to do was lay hands on this Rebetsu, giving the army the impression that it was because of Ankhemah's beating and nothing more. If he moved quickly they could have the man in court today. He gave orders and scratched a note, addressed to Remekh at the Compound of the Lion, and sent that off.

He'd like Pahotep and the others to be here to hear what this Rebetsu had to say—should they be able to lay hands on him. Atepmut wouldn't be pleased to hear that yet another soldier had been transferred the previous day—particularly as he hadn't believed it the first time. So the man better be available. He'd let the Lord know if—or when—that occurred.

He started the next case while he waited for results. The message given to him towards the end of the day left him feeling that he'd like to bite someone. The messenger came from the army with a neatly scribed note. It admitted that Rebetsu was one of theirs, that he was at present in Hanish, but regretted that he was unavailable—just that and no more.

Pahotep, who'd come to the court with Remekh and his sister, was shown the note and snorted vulgarly.

"Unavailable! I daresay he is, for by now rumors have gone back the other way. The officers will have heard what Rebetsu said to the girl, what Hanish's people are saying, and the last thing they'll do is hand the man over to be interrogated on exactly what he meant by his threats. But it's strange. After all, he could be told to claim that it was all a mistake, that he'd just yelled threats to scare her and that he and his friends were drunk and talking wildly."

Khepera pursed her lips. "I don't think so, my brother. They have the example of Renzai. He, too, knew more than he should, and he talked when he felt that the army had abandoned him to his fate. They risked much by silencing him as they did. They wouldn't want to do that again—knowing that we'd be watching for such an attempt."

Remekh nodded. "Let me scribe a letter asking why Rebetsu is unavailable, and asking when he will be able to attend this court to answer a complaint against him. They may also say that the beating of a whore is not a matter for the courts, therefore I shall say that it is a matter of theft, which is."

Atepmut looked puzzled. "The girl did not say that they stole anything."

Remekh smiled. "If I hire a porter and after he has done the work I refuse to pay, have I not stolen from him?"

Khepera giggled first, followed by loud, hearty roars of amusement from the judge and Pahotep.

"Yes," agreed Atepmut. "She said that they used her, beat her when she demanded her money, and departed. That is theft, as you say." He grinned unpleasantly. "And theft from a civilian, no matter what the officers say, is a matter for the courts. I can demand that they produce the man or explain to my satisfaction why he cannot be brought to me."

If Atepmut had been annoyed by the original response to his demand he was utterly infuriated by the reply which arrived next day. He read it, spluttered, turned red, purple, and white in turn, and leapt to his feet. Yelling for his guard, he swept out and almost ran through the streets to the Lion compound. There he asked for Pahotep and Remekh, who came quickly, along with Khepera and Shardis, who were visiting.

"What is it, Wise One?"

In reply the note was thrust into Remekh's hand, who read the important portion of it aloud.

"As previously stated, the soldier Rebetsu is not available for the justice of the Domain of the Lion. He has committed theft from army supplies and is imprisoned while we convene our court to judgment. As a soldier, his offense against his employers takes precedence. It is anticipated that on a verdict of guilty he will at once be executed.

"He has stated that he was alone when he committed the offense against your complainant. As you have no name or clear description of the others claimed to have committed the crime we regret that we are unable to assist in their apprehension."

Shardis couldn't help it. She giggled. Khepera smiled down at the girl, her expression wry. "Yes. They have us nicely."

"My grandfather would say that there's always a way if you aren't too fussy." Shardis's eyes sparkled wickedly. "You could arrest a soldier who matches the description of one of the offenders, take him into the judge's court and charge him. Get someone to agree that he looks like one of the men, and when he panics—well—soldiers know all the gossip. He'll know who was with Rebetsu. If he's scared enough he'll tell you their names."

Pahotep looked at the judge. "An interesting idea. If we do most of it in private and keep the man in the cells, his officer may assume that he's just gone off drinking. If we get a name we may be able to grab the man before the army finds out we know he was one of those involved."

Atepmut looked grimly pleased. "And once we have him, he'll talk."

"Yes," Pahotep agreed softly, "he will. He'll tell us everything he knows, everything he guesses, and then he'll start on the sins of his childhood. If my kin, my city, my people, and my Goddess are all in grave danger, there is nothing I will stop at and no path I will not take to prevent it."

Most of the plan fell out as hoped. The seized soldier, terrified, gabbled names, two of them, and was placed in a comfortable room with ample food and several containers of very strong wine. He immediately got drunk and stayed that way.

Of the men he named, one came into the city the next day and was taken. He proved to be a stolid man, rather stupid, and all they could wring from him was that his companion, servant to one of the senior officers, had told Rebetsu and this man that the army would soon take over the city. After which there'd be gold and women for all. When asked how he knew, he laughed and said that you heard a lot when no one knew you were there, and who paid attention to servants who were always in and out.

Their prisoner believed the servant eavesdropped on his master, something he often did. It had been useful in the past, but he didn't really believe it this time. And anyway, no one would give ordinary soldiers gold or slaves no matter how much of either was available.

He hadn't been much damaged, so they got him extremely drunk as well, and hauled him into court in the morning. His eyes were still crossing as it was hammered into him that he'd got drunk, made a beast of himself, started a fight, and spent the night under a table in a tavern. Since he was a soldier and little damage had been done, he was being discharged with a caution and a complaint to his commander.

The other soldier, too, was discharged with apologies. Inquiries had been made and they knew that he was innocent. In reparation for his imprisonment he was presented with a large jar of good wine. He promptly found a quiet corner away from the court and became drunk again. Eventually the army retrieved him, and once sober he was too bright to tell his officer that he'd divulged the names of comrades.

However, the army had already demanded the names from Rebetsu, having traced rumors to him. One officer straightened abruptly as soon as the second name was spoken.

"My servant!"

"Who listens at doors," another added cynically.

"Probably," the first acknowledged.

"Get rid of him, and do it permanently."

Finding items of value in the servant's belongings, charging him with theft from an officer, and executing him the same day took care of that. In the city, Atepmut waited for the soldier in vain. He went home that night and cuddled his cat while sharing his meal with her. It was amazing how she reduced his blood pressure, especially when all about him people were foolish.

"A clever idea," Khepera told Shardis, "but I think the army found him first." She sighed. "It's not good; the city is becoming agitated. People talk, and every time the story goes by, another layer is added."

"The last one I heard claimed the army is going to raze the city," Shardis offered. "We in the temple will be sacrificed to Aten and they'll burn us all alive, along with Bastet's statue and all the cats."

Khepera winced.

"They say that no one's going to lay hands on the Goddess and Her children, and they'll fight before that happens. That you might as well die fighting. And some hint that maybe we should get in first."

Khepera shut her eyes and bit back a groan. If the army were attacked, that would be all that Pharaoh required to send in troops. People's fears *could* become a reality. She reflected, as once again at midday she hurried through the streets to her brother's compound, that if this continued she'd at least be very fit when she died.

Shardis scurried at her side, keeping her mouth shut. Shrine's Lady was upset and she didn't want to make things worse. Not that she would, because everyone else was doing that. Once they saw Pahotep she'd better tell him what she overheard while out shopping very early that morning, a suggestion that maybe they could appeal to Pharaoh. He couldn't want to murder his loyal subjects, so it must be a plot by the army, and if Pharaoh knew about it then he could prevent it.

She told the Lord of the Lion Domain, but it was already too late. The letter had been scribed two days before and left the previous day with a family member traveling to trade in the capital. He traveled light and wasted no time in his journey.

* * * *

Akhenaten read the long, poorly written letter, smiled viciously at the opportunity afforded him, and called in priests of the Temple of Aten.

"I have here a letter, supposedly from a number of people in the city of Hanish. They say that I must not attack their city, that it is not right for a ruler to murder His subjects. That I should show respect to the Goddess or She shall punish me."

The priests of Aten sucked in their breath in mingled horror at the blasphemy, and pleasure at the opportunity.

"Exactly," Akhenaten confirmed. "There is no God but Aten. And little people, peasants, do not say 'must' to Pharaoh. This city and the Domain of the Lion in general need to be taught that it is *I* who rule. The Theban Regiment is outside Hanish. What other regiment is nearest?"

An officer came running with the records. Akhenaten read them and considered. "The Regiment of the Domain of Striking Hawk obeys Pharaoh. Let them join the Thebans."

"With what orders, Lord?"

"Surround the city, allow no one to enter or leave. Once starvation begins to bite, we shall see who says 'must' to their ruler."

Three High Priests moved forward. Syamekh, High Priest of the main Temple of Thoth, spoke quietly to the infuriated Pharaoh.

"Lord of the Twin Rivers, holder of the Cobra Throne, great Ruler whose Light Rises in the East and Sets in the West. Such a thing is unheard of. The city—a city of Napata—is not in open rebellion. The letter may be from some mad or disaffected fool alone. If You do this, the city may rebel, and Domains shall say that they were justified."

Amun's High Priest agreed. "Great One, the Lords of the Provinces would see such a move as a threat. Against a small, poor, obscure domain, far to the southwest, You send two regiments with orders to starve the city. For what? Some madman who claims he is oppressed by the army? What if he tells the truth? Are the Lords to hear that their Pharaoh suppresses Truth?"

Akhenaten looked at the third man. "You are High Priest of Aten, what advice do you give me, Khamay?"

Khamay spoke smoothly. "Such a letter is an intolerable insult, Great Lord. Yet if it is the words of a mad fool, shall You not look foolish if You take them seriously? Would it not be better to discover the truth?"

Akhenaten considered. "How would you suggest I do this?"

"The names of those who wrote are inscribed on the letter. Let the army go into the city and find all of those names. Let them be questioned severely, if this is some conspiracy against you, then all shall be known."

Syamekh shook his head. "If You send the army into the city to drag away everyone of similar name, You will have hundreds to question. If many who are innocent are tortured or killed, what does that say of Pharaoh's justice?"

Akhenaten shot to his feet, bellowing with fury. "I am Pharaoh. I am the great and mighty ruler of Napata and of all the lands beyond!"

Syamekh regarded his ruler and mentally snorted. That might be true, but the spindly-legged, fat-bodied ruler, his high-pitched voice rising higher still in rage, and his white-rimmed, popping eyes, resembled nothing so much as an infuriated swamp-frog. Still, even frogs could poison. This business must be reined in before the prophecies of the dreamers in the Temple happened in the wrong way.

"You are indeed the Great, the Mighty One," he agreed soothingly. "Your tread shakes the earth, Son of the Sun. Who shall say You nay, or protest any decision You make? Yet, wisdom urges caution. Let men be sent to Hanish, yes. Perhaps I could send priests, for the wisdom of Thoth is widely known. If we found these foolish men, they could explain their words."

Akhenaten settled back on his throne. Syamekh saw Khamay move forward and hiss into a royal ear. An oily snake in the grass, that Khamay, and a dangerous one. A hidden viper that struck unseen and without warning. Syamekh wondered what the man was saying.

Akhenaten listened closely, then nodded to the High Priest of Thoth. "Y-e-e-s-s," he said, and continued, more decisively. "Yes, let it be done. You may make all suitable inquiries about this letter and recent events in Hanish, but go yourself."

Unheard of! To send the High Priest of a great Temple on an errand like a child sent shopping? Yet, it would be a chance to confer with Remekh, and he could spin out the time, travel slowly, and take a moon or even more to find the man responsible for this stupid letter and to be certain that he had the right person. Yes, it could be useful. Yet why did he have the feeling of a second sandal poised to drop?

He bowed. "Great One, at Your command I shall go. Let an exact copy be made of the letter that I may take it with me and truly inquire— as is Your will."

Pharaoh waved at a scribe. "Let it be done as the High Priest says. Make three copies, in case one is lost. Syamekh shall carry the original one, two copies shall go with a priest of Aten who will accompany him— I trust you to find a suitable man, Khamay—and the third copy shall be in the possession of the Commander of the guard."

Syamekh growled silently. There went one possibility. If he lost that Amun-cursed letter on the journey he could have procrastinated for quite some time. Oh, well. He departed the court to prepare for his trip, still wondering why Pharaoh had been so complacent about not sending another regiment.

He discovered that when he reported to the city gates with his own group of temple guards. The Regiment of the Domain of the Striking Hawk was drawn up in rows that filled the area in front of the open gates. Pharaoh stood surveying them from his grossly over-ornamented chariot. Behind him, Khamay smirked as his gaze met that of Amun's High Priest. He looked exactly like a cat that, despite all precautions, reached the milk pitcher. Somehow, Syamekh thought, the thrice-damned man has earned that look. He waited to hear how.

6

Pharaoh, whose reedy voice was not suited to being heard over distances, signaled to his speaker. The bull-necked man stepped forward, and in a voice that matched his size, announced his ruler's decision.

"Thus says Pharaoh. 'The city of Hanish of the Lion Domain has appealed to me for justice. Far away and the least of the Domains, yet are the people of that domain dear to me. That their complaint may be fairly and honestly judged and recompense made at need, I send my most dearly beloved Syamekh, High Priest of the Temple of Thoth, to be my judge and voice in this matter.

"'Yet the journey is long and the road hard and dangerous. That he shall arrive unharmed I send with him the Regiment of the Domain of the Striking Hawk, to guard and protect him along the way. May all the Gods go with Syamekh and may he return to his temple once again to share his wisdom with those in need.'"

Syamekh schooled his face to a blank smile of appreciation. That was the other sandal all right. Nothing he could do about it either, for it was within the customs—just. No wonder the ruler had given in so easily. Khamay had to have come up with the idea, because Akhenaten wasn't that smart. And what was worse, he suspected that Akhenaten—or Khamay—had given secret orders to the Regiment's Commander to be carried out on their arrival.

Syamekh mounted the donkey held for him and joined the procession as it marched off down the road. He looked back once to see Khamay's hand lifted in a sweetly polite farewell. He ignored it, since he couldn't make the return gesture he would have liked to.

It would take weeks to arrive at Hanish anyhow and that gave the Lion Domain more time. On his own, with only his attendants and guards, Syamekh would make the journey in half the time, but a regiment on foot travels far more slowly. Not that Syamekh minded; so far as he was concerned the time spent was all to the good. It gave him time to do something that Khamay—for all his low cunning—hadn't considered. Halfway along the road to Hanish one evening, as the regiment made camp, he summoned a man of his guard—a devoted, devout, and sensible youth who was also a minor priest—handing him a small, sealed scroll.

"Tiaahn, I want you to take this to the priest of Thoth, Remekh, residing currently in the House of Pahotep, Lord of the Lion Domain in the city of Hanish. The scroll must be given into his own hands." Tiaahn nodded, accepting the scroll. "And take this silver chain. Break off links to pay when you must."

The chain tapered, one end having links that were thick and heavy, the other having thinner, lighter links. Together they added up to an amount that would keep a man without expensive tastes for a year in a medium-sized city.

Tiaahn's eyes widened slightly. "High Priest Syamekh, that is too great a sum."

"No, it may not be: hear me. You go in secret, you go with all speed, and it is important that nothing delays you. When your horse is exhausted or goes lame you are to buy another. You are not to bother halting early and cooking for yourself: take a room in some village once it is too dark to ride. If you think it unlikely there will be a place to stay around dark, then buy food along the way and eat when you camp. You understand me? There is to be no delay. I require you not only to lay this scroll in Remekh's own hands, you are to return with a reply—if there is one he can make quickly. If not, then return with an acknowledgement that he has received my information. This must be done before the regiment reaches the Lion Domain's borders."

Tiaahn stood holding scroll and chain. "And I presume, High Priest, you prefer that Khamay's men or the regiment know nothing of my journey?"

"I prefer that absolutely no one around us knows anything whatsoever of your journey," Syamekh said dryly. "All of them have their own agendas, including some supposed to hold only the interests of their masters in their hearts. I suggest that you leave …"

Tiaahn chuckled softly. "Wise One, I know how to disappear without such spies noting my departure. Let you be angry with me, threaten and curse me, and leave the rest to me."

He secured the chain about his waist with a cord, leaving a few links unsecured at each end. The scroll he placed in his waist pouch. He bowed low to the man he respected and loved, took his leave, and packed two small saddlebags which he placed by a carefully chosen horse. After which he left to enjoy the debauchery of a nearby village. The women weren't too bad. He took one to her room, enjoyed an hour, and paid—a little more than expected, so that if any asked she'd talk—and went to find the inn.

The beer there was an abomination to Thoth and good taste. Tiaahn apparently imbibed huge quantities before becoming too drunk to walk and falling asleep in a corner. Thanks be to the Lord of Wisdom that he hadn't actually drunk more than an initial mouthful of the noxious brew.

He remained firmly asleep until Syamekh came storming into the building. The High Priest might have accepted that Tiaahn had made a fool of himself for once, had he not been forewarned. As it was, he heartily approved the ruse but raved loudly and angrily at the young priest.

"You drunken sot! Is this how a priest of Thoth behaves?" He appeared to lose his temper completely and kicked the young man. Only someone standing almost on top of them would observe that the vigorous kick did not land. Tiaahn rolled over, wailing protests and excuses. "Forgive you? Excuse such behavior?" Syamekh kicked again and his victim howled louder.

"High One, Lord, I am sorry! It shall not happen again, do not send me back."

A couple of watching officers, in for a quick drink before the regiment departed, called encouragement to the outraged Syamekh. "Send him back!"

"No, keep him here and make him walk."

"Send him back for a whipping. Boys learn through sore backs."

Syamekh grabbed Tiaahn roughly, dragging him to his feet. "That last sounds like a good suggestion to me, you disgusting piece of filth. You'll carry a letter back to the temple telling them to whip you soundly. Then you'll return to me with a letter from my scribe to say that it's been done. You'd better make both trips before we reach Hanish. Riding one way in expectation and the other with a very sore back will remind you of what happens to those young priests who forget their position."

Tiaahn sniveled. "But Great One, no mount can make such a journey in time."

Syamekh smiled evilly at the cowering youth. "Then you'll receive a whipping from me when you do return—for failure to obey my orders," he snapped, to mutters of approval from the listening officers.

Tiaahn opened his mouth to argue or plead and Syamekh shoved him towards the door. "Out! Do you think I have nothing else to do but seek out drunkards and discipline unruly priests? You'll be on your way immediately. No, no time to eat, and I'm sure your stomach will thank me for that anyhow. Go, at once, or you'll be riding *both* ways with a sore back …"

His angry words faded from the listeners' ears as he drove Tiaahn out of the building and toward the horse-lines. He kept up the pose until the lad was safely mounted, with all his required small travel items stowed safely.

He spoke quietly. "You have everything you'll need?"

"I do, Master."

"Thoth speed and protect you." He lifted his hand and pronounced a blessing, one addressed directly to his God, and from His High Priest for another of the God's sons. "Go quickly, the regiment moves off soon and the scouts will move ahead."

Tiaahn looked down at the man he honored. "Master, if I do not return, then I am dead. Only that will keep me from your side." He kicked his mount into a brisk canter and vanished down the road in a cloud of dust.

Once out of sight he swung in a wide circle across country and turned again in the direction of Hanish, avoiding the regiment, the sharp eyes of scouts, and—so far as possible—the beady-eyed nosiness of local peasants. He'd made sure to obtain bread and cheese, and in the breast of his robe he'd also stowed a small quantity of dried meat. Tiaahn continued to make time, riding alternately at a fast walk and a canter. He slowed his sweating, utterly weary mount to a slow walk in the early afternoon and ate the bread and cheese.

Ahead he saw a small village. It would not be on the regiment's line of march, for that was to his west. Nor did he have to worry about exhausting his own lighter, better-bred beast, as that had been left behind. Instead he had taken a sturdy horse that was used to bearing a large and heavy man—which Tiaahn was not. It would last a day of hard riding, after which he could exchange it and not regret leaving it with some peasant. He studied the village and decided against a halt of more than a few minutes to allow the horse to drink. Although …

He rode in, eyes busy, and briefly his expression showed triumph. There! A pair of horses tethered to the door of what was clearly another inn. He took his mount to drink, paused briefly around a corner, hidden behind his mount as he walked it before entering the tavern. Once inside he approached the owners of the beasts outside. In less than an hour he was riding out of the village on one saddled animal, the other following meekly. The owners had assured him that either would follow the other. They were accustomed to being ridden together.

Tiaahn pushed them hard. They had little breeding, but their stamina was considerable, the more so, as, as with the earlier mount, he was riding animals used to a much heavier rider. He continued until almost dark, found a sheltered spot and hobbled them to graze before lying down wrapped in his cloak to eat the dried meat. He was thirsty, as he'd emptied his water-skin between himself and the horses during the day, but he'd find water or a village in the morning. Looking for either now would waste time.

He was on the move again at first light, changing the mount he rode every hour or so as he continued to push forward. He should be well beyond the regiment's scout range by now, but he must stay off their direct route. Peasants talked. So little happened in their lives that the arrival and departure of a stranger would be discussed for a year. Still more would they talk about a stranger with two horses, both of them showing evidence of hard riding. And it was that sort of information for which scouts listened.

He found a small village soon after he set out that day, a mere handful of mud-brick houses. It had a well and he was able to buy bread and cheese before riding on some distance. The bread was coarse and full of husks, and the cheese was of poor quality, but it was food and he ate it knowing that he wouldn't find better any time soon. He allowed the horses a brief rest while he ate, then mounted and continued his journey.

A day later he swapped the leg-weary, staggering beasts for a single mount, better bred and faster. That too was left behind, as were others, but Tiaahn kept going. Syamekh had accepted the seven-year-old son of a peasant into the temple because the boy showed promise—and genuine devotion to Thoth. There'd been some who had protested, but the High Priest was, while a kind and gentle man, a man too who was master in his own shrine. His own predecessor had taken in a peasant boy now and again. He'd said that they were often more genuinely devout—and they knew the meaning of hard work.

Syamekh had followed that habit, seeking out suitable lads of ten to twelve and offering them a chance to rise. Tiaahn's family had loved him, but they knew a peasant's life. In the fifteen years he'd served his master he'd seen his parents die of unrelenting toil. His two older brothers and one older sister had either died from disease or been killed in accidents, and his younger sister had married a trader and he never saw her. His younger brother had joined the army five years ago, and while Tiaahn didn't know for sure, there was a rumor that he'd died, too.

Syamekh had saved him from all that, provided an education and a trade—since his protégé could now read and write well enough to hire as a scribe at need—and made a confidant of him when he found the boy could keep his mouth shut even under substantial provocation. And now, for the first time, Tiaahn had been given an important mission. Something he could do to show his beloved master his gratitude. He changed mounts at another small village, and this time halted long enough to drink beer that wasn't too bad and listen to advice on the road ahead, since at dusk the previous night he'd passed into the lands of the Lion Domain.

The innkeeper knew of Hanish. "It's a far distance, but stay on the road; it leads right to the city. I was there once five floods ago." His eyes widened in awe. "A great city it is, too. I went to the temple of Bastet for a blessing. You know the Lion Lord's own sister is Shrine's Lady. You could go there, an' get blessed as well." He considered Tiaahn's temple insignia dubiously. "Least, you could, if you don't have a problem with the Goddess, Lord Priest?"

Tiaahn shook his head. "I serve Thoth," he assured the man. "But he and the Lady are not enemies. Nor is a blessing from her to be despised."

Actually, it was useful advice. If the Lion Lord's sister ran the temple of Bastet, then if Tiaahn was unable to find Remekh he could perhaps approach the temple of Bastet and ask there. From what his master had told him of events, and from the rumors Tiaahn picked up, and from soldiers of the regiment as they traveled, Shrine's Lady should also be aware of coming trouble. She'd have an interest in seeing that a scroll from Syamekh reached the one intended to receive it. He accepted clear directions to the Temple just in case and departed, having paid for all services received generously, but not so much as to cause undue talk.

Two days later he stayed the night at another village, long enough for his clothing to be washed and dried, to eat and sleep well, and to exchange his mount—for the final time, he hoped. In this he was right, for the earlier innkeeper's directions were accurate, and he rode into Hanish an hour before dusk the following night.

He decided to find out what he could, while also allowing himself some latitude against the urgency of his journey. If he was required to answer questions and make long explanations to the Lion Lord, as was possible, it would be better if he'd had a good night's sleep, some knowledge of what was occurring in Hanish, and food on which he could gather energy.

He stabled the horse, took a room, and had a convivial evening—listening to all the gossip while apparently drinking heavily. He didn't like what he heard, and he feared that Syamekh wouldn't either. The Theban regiment were Pharaoh's men and not raised from one of the domains. If they were behaving this way it was because—as Syamekh feared—Pharaoh planned to wipe out the Lion Domain as an example to the other, larger, more powerful domains.

The Domain of the Striking Hawk was bound tightly to the current ruler, too. One of Pharaoh's half-sisters by a lesser wife had recently wed the Lord there and the Striking Hawk regiment would do whatever

Pharaoh ordered—no matter how brutal, outrageous, or possibly unlawful the orders might be.

Tiaahn rose early, checked that his mount was well fed and cared for, ate a hearty breakfast, and then set out for the Lion Compound. In the breast of his robe he carried the scroll, and within his own breast he carried the hope that whatever information he brought would save the people here—because otherwise he was afraid all of them were doomed.

To his surprise he found that Remekh had left orders that if one came asking for him, such a person was to be shown in while Remekh was summoned. Tiaahn stood respectfully as an old man entered.

"Lord Remekh?"

His mouth opened slightly as three others entered behind the old man. One was a man of about fifty, vigorous still, dressed in clothing that indicated nobility. The woman with him was perhaps ten years older, her robes those of a High Priestess of Bastet. Behind her came a girl in the clothing of a junior priestess of that Temple. Her gaze met his and she winked.

* * * *

Shardis was finding life interesting. She worried about what could happen, but she was confident the adults had ideas that would save them all. Besides, why shouldn't she enjoy life until things went bad, anyhow? Khepera said that she wouldn't be taken and abused as a slave or tortured for possible information by the priests of Aten. If it worse came to worse, Shardis would die painlessly and find a new life in her next incarnation. Khepera promised that. She focused her attention on the people in the room. The young man looked nervous, so she winked and saw the flicker of acknowledgement. He offered a scroll to Remekh, who noticed the young man watching her.

He leaned towards Tiaahn and spoke quietly. "She is Priestess in the Temple of Bastet. A clever and intelligent child. It is good she hears what is said."

Tiaahn bowed, proffered the scroll again and it was accepted. Remekh untied the tape and glanced briefly at the opening address—which in this case introduced Tiaahn and named Syamekh as the sender.

"Sit down, boy."

The others were already sitting: the old priest on a stool, the two adults on a long divan, and the child on the floor at the woman's feet. Tiaahn sat on the floor and waited silently. Remekh scanned part of the scroll quickly and, returning to the beginning, read it aloud.

"'Written on the road to the Lion Domain by Syamekh, High Priest of the Temple of Thoth. Be warned, my brother in the Temple and in the service of our God. Half a moon ago I attended Pharaoh, who had received a letter from your city and spoke thus in the great court before all.

"""I have here a letter from a number of people in the city of Hanish in the Domain of the Lion. They say that I must not attack their city, that it is not right for a ruler to murder his subjects. That I should show respect to the Goddess or she will punish me."

"'The priests of Aten replied, "There is no God but Aten. And little people, peasants, do not say 'must' to Pharaoh. This city, and the Domain of the Lion in general, need to be taught a lesson, Great One, Lord of the Twin Rivers. The Theban Regiment is outside Hanish, what other regiment is nearest?"

"'An officer came with the records. Akhenaten read them and spoke again to all before Him. "The Regiment of the Domain of Striking Hawk obeys the Pharaoh. Let them join the Thebans."

"""With what orders, Lord?" asked the priests of Aten.

"""Surround the city, allow no one and nothing to enter or leave. Once starvation begins to bite we shall see who still says 'must' to their ruler."

"'Therefore, old friend, I write to warn you and those about you. I spoke against such a thing, saying that there was no proof this letter was sent by any but a madman or a fool, and that it was not right for a ruler to slay his subjects who had done no evil. For my speaking out I, too, travel with the regiment, having orders to seek out those who wrote this letter and ask of them how they presume to give orders to Pharaoh. In truth, once I received true copies of the letter and read it myself, I know that it did not say as Pharaoh claims. It is foolish and imprudent, but it makes no such demands.

"'However, I believe that Akhenaten plans to use it as a weapon against Hanish and the Domain of the Lion, and reduce them to nothing for their supposed treason. The reasons for this you already know, but now is the time that we feared, when temple strives against temple. I will do all that I can to delay events and speak against this folly, yet I believe that the demands of Pharaoh will be carried out. The regiments are under His command and will obey Him, no matter what orders they are given. Moreover, soldiers given free rein against a city will not hold back even if that outcome is horror. If all else fails, the portal stands, and it may please you to pass it lest what befalls those of the Lion Domain is worse.'"

Pahotep spoke quietly once the old priest was finished. "You trust this man?"

"I do. We feared this day might come." He rolled up the papyrus again and retied the tape. "Syamekh's predecessor was my good friend, and Syamekh too is trustworthy and a sensible, moderate man. He seeks for his God to be strong in all the lands of Napata, but as not a God alone. The Priests of Amun are greedier, but even they do not wish to destroy the other Gods. Syamekh saw the direction that Akhenaten and the priests of Aten-Ra began to tread almost three years ago, and wrote to me at that time, warning of the possibilities and dangers.

"The priests of Aten are fools, for the ordinary people will not give up their gods. Throwing down the Temple of Bastet and destroying the inner shrine will not convince others who worship the smaller gods to turn to Aten. Instead, it will persuade them to stand against this, lest their gods become angry. Civil war will likely weaken us, indeed that is what both Syamekh and I fear. There are strong countries about us who presently bow to Pharaoh. If Napata grows weak, they will rise against us."

Khepera shivered slightly. "I have read the histories. Yet the Hyksos rose and were crushed in a single battle."

"Because they rose too early against a Napata that was unified and strong, and ruled by a Pharaoh who was a soldier. Ahmose was a fighter and the son of a strong woman, who was daughter to another. He could give battle, knowing his mother and grandmother stood behind him, and that Napata would hold even if he fell."

"This time it is not so," Pahotep said thoughtfully. "Akhenaten is no soldier to lead his regiments into battle. His wives fight amongst themselves for precedence, as do his children. His parents are dead, he has named no heir, and he trusts no one save this priest of Aten. An ambitious man, yes, but if the army falls and soldiers of the enemy swarm across the land, such a man gathers all he can carry of his wealth and flees."

"Do you mean the priest or Pharaoh?" Remekh asked.

"The priest, but you have been in Pharaoh's court. Do you believe he will fight? That he will stand as shield to his people and die at need to save them?"

Tiaahn sucked in a breath. That was treason. And yet … And yet, he could not dissent. He, too, had seen enough of the ruler to believe that this man spoke truth. Akhenaten was a physically weak man of no known courage. He loved beauty, his chief wife, his God, and luxury. To keep most of those—the last in particular—and if his life were at risk, he could well betray everyone and scuttle away to safety. Remekh's gaze met his and he knew that the priest had read his thoughts.

"Tiaahn, you have spent time at the court. You know the thoughts of your master and you are in his confidence, or so he writes. What can you say of this?"

Tiaahn hesitated, then made up his mind. He wouldn't speak treason. But he'd listened to the soldiers. To report that would be doing no more than repeating common gossip—and that would still tell them all they needed to know.

"I traveled with my master and the Regiment of the Striking Hawk for half a moon," he said carefully. "Often I sat around camp fires with common soldiers of no rank. They talked and I listened, and I can tell you this. The soldiers believe that they are coming to Hanish to sack and raze the city. They talk of having slaves of their own who they can send to aid their families. They believe that with the whole of the Lion Domain trampled into the dust, slaves will be so cheap and plentiful that even common soldiers will be able to own several. They expect to loot with impunity, to rape and slay with the sanction of Pharaoh."

Remekh smiled. "Well told, lad. Now I shall tell you something neither you nor your master knew. Pahotep, Lord of the Lion Domain, received a threat from Pharaoh two months ago. This was sent directly to the Commander of the Theban Regiment. He sent an officer to the Temple of Bastet, one who broke in on the dawn prayers to the Lady to deliver his message."

Tiaahn bowed his head respectfully. "Will you share the warning with me, that I may return to tell my master?"

Remekh nodded. "'Thus said the voice of Akhenaten. That the God spoke to Him two years ago saying that all the world should worship the sun and the sun alone. Then said Pharaoh, my words that this should be so have been ignored and rejected. I shall show my people that Sun-Lord Aten-Ra is ruler over all the lands and that His power shall not be denied. In four moons the river floods again, before then shall the priestesses of Bastet attend His Temple and bow before Aten-Ra. They shall pray to the Sun before all the people—or Bastet's Shrine shall fall and those who support the Goddess shall be as the sands that blow. Here—and gone.'"

Tiaahn could hardly believe what he heard. Pharaoh, even Pharaoh, could not demand that one God bow to another. Another portion of the threat struck him and he looked up.

"Four moons he gave and two have gone. In another moon the Striking Hawk will be outside your gates. What will you do?"

Pahotep stared at a wall painting that showed the Goddess stooping over a wounded soldier who wore the insignia of the Lion Domain. It had been painted to celebrate Kahosen's deliverance in battle, and to mark the keeping of his oath. In the background the Temple of Bastet could be seen, with a golden cloud in the shape of the Goddess hovering above it.

"I do not know, and with the new information that Tiaahn brings there is another problem. If the Striking Hawk Regiment is ordered to surround the city, how then would Bastet's priestesses travel to Thebes or to Pharaoh's new city of Amarna? Will they be permitted to depart, or is this another way to keep them here and claim that they have not come to bow before Aten as was required of them?"

He stared around their small circle. "That seems to me like the cunning of one who wishes to be sure we give a pretext for our own destruction, one that can be cited in Pharaoh's courts as an excuse for his actions. But we have a moon remaining to consider our choices, at least."

"Are there any?" Khepera asked quietly. "Have we any choice save to surrender and be slaves, or fight and die?"

Remekh stood, holding up the scroll. "There is one other. When Syamekh says that if all else fails, the portal stands, and it may please us to pass it lest what befalls is worse." He paused and looked at them. "When he says that, he does not speak of death and a judgment and our reincarnation."

Khepera caught her breath. "He speaks of the dreams of Amatsunake?"

"Even so do I believe," Remekh confirmed.

There was a long silence as all but Tiaahn considered that. At last Pahotep answered his sister's questioning look.

"If there is no other choice and if the portal will provide an escape for all my people. I will not flee and leave them to the vengeance of Pharaoh. If Bastet approves our departure, if the lands beyond the portal are such that we can survive, and if the portal can even be opened. If it can and will accept us all, then I may agree. Remekh, let you search out further wisdom for this purpose.

"Tiaahn, rest the remainder of today. Tonight return to your master with all haste, tell him my words, and beg his aid in this once he arrives. Ask him to delay those who would act against us—as and how he can. Khepera, return to the Temple with Shardis and ask Bastet's will. And may Pharaoh change his mind so that we must not depart the land we love and be forever exiles."

He waited, but there was no reply. None there truly believed that could—or would—happen.

7

Tiaahn spent the rest of his day and his night in luxury such as he had never known. But as Remekh said, he might as well enjoy it while he could—which Tiaahn did. The old man spent his night writing, putting down all that he knew of the events in Hanish, possibilities arising, and his further theories regarding Amatsunake's knowledge that might save them.

He and Syamekh had discussed the latter in the past, both in person and by letter, and wondered if a portal might—or could—be opened as the sage claimed. They'd considered a few of the dangers, and been dubious. Now it looked as if they might learn about the dangers firsthand.

* * * *

Their dangers were both greater, and other than expected. Khamay had overplayed his hand and Akhenaten was in a chariot on the road with his elite guards, ten days behind the Regiment of the Striking Hawk, but moving slightly faster despite the luxury demanded at each stop. It had begun in private.

"Great One, word has reached me that the regiment travels well. In two moons at the most they will be in Hanish. The High Priest of Thoth—Aten curse him—remains with them."

"Good." Akhenaten considered the journey, the new sights, the excitement, and the peasants who would line the road cheering him were he with the regiment, and felt briefly wistful. It was from that vague dream of importance that he spoke.

"Perhaps I should have gone with them. Ahmose led his men into battle in his day; he has battle honors on half the stelae in Thebes. I am Pharaoh, and am not less than he. I could also lead my men and raise stelae to my victories."

Khamay was horrified. Akhenaten was a spindly weakling untrained in war, and—as all knew but none discussed, at least not where they could be overheard—he was also a coward, a dreamer, and a hypochondriac. He whined at the slightest scratch, convinced himself he was dying if he had a cold, and required pampering at all times. The idea of him on the battlefield was on a par with expecting a rabbit to lead a herd of gazelle to attack a lion. For the first time in many years, Khamay spoke without censoring his words.

"Lord, Great One, You are untrained in the arts of war. How would You conduct a battle? You would be killed, and who then would rule the land and glorify the God?"

He might have got away with the latter half, but the first part pricked Akhenaten savagely in his pride.

"Untrained? Do you mean that I could not arrange a battle, would not know which orders to give? Or perhaps you believe that my soldiers would not follow their Pharaoh?"

Khamay winced. Of course this idiot couldn't arrange a battle. He couldn't arrange a party in a tavern!

"Great One, the men would follow You anywhere You led." Ah, perhaps he hadn't put that very well, either.

"Anywhere I led? You mean that if I wasn't leading they might not obey my orders?" Akhenaten had drunk a little too much the previous night. His head hurt and his stomach felt sour—his mood was shifting to match it by the second.

"By the One God, Great One, no! The men would obey Your orders or die." Khamay despaired at what was coming out of his mouth. He was digging this hole deeper by the sentence.

"Oh, so now I must threaten them with death before they will obey me?" Akhenaten leapt to his feet, his voice a high-pitched squeak, his version of an outraged roar. "By Aten, you shall see how my soldiers rally to my call. Summon my personal guard! We ride for Hanish. Today. *Now!*"

Khamay protested and was overruled. He explained that it took far longer than an hour to make arrangements for Pharaoh to travel, and was overruled. He pleaded that Akhenaten would not like the privations of the road and his wives would be outraged. In return, he was told that wives would not be required on the road, and was he suggesting his Pharaoh wasn't enough of a man to handle minor discomforts? He was, of course, but he dare not say so. In any case, he was overruled. Khamay hastily tried to excuse himself from being swept up in this madness and was overruled.

Preparations took longer than an hour. It was, in fact, mid-morning the next day when they set out, Akhenaten leading in his favorite chariot. One hundred of his elite guard rode in columns on either side and behind him, with a straggling baggage train panting in the rear. Khamay rode in a chariot behind his master. He'd protested at that, for he loathed chariots and preferred a horse litter. But a litter could not keep up with Akhenaten's *glorious, triumphant, procession to battle.* Khamay saw the dangers of further protest from the look he received. He shut up and rode in the chariot.

He expected Akhenaten to surrender and return to his city with every hour that passed. It took a couple of days, but then he realized that Pharaoh was having fun. As quickly as everything had been assembled for this idiot procession, nothing had been omitted. Pharaoh had all his luxuries. He slept in soft bedding on a pallet in a fine tent. He ate and drank as well as he ever had—and someone had been very clever.

Khamay had no idea who, but unlike Akhenaten, this person *could* arrange a party. They'd made certain that scouts went ahead to every small village to tell the people to turn out and salute their ruler. And the people obeyed. They lined the road in small clumps of waving, bowing, loudly cheering peasants. Tossing flower petals before their ruler when they could find them, laying greenery across the road when they couldn't. Crying blessings, and shouting of their ruler's courage as he went to war. He listened to the current cries.

"Pharaoh! The Lord of the Sun goes to War, Honor to the Pharaoh! Aten bless Your courage, Great One! Defender of the God, Thy bravery is that of the Lion!"

Khamay's snort was hidden in the renewed noise as Akhenaten slowed to toss small scraps of silver to his subjects. They scrambled for them, shouting their praise and gratitude even louder. His idiot ruler would tire of this journey, he was certain of it. It only remained to ensure Pharaoh kept his pride still, when he turned back.

Akhenaten rode on. He adored the shouting peasants who adored him. He loved the idea that he was a rough and ready soldier riding to battle, with the courage of a lion in his heart and a song on his lips. The camp resounded to martial music and that was as it should be. Pharaoh went to war and he, too, was a soldier. He lay on his comfortable pallet at night, half-waking now and again to the challenge as the guard changed, and reveled in it all.

For the first time in his life, he felt like a true man. He should have started a war a long time ago. Once he'd dealt with this stupid Lord of a small, stupid, Domain that had dared challenge their Pharaoh, he'd take an interest in other lands. There were the Hittites and the Cymoryans, both unruly people. A good beating would bring them more into line. He woke sufficiently to summon his scribe.

"Write thus: I, Pharaoh, ride to war against a rebellious domain. Once they surrender I shall consider other lands that do not honor Our Throne and the Sun God as they should. They shall bow to Us both or be thrashed as a puppy is punished, to teach it manners and whose orders it obeys.

"Send a copy of that to Khamay, High Priest of Aten, that he may know my will."

Khamay read the copy of this decree over breakfast the next morning and groaned. Then he drank more wine and reflected. Despite this martial nonsense currently consuming him, Akhenaten remained a coward and a hypochondriac. All that was required was to make sure that he survived the upcoming battle, but suffered a minor injury: something messy and painful, but ultimately harmless. He'd run all the way back to his city and never set foot outside it again.

It wasn't actual war Pharaoh wanted, Khamay thought. It was the feeling of being a great leader of men, a soldier amongst soldiers. Khamay could make sure that Akhenaten had that without starting wars. He'd set up a special guard, one who would pretend not to recognize Akhenaten when he came amongst them wearing a soldier's garb. The ruler could swear, toss dice, drink unwatered wine, talk about women, and be a man amongst men all that he liked—so long as he was safe, worshipped Aten, and saw that all his people did, too, As long as Khamay became ever more rich and powerful.

He smiled briefly as he watched his ruler scatter another handful of silver scraps to wildly cheering, bowing peasants. He could even arrange small excursions outside the city so Akhenaten could do that too, since he enjoyed it so much. He glanced up at the sun. From what the scouts had told him earlier, they'd catch up with the Striking Hawk regiment by tomorrow night, and thank the God for it. He could delegate a lot of his work to the lesser Priests of Aten who traveled with the regiment.

His smile widened at the thought of Syamekh's dismay when he saw who joined them. He'd get some amusement out of this journey, after all. Twisting the High Priest of Thoth's nerves until he cracked would make this impossible trip worthwhile. Khamay chuckled to himself. Thoth's priests—the priests of Amun, too—were conspiring against him. Let them try. He would win in the end. He was smarter, more cunning and devious—and Pharaoh listened to him. Let them all beware; Syamekh in particular.

* * * *

Syamekh would have been slightly less upset than Khamay hoped. As it was, he was oblivious to Khamay's arrival—for a very good and sufficient reason: he wasn't there. Pharaoh had set out ten days behind the regiment, but a gap of that size is not closed in ten days, since those ahead are also moving. In fact, there was something of a coming to-gether, as the regiment neared the Lion Domain's borders when Pharaoh caught up. And the night before that, Tiaahn reached his master to give him the scroll penned by Remekh and tell him—very quietly—of all that had been discussed.

"Master, has all been well with you?"

Syamekh smiled. "Yes. Come to my tent and have something to eat. I'll post the guards further out so we are safe to talk. I always have my tent on the edge of the camp, so that can be done at need."

He called to a servant to bring food and wine, and led the way. Once inside, he spoke severely to Tiaahn (allowing it to appear that his original annoyance at the young man had lessened slightly and that, after all, Tiaahn would not be beaten again since he'd been thrashed in Thebes) as the platters and pitchers were laid out. That information would be gossiped about and would satisfy those who might wonder at Syamekh's hospitality. Once the servants were gone, he nodded to his junior.

"You look well, if weary. You found Remekh?"

"I found everyone you wished me to, Master. We talked, I told them all I knew, and Remekh sent a scroll." While they ate, he talked between bites. "Remekh called in the Lion Lord, his sister who is High Priestess to Bastet, and a child who accompanies her."

"A child?" Syamekh looked surprised.

"A clever and devout child, so I was told. She is about fourteen floods of age, and …" He considered how to put this. "It is possible she is being groomed to be High Priestess when Shrine's Lady departs. It was mentioned that the matriarch of the temple cats favors her, and the child was present during all of our discussions. She spoke little, but she appeared to understand what she heard."

Syamekh nodded. "And no ignorant child would understand political maneuverings. Nor would they have permitted her presence unless there was good reason. I suspect that you are right. Interesting." He considered that. "Yes, very interesting. How old is Shrine's Lady?"

"Perhaps sixty floods, Master."

"The child is not related to her?"

"I do not think so. The Lady Khepera is clearly of the old pure Napatan blood, and the child an outland cross. She is fairer of skin, and her hair and eyes are not black. Nor did the Lady seem more than fond of her; there was no doting such as a grandmother might make."

Syamekh chuckled softly. "Well noticed."

"No great credit to me, Master. I looked for it. I wondered until Remekh hinted to me why the child was present. But here is the scroll he wrote. And they talked of a portal that might be opened to allow them to escape."

"What did they say?"

"The Lion Lord said that if it could be opened, if it would permit all his people to flee, if they could survive when or where it took them, and if there was no other choice than to stay and die or be enslaved, then they would go."

Syamekh thrust down a sudden impulse to shout his satisfaction. Nothing was certain, but he and certain other priests had feared this day since dreamers in both temples began to dream of a Pharaoh gone mad, of domains destroyed in civil war. Of surrounding countries breaking free to turn on a greatly weakened Napata and make war.

They awoke to tell of shrines and temples that burned, priests who were slaughtered, and a people and a land weakened from within, then destroyed by enemies from outside their lands. And all the dreams began with the destruction of a small, obscure domain in the southwest—The Domain of the Lion. In all the dreams, this was the spark that lit the fire. Other domains would rise up against the wrongful destruction of one of their own. Some would stand behind the ruler, others against him, and the land would burn.

Until it actually happened, however, that fate might be turned aside, but a wise man took precautions. For a decade, Syamekh, Remekh, and Amun's High Priest had exchanged letters. They laid plans for a number of possibilities, intending to mitigate the destruction at the least, prevent it wholly at best. Syamekh re-read the scroll, and sighed silently. It looked as if the worst was about to arrive. He should find an excuse to travel to Hanish as fast as possible now. That would give him time to consult with Remekh. All he required was a good excuse, and he'd just thought of one.

"Tiaahn, see if you can find the commander's second-in-command. I need to talk to him."

"Yes, Master."

As he hurried away, he could hear Syamekh giving brisk orders to the servants and temple guards, something about preparing for a swift journey. When he returned with the commander's man, Syamekh stood in the middle of a whirl of people packing.

"Greetings, Noble Tahrishep. As may have come to your ears, Pharaoh gave me a letter from certain citizens of the city of Hanish. Now that we are closer to this city, it is my duty to travel ahead to make inquiries on this subject before the disruption caused by the regiment's arrival."

The noble Tahrishep blinked. He did know of the letter, for his superior had a copy. And it was true that the arrival of even a peaceful regiment outside a small city caused disruption. The arrival of the Striking Hawk regiment to join that of Thebes would almost certainly cause not only disruption, but havoc, panic, and chaos.

"I can see that," he agreed. "It would be easier to find the citizens who sent the letter if everyone in the city is not running in circles."

"Quite so, noble Tahrishep. You have the wisdom of a commander of men. Therefore, since the city is only another twenty days' travel, it is my duty to go ahead and do as Pharaoh commanded."

Tahrishep bowed. "The will of Pharaoh is the will of His soldiers. I shall tell my commander of your plans. When will you depart?"

"At dawn."

"Very well. May your God watch over your road."

He bowed and marched off, to become embroiled in a dispute amongst officers that caused him to forget Syamekh's plans. Not that he thought them important anyhow. So a pampered, over-fed priest traveled ahead to do something Pharaoh wanted. The priest was taking a few guards and servants, and a handful of baggage animals. Nothing in that plan was of major importance, or anything that his commander had to know without delay.

On the camp edge, Syamekh left not just at dawn but a little before. In the half-light he walked his mount quietly along the grassy side of the winding, rutted road, making neither noise nor dust. Behind him trailed twenty baggage mules—none overloaded, fifty guards—all silent, and twelve servant priests—all irked at the early start. Tiaahn stayed well behind, watching to see if anyone noticed or followed them. No one paid them the slightest attention.

Syamekh smiled as Tiaahn cantered up mid-morning.

"No one in sight?"

"No one. Camp broke an hour after we left. They're on the road behind us. Master?"

"Yes?"

"When I came this way before, I was advised of a shorter way. It isn't practical for a regiment, but it could save us two days."

"Then when we reach that place, take the lead and we'll follow. The more time we save, the better for those in Hanish."

They camped that night and while everyone was weary, no one was exhausted. The same could not be said for the High Priest of Aten, who was exactly the sort of priest Tahrishep believed. He sat in the chariot since he was too exhausted to stand, as Pharaoh thundered into the regiment's camp. Trumpets alerted the guards, who, hardly believing, rushed to inform the Commander that—if they were correct and it was hardly likely—some fools were announcing that the Lord of the Two Rivers was about to enter their camp.

There was considerable confusion, which lasted for a good many hours. In the midst of it Khamay staggered from his seat and went in search of his priests. He brushed off their greetings and exclamations.

"Where is Syamekh?"

"He always camps in the same place, to the far side of the horse lines, High Priest."

"Show me."

They did, to find it deserted. No one seemed to know where the High Priest of Thoth was at the moment. Khamay stamped to the commander's tent.

The commander looked at him blankly. Must be polite to the man, for he had great influence with the ruler, but how could the commander be expected to know where some priest had got to? He wasn't part of the regiment, just traveling with them for his safety.

Tahrishep heard the question. "Ah, High Priest, I can tell you." He turned to his commander. "I regret I had not time to inform you of this. I have been busy. The priest approached me last night to say that he would ride ahead. He had orders from Pharaoh to make inquiries concerning a letter. He felt he should investigate before we arrive and there is some—disruption."

The corners of the commander's mouth quirked upwards a little. "I see. There is your answer, High Priest of Aten-Ra. Your colleague has gone ahead. You'll meet him in Hanish."

Khamay glared at Tahrishep. "How long to reach the city?"

Tahrishep had no time for civilians. Besides, he didn't like this one, and Syamekh—while a priest—had at least been courteous.

"He thought twenty days, High Priest. Myself, I think he'll be only a day or so before us. The roads are not good, and it will take us perhaps another twenty-five days."

Khamay smiled finally. "My gratitude for your information, noble officer."

His tone was faintly sarcastic, but these idiots wouldn't notice that. Soldiers were stupid or they wouldn't be soldiers. He left the command tent, not noticing the scowls that followed him. His personality was not the sort that won friends—but then with his power he didn't care. Syamekh wouldn't be able to arrive early enough to cause any trouble, and that was what counted. He would have been less pleased and more enlightened if he could have seen his enemy.

* * * *

For ten days, Syamekh and his men traveled at a speed that would have surprised Tahrishep, who considered all priests soft and out of condition. Syamekh had given the figure of twenty days so that it would be passed on. He'd always known he might need to travel more quickly and quietly brought along five extra baggage mules—big, strong, fit animals—and when they packed that first morning, the loads for the original fifteen were split among the current twenty. They could move faster, need fewer breaks to rest, and continue on the road for longer.

His guard had an additional twelve mounts, as well. Carefully selected to be nothing much to look at, but the sort that could stay with a fast pace. If a beast went lame, it could be left and one of the spare mounts saddled. They moved at a steady pace, allowing the mounts and pack animals to rest at intervals. Nonetheless, they made almost twice the regiment's speed. The short cut put them a further two days ahead. Hanish appeared on the horizon ten days after they'd separated from the regiment.

Syamekh halted his men as soon as the city came in sight. "Set up the small tent. We'll eat and allow the animals a rest, and Tiaahn and I must change into official robes. I want no one to think that we priests belong to the Sun-God." He grinned wryly. "Where possible, I prefer not to be pelted with rotten fruit."

Tiaahn nodded agreement and a small ripple of laughter went around the group. The tent was used for its intended purpose, and the horses and mules were rubbed down and allowed to drink. Syamekh emerged from the tent in his priest's garb and looked towards the city. They would be there well before dusk. They could find an inn, stable the beasts, bathe, and Tiaahn could be sent to inform those who needed to know that Syamekh had arrived. After that, events were in the lap of the God.

8

Pahotep heard the news of Syamekh's arrival with relief. He sent servants running to tell Remekh, and to ask Khepera to attend the compound. He had no idea of what help this High Priest could be, but he was Remekh's comrade so he probably wasn't useless. He might have more up-to-date information, and it was possible that together he and Remekh could find a way out for all of the Lion Domain. He thought of that as he gave further orders. His servants blinked at some of them, but obeyed.

Syamekh entered almost two hours later, with Tiaahn close behind him. Pahotep considered the young man and nodded.

"Welcome to both of you. I expect, High Priest, you will wish to have your assistant with you. Rooms have been made ready. Remekh tells me you need space, peace, and privacy to research, and all you need shall be granted. Only tell what you wish and it shall be done."

Remekh arrived and greeted everyone, followed by Khepera's arrival with Shardis. Pahotep had wine and food brought in, guards stationed down the corridor where they would not overhear the discussion, and Pahotep waited in some impatience.

Remekh spoke to the point finally. "It is fortunate that I had already been researching Amatsunake's work." He turned to Syamekh. "I believe some of his dream discoveries may tie in with Kahosen of this House. There are scrolls here from Kahosen's time, and they explain something we had never understood. Amatsunake was here for almost five years as a guest of Kahosen before he returned to his temple and died there. Kahosen liked the old man sufficiently to allow him quarters at court, a pension, and assistants so that he could study."

He held up two scrolls. "In these he has gone farther than we realized. He has left calculations, diagrams, incantations, and many accounts of dream journeys."

Syamekh's face lit with excitement. "Is there enough information to open a portal?"

"Apparently Amatsunake came here because he thought a portal might be opened from this place. The land and its aspects are propitious according to his records and, most interestingly, the Temple and Shrine of Bastet lie in the center, so I believe there may be a chance. It will require further investigation, but—how far ahead of the regiment are you? How much time might we have before they arrive?" Remekh questioned.

Tiaahn answered. "After they arrive they must settle in, make a longer-term camp to check their gear and battle order—even if they do plan an attack the day after—and they'll first approach you, My Lord, with the formal announcement of intent." He looked at Pahotep. "After that, it depends on how long you can keep them talking."

Syamekh's look was sour. "Not long. Khamay has been given much of Pharaoh's power, and he has his own sword to sharpen."

"Never mind politics, we'll have to deal with that once the regiment arrives," Pahotep said impatiently. "What I need is information. How long before they appear?"

Tiaahn calculated. "I would say another fifteen days at the least, Lord. It depends on their speed, but so far as I know we are certainly that far ahead of them and I think it unlikely they'll speed up. If they slow, then we could have more time."

Khepera inclined her head, acknowledging Syamekh. "I do not know how much you know of my Goddess, High Priest. She has been worshipped in Hanish long before Kahosen. Before his vision we already had a small shrine and several priestesses. They specialized in healing—and," she paused significantly, "in dreaming for those who required information or suggestions as to a path to follow to achieve desired results."

Syamekh looked thoughtful. "That was written in some of our scrolls. But they said that the line of women who dreamed had died out. Are you saying this is not so?"

Khepera smiled. "I am saying that we have a true-dreamer in Bastet's Temple. So far she has dreamed only small dreams, little of major use, or of more than a few days into the future. I believe her ability was sent to us at this time for a reason, and I think you can make use of her." She motioned to Shardis who stood and walked over to stand between Syamekh and Remekh.

"I only discovered this recently. Shardis dreams true. Now and again she has been able to tell us of the future, but she also has an odd form of the talent. In this other type of dream she does not recall what she dreams, but if while she dreams she is touched and asked what she sees, she will answer."

Remekh looked at the girl, who stared back unafraid. "That is a linking talent. It is rare, very rare. But with someone who can link touching her, they may be even able to see her dreams. A number of priests and priestesses in several temples, including my own, would be able to link with her."

He held up a finger in warning. "This ability is listed in the scrolls in the great Temple of Thoth. But have a care with this gift. It burns out. It arises, they say, only at such times as there is great danger to a wide area, and once the danger is passed, the gift disappears, often never to return."

Syamekh nodded. "I, too, have read that. But you overlook a point, old friend. If the child has the gift, then what does it tell us about this time and place?"

Khepera's voice dropped to a soft near-whisper. "That great danger threatens us. That such a gift may be invaluable in opening this portal. If the gift has appeared, it is likely that we *must* open the portal and chose a new land in which to survive."

Syamekh bowed his head. "Even so, Shrine's Lady." He turned to Shardis. "Will you help us?"

"Yes."

"That is all? Just 'yes'?"

"Yes."

Smiles surrounded her.

Shardis looked at Khepera. They assumed she was only a child who did not understand the serious threat against Hanish. She understood. She had dreamed for the last three nights and knew what she would be asked to do today. In her dreams the Goddess had asked first. If she said yes to the Lady of Claws, after seeing many things that might come to pass—and how those she loved could die—then she need say no more than the single word when asked by people.

She spoke gently into their discussion, the words cutting through Tiaahn's description of how they had left the camp. "Pharaoh arrived there the night after you left."

"What?" Khepera was stunned.

"I dreamed. I only just remembered." She hadn't, but the Goddess told her she would know when to share what she had dreamed five nights earlier, and she had waited.

"What did you see?"

"He rode into a camp in a chariot. A fat man came with him in another chariot." She described Khamay very accurately. "He was angry and tired but he asked for Syamekh, and he was angrier when he found Syamekh had left camp. There were lots of guards and a whole lot of baggage." She looked at Khepera. "That's all I remember."

It started another discussion. Kahoret entered in the middle, leaning heavily on Neshang's shoulder. Pahotep studied the pain-filled way he still moved and sighed.

"I suppose, cousin, that now you're here, you may stay, but I hope you have a contribution to pay for your suffering?"

Kahoret smiled as Neshang lowered him to a seat and sat cross-legged on the floor before him. "I may well have, cousin. Listen, I've been a soldier for quite a few years. I've heard everything that's been happening and one thing is clear to me—as a soldier. This portal is our only chance if Pharaoh comes against the Lion Domain. Let you, cousin, Khepera, and your advisers try to hold off death, disaster, and the armies of the ruler. But if all that fails and we must flee, then there are preparations that should be made."

Shardis nodded. "Gather beasts," she said. "I dreamed that."

Kahoret looked at her approvingly. "Yes, you'd know anyway. If danger comes to a village, you pick up everything valuable and portable, run and hide, don't you?"

Shardis shook her head. "Grandfather said if you have things already hidden away and you run to them, then you don't lose them when thieves come."

"No, you don't." He turned to Pahotep. "That's even shrewder. Tell the people that it's a precaution, but before the regiment is due, have them drive their beasts to the other side of Hanish, close to the city. The Wadi of Baboons would be a good place. It leads right to the southern gate on that side, but the land about it is very rough. Soldiers may surround the city, but they are unlikely to place men down in the wadi. The animals can be driven fast through there and into the city. The bottom is a layer of sand, not so deep they will bog down, but deep enough to cushion their hooves—meaning that they can move swiftly and without stumbling—and in greater silence."

His cousin nodded slowly. "That seems sensible. What else should I have the people do?"

"Tell them to gather all their portable valuables, and bring them for safekeeping to the Temple. Gold, jewels, silver, weapons. Anything easily carried and of value should be stored there. Khepera's priestess can keep tallies so we know who owns what. But if we must use the portal and the Temple is the center, then we'll have the valuables right there." He smiled. "And tell the women to bake."

The men stared at him while Khepera laughed. "Yes, brother, tell them to bake. Not the usual baking, but journey bread. They should make cheese, too, hard cheese, not the soft. And they are to dry as much meat as they may lay hands on. They're preparing supplies that will last without rotting for moons, and they are to be stored carefully. Let them suspect that you fear a siege. It could be true, and we'll be prepared for either event."

"Yes, and tell them to make up packs that they and all their family can carry, and packs for any beasts they can load. Let each pack have a few valuables, clothing, bedding, and something in which to cook," Tiaahn added.

"No child will be able to carry that sort of load," Pahotep protested.

"No, but they can carry a few scraps of silver, a gold ring perhaps, and their clothing wrapped in a good blanket. That weight even small children should be able to bear if they are healthy and have seen five or more floods."

Shardis piped up. "I was that old when I first came to the Temple and I could have carried a pack like that for a flood before."

Pahotep threw up his hands. "Then it is done. Once we're finished talking today I'll have my guards go quietly to all the villages and about the city. Fifteen days before the regiment arrives, you think? Hmmm, I shall send scouts to watch for the army. A regiment will travel here by the main road, for the land becomes rougher the closer you are to Hanish. If they want to keep the regiment together they'll have to use the road. We'll know when their scouts approach."

He turned to Kahoret. "How far ahead will they send scouts?"

"No more than two days ahead. Likely only one, but count on two." Kahoret recalled what Shardis had said. "On the other hand, if Akhenaten is with them, they'll opt for safety. Count on three days, better not to take chances."

"Good. I'll suggest people start taking precautions as soon as our men have seen Pharaoh's scouts five days away and returned to let us know. Now, what can we say to our beloved ruler when he arrives? What protests can we legitimately make, and what about this letter?" Syamekh removed the copy from his travel-pouch and read it aloud again.

Pahotep groaned. "Idiots! I know two of those who signed it. Merchants, worried about the increasing trouble with the Theban Regiment. One of them had a stall overturned in the marketplace during a brawl between soldiers. Most of his goods vanished by the time my guards broke up the fight. The other …" He grinned. "That horse-faced son of his was propositioned by a soldier—a man with little taste it would seem—or one with a sense of humor. The boy panicked, rushed home to his father and exaggerated. I looked into the matter, but no harm was done. No one laid a hand on the lad and probably never intended to do so."

"Lad? A child?" Syamekh asked.

"No, I say that because it seems to be how his father thinks of him—it is certainly how he speaks. Always 'my boy' this, 'my young lad' that. In fact, the young man has seen twenty floods of the great river, or even two or three more."

"Old enough to handle a proposition, then?"

"Apparently not." Pahotep's tone was tart with annoyance. "And now his father went over my head to Pharaoh. Of all the stupid, idiotic … How does he think any ruler is going to react to being told his job, or to the suggestion that he's breaking his own laws? Can't we round up the ones who signed this and have them waiting when Pharaoh arrives? Tell him I formally renounce my rule over them and that for their insult to the Great One they are his to do with as he wills?"

"It might buy us time," Remekh said thoughtfully. "Particularly if they be given a huge show trial. Atepmut would love that."

"And if they are convicted?" Khepera asked quietly. "If they insulted Pharaoh deliberately then it's treason. You know some of the penalties that can be invoked for that."

Everyone shivered.

Pahotep looked at his sister. "Better five fools die than everyone in the Lands of the Lion dies or is enslaved," he told her. "If they're convicted, I can ensure they're given a quick death. But Remekh speaks truly, it could buy us quite a lot of time. And then too …"

"Then, too," Syamekh cut in. "Akhenaten loves luxury and he'll find less of it than he's used to here. I doubt he brought any wives. He also bores easily, and once the trial is over there is the chance that he'll pack up and go home—especially if the letter writers are convicted, and if we all grovel enough to make him feel like a real ruler and a true man."

Kahoret stood, his hand on Neshang's shoulder for support. "It is the start of a plan, but I think you should still warn the people to prepare. It's early in the season to move the animals to the far side of the city, but farther out there'll be grazing, and they'll be in position to move into Hanish quickly if something goes wrong. The people should still make up packs as well, but they could leave preparing the journey food until we get some idea of Pharaoh's intentions."

"People don't like to doing anything twice," Shardis said. "If it doesn't happen immediately they think it won't happen at all. If you make them bake and pack and then say it wasn't necessary, they won't bother the next time you tell them to do it."

Kahoret grinned. "She's right. So we move the beasts and leave them, we tell the people to make up packs but say they are to be left waiting, that way even if things drag on they're still available. Those with wealth can afford to leave packs sitting, those who're poor can pack in minutes. Baking can be left. Most of that would take a day or two, and with the Goddess's aid we'll have that much warning. Or I'll pray it's so," he added soberly.

"Right, let's get started. Sister, be ready for the wealthy who begin bringing valuables into the Temple. Organize your priestesses to list everything brought in with three tallies: one for the owner, one for the Temple, and," he grinned, "one for my domain scribes, in case of argument."

"I'll have Isara do that; she loves organizing and she's good at it. It'll also keep her from trudging about wringing her hands and prophesying doom," Khepera added acidly.

She liked Isara, but after the business with the war leopard, she needed someone strong within the Temple to back her. Now might not be the time to disrupt Temple protocol, but no time was good, and if anything happened to her in the next few moons, she didn't want Isara throwing away all they had.

She couldn't yet announce Shardis as the next Shrine's Lady, although she'd known from the day she found the child that was what she'd become. It was still too early, for the older priestesses wouldn't follow a girl. She would have to decide what to do soon. Isara had never been formally announced as Second in Power, only assuming that position when Khepera was absent, and the priestess wasn't a spiteful woman. If the right person was chosen formally as heir, Isara would obey her without question.

Khepera departed, the girl following, while Pahotep turned his attention to his cousin. "Return to your bed. If you have any more soldierly insights, send Neshang. Remekh, you and Syamekh and Tiaahn, if you will, may retire to your rooms. I'll round up these five fools and talk to Noble Judge Atepmut."

Pahotep sighed. All he'd ever wanted to do was run his domain without disorder, see that his people were kept safe, and worship his goddess. It occurred to him that the Goddess probably had the same duties—barring that last. He hoped that she'd aid him in his.

9

The city hummed as busily as bees in rich pasture. In the far villages, sheep and cattle moved to the south as small streams of them gathered into larger rivers. Herders arrived and waited at the southern pastures; it was early but there was grass and there could be more if it rained. A lot of prayers went up that it would, and it seemed the Goddess heard. There was rain: a long, steady, soaking fall that brought the grass leaping upwards with the rising sun. Oddly, it fell only in that one area.

In their houses, people made up packs, and held back the animals that would carry possessions, or those who could not travel on their own.

Packs accumulated in house corners, were tripped over, moved, tripped over and moved again while people cursed packs, rulers, and life in general. Old people talked—they were the repositories of the ancient stories, the ones who remembered tales told by grandfathers, some tales handed down from *their* grandfathers—and some granddaughters who listened made further preparations.

It was within the memory of that fifth generation before the present day, that men of the Lion had gone with Kahosen to fight the Hittites. It was within that same memory that some of the wild tribes of the south had come north to attack enemies they believed were weakened.

The city merely closed the gates, but villages in the path of the tribes had no gates. Many died quickly, and others wished they had. The people of the smaller, poorer villages could not read or write and they had no scrolls telling of the domain's history. But they had memories which were passed on, and as always, while some ignored the stories, others heeded them and prepared. Their families would have the better chance of survival. Evolution favors commonsense and a willingness to learn from history.

Over it all Pahotep watched. He rode quietly through the gathering herds, talked to the herdsmen and headmen of small villages, and worried about what would happen to his people. Where were Pharaoh and his soldiers? Would Akhenaten listen to the Lion Lord? Or would the priest of Aten-Ra sway him to attack Hanish without talking first? Pahotep looked at the people as they moved their herds, opened their marketplace stalls, lived their lives, and feared for them at the hands of a man who was a self-centered, pampered fool.

* * * *

Khamay rode his mount beside Akhenaten and smiled, a small vicious smile of pleasure and—he thought—of triumph. He had managed to poison the ruler's mind sufficiently that even if the Great One parleyed with the Lion Domain, the negotiation would end in an ultimatum, one that no Domain Lord would accept. Akhenaten could legitimately fall on the lands of the Lion and take all that was portable. Khamay would ensure that a fair proportion of the loot accrued to the Temple of Aten—and to himself.

"You believe that they plan to join those who would oppose me in this matter, Khamay?" Akhenaten sought reassurance.

"Oh indeed, Great One. They have not Your vision, Your wisdom, or the favor of the God as You do." Khamay provided it.

"They are a small poor domain, and far from Thebes. There is little harm they could do."

"All true, Wise One. But they can urge, encourage, and support the belief of those who worship Amun that their cause is right. That Aten-Ra is no more than one God amongst the others, and no more powerful."

The Pharaoh scowled. "Untrue. He is preeminent. Lord of the heavens. He shall have his rightful place as the one God. All shall bow to him and once they have done so, once they have had time to understand what he is, then …"

"Then He shall rule everything," Khamay cut in softly. "Best that You not reveal Your plans as yet, Great One. As You have discovered already, there are fools who have not Your far-seeing wisdom."

Akhenaten puffed out his spindly chest. "Even so, Khamay. But," he glanced about him and rode closer to the High Priest even as he lowered his voice, "once all bow to Aten and the people have had time to become used to the order of things, then we shall have no need of other Gods. Isn't that so?"

"It is, Wise One. Once those who foment discontent are broken to Your harness then Aten shall reign supreme. There shall be no other Gods, and You shall be the Great One, the Divine Son of Aten-Ra. Your name shall live a thousand generations. Your descendants shall rule all the Lands and worship You after Your great Father."

Akhenaten smirked. "I shall ascend after my death to sit at my Father's right hand. Together we shall watch over my lands. My undying ka shall protect my people and they shall pray to me."

"That is so, Great One. Your tomb too shall outlast that of all other Pharaohs. It shall be marvelous, a thing at which all the people wonder."

"Yes. I wonder how much wealth the Lion Domain will give me in fines for their rebellious behavior. If the sum is sufficient, I could build my city more quickly. I plan to name it Armana, you know."

"Yes, Wise One, so I have heard."

Akhenaten jerked his head around to stare at Khamay. "Heard? From whom? I have told no one! Are there spies in my court, eavesdroppers in my walls that you know of a thing only I know?" He bared his teeth in a snarl. "By Aten, if there are those who spy on me I'll find and exterminate them! Tell me now, priest, how is it that you know the name of my city that will be the jewel of all lands?"

Khamay hid his dismay. The man was becoming crazier by the minute. Would his plans to make himself rich and powerful on the back of his master's infatuation with Aten founder on the rock of that obsession? He made his voice quiet and soothing.

"I do not say that there are no spies, Great One. Assuredly some of the Domain Lords will have men at Your court that report what You say. Yet the name came from no spies. You told me in a moment of Godlike inspiration. Do You not recall? You said that Aten Himself had come to You in a dream, called You his son, and told You the city's name. You said it should be called Armana, and it would be a monument to You and the God forever."

In fact, Khamay reflected, Pharaoh had merely said the name in the midst of a long talk about the city. The Temple to Aten that would be its center, with the grand palace surrounded by ponds, airy walks, and raised balconies to catch the breezes. But Akhenaten did like to think that all his ideas were inspired. And the man was quite suggestible, if you put your suggestions the right way. Khamay schooled his face to an admiring and awed look.

"Oh, yes, of course. Yes, how else would you know? You are not one of those who spy on your ruler. I trust you, Khamay. You shall always have a place at my side, even when I ascend to be with Aten-Ra."

A most unpleasant shiver slide down Khamay's spine. His ruler was likely to die long before his high priest planned to depart the earth. The murder of wives, pets, slaves—and certain individuals the ruler felt that he would require with him in the afterlife—often marked the death of a Pharaoh.

Khamay would rather live comfortably—if unmemorably—for another twenty or thirty years. He had no desire to meet the strangling cord prematurely; he intended to die at a great age, mourned by all his friends and junior priests. His smile was sickly—not that Akhenaten noticed.

"You do a humble man more honor than is justified, Great One. I am but a vessel of the God. You will live for many years and I will be an old man, failing in health and wisdom. I would recommend a younger man who may sit below Your seat by the God. One who would never presume on Your favor."

"You may be right, Khamay. It is good that you think of your ruler and not your own aggrandizement."

"I think always of You, Wise One. The God commands me."

Khamay hid a relieved sigh. That had Akhenaten off the subject just now, but the man was obsessive. You could turn his mind to other ideas temporarily but he tended to come back to them sooner or later. And that was one thought Khamay would prefer that Pharaoh forgot. He'd have to make plans as soon as this campaign was over and they had what wealth the Lion Domain possessed. It could be tricky, but perhaps he should start influencing his ruler to consider naming a successor. Suggest a man who'd be guided by Aten's High Priest. Then if Khamay was to be added to the tomb-goods, the new ruler would countermand that.

"Great One?"

"Yes?"

"Have You considered taking a new wife? It is two floodings since the beautiful one died." That had been when Pharaoh turned to Aten, when grief had given way to a single-minded fixation, and it was possible that this would be loosened a little if a new woman shared Pharaoh's bed.

"Why?"

"Well, Wise One, You have never spoken of Your heir. If You do not sire sons to take the throne after Your death—may that be long averted—then there could be strife in the land."

"I shall be sitting with my Father. There shall be no strife. I shall forbid it."

Really, the man was becoming crazier. "Of course, Great One, but the people depend on Your wisdom and guidance. Is it not better that they should know Your wishes clearly?"

Akhenaten considered his words. For himself, he'd like to see any-one on the throne but the man most Lords of the Domains would chose if there was no clear succession.

Ahmose was Akhenaten's younger half-brother by a subordinate wife of his father's. She was not of the bloodline of either Akhenaten or his sire Amenophis the Third, but she could trace her lineage back to the Ahmose, who in a single battle had defeated the Hyksos. That combination would be sufficient for the Domain Lords. This generation's Ahmose was young, sensible, intelligent, good-looking, practical, and thought that the Gods should be worshiped and otherwise a man left them alone. A perfect ruler so far as most of Napata was concerned. If anything happened to the current Pharaoh in the next few floodings and he died without stating his heir, there was a strong likelihood that Ahmose would take the Cobra Throne.

Khamay really didn't want this to happen. Apart from knowing that the man disliked and distrusted him, Khamay would lose much of his power. And if Akhenaten left an order that his High Priest was to join him in the tomb as chief adviser, Ahmose was not the man to prevent that. Khamay reconsidered that thought. Truthfully, Ahmose would probably make certain that it happened—even if his predecessor hadn't left specific instructions. No, he must persuade Akhenaten to name an heir, and take another Royal Wife as well.

"There is Tashotet, Wise One. She is young and she admires You greatly. I have seen her watching You when You give judgments."

The girl was young, and better yet, she had something of the look of the Beautiful One who was gone.

"Perhaps. Yes, you may be right, Khamay. I should consider a new Royal Wife. But not now. I am hot, tired, thirsty, and we shall camp for the night."

"Right now, Great One?"

"Of course now. That is what I said. I want to bathe, rest in the shade—and get off this Aten-damned horse for a while."

Khamay walked his mount back along the column of soldiers to pass on that order. The regiment's commander said nothing, but his look was eloquent. Khamay shrugged.

"I know. It's another two hours before we'd normally camp, but it's his order. He wants a drink, a bath, shade—and from what he says, to ease his sore arse on some soft cushions."

"Don't we all?" The commander was resigned to obedience. He had no choice; the word of Pharaoh was his order to obey. But as he passed the command up and down the line, and as the regiment swung off the road to make camp far too early, he muttered irritably under his breath. A journey that should have taken only another fifteen or twenty days from the time that priest of Thoth had gone ahead—and which now looked likely to be twice that if his ruler didn't stop camping early and pampering himself.

* * * *

In Hanish the population hoped that the pampering would continue, or rather, that hope *would* have been so—if they'd known why it was taking so long for the Striking Hawk regiment to arrive. They didn't, but they weren't complaining—or not too loudly. In the time given them thus far, they had most of the sheep, goats, cattle, donkeys, and breeding horses safely hidden on the far side of the city, in the rough lands around the Wadi of Baboons.

A large group of skilled masons went to the roughest area of land near the Wadi of Baboons, land within half an hour's walking distance of the back gate of the city. Under Pahotep's orders and Khepera's supervision, they added a complex of twenty rooms driven deep into a cliff face. This would have two disguised entrances, air holes driven into adjacent caves, and would hold some five hundred children and fifty adults to care for them. Water jars would be held in niches there, and grain and other suitable food placed in storage.

If the city was about to be surrounded, the children of outlying areas would be brought here. After the army left, they would be able to regain their inheritances, or if not, they would not be enslaved and could, in time, find other homes.

Kahoret took Neshang and ten of his own men to round up the letter writers. They were not happy and said so in long, loud, whining tones that set everyone's teeth on edge. When the protests were made for about the twentieth time, Kahoret turned sarcastic as he recited their own words back to them.

"We have done nothing wrong. Why are we seized and dragged to the Lion Court? What charge is brought against us? How about promiscuous letter writing, mailing without license, and failure to declare lack of intelligence? How about endangering the city of Hanish and the entire Domain of the Lion?"

The merchant, Aashep, gaped at him. "What?"

Abruptly Kahoret lost all patience. "You halfwit, did it never occur to you that rulers don't like to be lectured? You and your fellow idiots sent a letter to Pharaoh, didn't you?"

Aashep drew himself up. "We did. We are citizens of Napata. Pharaoh allowed the Theban Regiment to get out of hand. They sit about outside the city, causing trouble, propositioning innocent lads, brawling in the market, insulting and threatening honest merchants until for fear of them prices are lowered."

And that was probably what upset this bunch of shopkeepers the most, Kahoret thought.

"The regiment answers to the ruler. He should know how they behaved, and then he'd call them back to Thebes. We did nothing wrong. We had a right to let him know what was going on."

Kahoret looked at the flushed face; the man was almost panting with anger and self-righteousness. Behind him the other merchants were nodding and mumbling agreement.

"Oh, you had the right," Kahoret said. "And Pharaoh has a right, too. A right to call your letter treason, to have you charged and if convicted, to have your sentence carried out here and now, before he returns to his palace." He stared at the gaping, suddenly terrified faces. "If you felt you had just cause for complaint, all you had to do was approach Pahotep. Or bring a case before Pharaoh's judge in Hanish, the Noble Atepmut." He snorted in disgust.

"Instead you write a letter suggesting that Pharaoh is breaking his own laws. That he's incompetent and can't control his regiment, that he's ignorant of what's going on, and that you, the clever merchants, are going to set him straight." Kahoret threw up his hands. "Now he's coming here, and you'll be able to do that. I'm just happy not to be wearing your sandals when you explain what you meant to an outraged ruler whom you insulted. But I don't think he'll be interested in hearing it. I hope you all have wills."

He wished he'd kept his mouth shut after that. The wailing and lamentations lasted all the way to the court cells, where the five merchants were locked up and a guard placed in the corridor outside.

The guards, too, wished to be elsewhere. The merchants turned from wailing about ill fortune to complaining about the lack of amenities, and they were equally irritating on that subject. That was substantially compounded when their families arrived, until the guards were undecided between earplugs and mass murder!

* * * *

Pahotep consulted Barhket, his scout commander. "There is no sign of the Striking Hawk as yet?"

The scout, a hard man in a hard land, was baffled. "No, Lord. I sent two men dressed as hunters down the main road to see if they could find any sign of the regiment. They traveled six days down that road and saw no one, neither scouts nor regiment. I have no idea what has happened that the Hawks are so delayed."

Syamekh, who was listening, chuckled. "If little Shardis is right, I may be able to enlighten you. Our great ruler, that soldier amongst soldiers, has found that the journey is long, exhausting, and not as much fun as he'd anticipated. I wager the regiment's commander by now is fit to be stewed. Akhenaten will have them camping earlier and earlier each day while he lolls in the shade, drinks heavily to alleviate his boredom, and has relays of servants carrying water for baths to cool his sweating body."

Barhket stared. "But Lord Priest, he is coming here. Surely he would not wish to be so long on the road that he gives us time to make preparations?"

"He won't care if you're making preparations to open the gates and deck him in garlands while dancing naked—or commit mass suicide in the Temple grounds. What he cares about is his comfort while he travels."

Barhket shook his head in disbelief.

"Listen, Commander of Scouts, you are thinking as a soldier of the Lion. Pharaoh is not and never has been a soldier. He's lived all his life in a luxury you cannot imagine. His will is the will of the Gods, so if he says to the regiment commander that they make camp early there is only one reply the man can give, understand?"

"Yes, Noble Priest."

"Yes, and that's what the commander says. 'Yes, Great One.' He may not agree, but he knows better than to say so." He grinned at Barhket. "As you do." He received a nod and a grin in return.

Pahotep smiled. "Commander of Scouts, return to your duties and be vigilant. On you and your men may depend the lives of the Lion Domain."

Barhket saluted and passed Kahoret in the doorway. Syamekh saw his exasperated expression and guessed the cause.

"Do I gather the merchants don't understand why they've been detained, don't approve, and are revolting?"

"Utterly!" Kahoret confirmed wearily.

The High Priest of Thoth snickered. "Make sure they're kept where we can find them. If we haul them out to Akhenaten the second he appears we may give him something to think about other than a siege or a concerted attack on Hanish. He's not a fast thinker at any time, and if we're handing over the criminals and swearing our eternal loyalty to the throne at the same time, it could distract him sufficiently to make him think twice about Khamay's plots."

"What else is he interested in?" Pahotep asked.

"His scheme to build a new city to the glory of Aten. He has the first couple small buildings up already and often rides out to spend a night drinking and visualizing the completed city. But nothing has been built on the place chosen, so there are no good roads. They'll have to be built once the heavier stones are ready to be moved on site, and I've seen some of the architect's plans. Akhenaten's going to bankrupt the country if he builds on the scale he intends. You might curry some favor when he gets here by offering skilled men and gold, if you can spare any."

"A little. We trade now and again with the men of Kush and the lands there. And," Pahotep smiled unpleasantly, "I can fine those letter writers down to the bone. Turn their fines into gold and offer that as well."

"Dead men don't need gold," Kahoret agreed. "And if they live, they can be grateful for that. What do we charge them with?"

"Atepmut will think of something. Tell him everything you think it's safe for him to know. Basically, those idiots have endangered everyone in the domain, and if we have to beggar them to buy safety, then I'd rather see them beggared than see all of my people lying dead in the streets."

Kahoret left and Khepera arrived to report on the work beyond the city. That went well: in another five days it would be completed and stocked with supplies. The children and adults had been chosen who would take refuge if the need arose, and the entrances cunningly concealed.

Time dragged on. The Commander of the Theban Regiment issued an order that his men were to go to the city during the hours of daylight only. They were to go in groups of no fewer than five, and they were not to get into trouble. A rumor about the infamous letter had come to his ears, and for all he knew the Striking Hawks were coming to order him back to Thebes, where he'd be demoted or even executed for allowing things to get out of hand in Hanish.

Since the rumor spread to his ordinary soldiers, they now shared the same fears, and behaved better when in the city on day-leave than they had for some time. The people of Hanish, unsure of anything at all themselves, also behaved. No one wanted an angry regiment to arrive—made still angrier by general disorder.

* * * *

On the road, Akhenaten almost enjoyed himself, now the pace had slowed and his time riding had shortened.

"How many more days before we come in sight of the city?" he asked Khamay.

Khamay made certain to know the answer to that question, for he was asked several times each day. "Another ten days, Great One. Unless we move faster."

"Certainly not. *I'm* a soldier, a man. *I* could endure it, but there are older servants and aged priests. I will not force them to hurry beyond what they can manage." He struck a pose, apparently aiming for a look of nobility of character and compassion for the lesser breeds. Khamay thought that he looked like a posing rat, fat with stolen grain, and smug about it.

He half-bowed in his saddle. "Of course, Great and Noble One. Your care for those about You is well known."

Oh, well, too bad about the commander who'd asked Khamay to suggest a faster pace. He'd just have to understand that if Pharaoh wanted to dawdle his way to Hanish, the whole regiment would dawdle with him—or suffer the wrath of the Divine One—a wrath Khamay had no intention of bringing down upon himself by any attempts at either insistence or the application of reason.

Of course, once they were a few days closer to the city, there was nothing to prevent him sending a couple of young priests ahead with certain orders. He quietly summoned two he considered sensible. Green, yes, but not the type to lose their heads.

"Make preparations to ride ahead to Hanish in three days' time. Do not dress as priests, do not make a fuss or appear obvious in any way. Once in the city, seek out the Temple of Bastet and enter secretly when the women have gone to bed. You are looking for letters that suggest rebellion against Pharaoh, communications with the temples of any God apart from Aten-Ra, and anything that suggests even the slightest collusion in fomenting unrest. Do you understand?"

"Yes, High Priest."

"Good, then go and make any preparations required."

He watched with satisfaction as they left his tent. If they found something and he brought it to Akhenaten, the city and the temple would be on the back foot from the start. It'd also annoy the Great One sufficiently to make him listen to his High Priest and any harsher suggestions on dealing with malcontents.

The two young priests departed wearing the casual, inexpensive clothing of minor merchants' sons. They arrived in Hanish a day before the regiment and their ruler, and scouted the Temple for two days. The second night after the regiment arrived, convinced that they had nothing to fear from a gaggle of women, they set out for the Temple.

* * * *

In the outlying villages of the Lion Domain people also prepared, but for most, they did not plan to go into the city. It was too large, too crowded, and far too expensive. They'd do as they always had done, and take their chances in the wilds. For many of the village children and some of the adults, there was the prepared cave. For the others there were bolt holes, caves natural and man-made, and their meager possessions and livestock could be safely hidden. The rumor that Pharaoh traveled with His regiment had spread—from whom and by what means was unknown, but peasants hear everything in time—and they understood the nobility.

"Won't sit about in this Bastet-forsaken spot forever," said Ferharate in his tiny village. "Nobles have got better things to do and they does them in comfort. All we has to do is stay out of their sight a while, an' once the army's gone we can come out and get back to the village."

"How long do you think we'll have to stay hidden?" His wife was calculating what supplies they would need.

"I don't know, do I? I'm not the Set-cursed idiot bringing an army here. But take all the livestock and half of everything else. That way if he comes we have to move only the other half."

It made sense. His wife accelerated her work and that of everyone else since Ferharate was headman. The women of the village cursed their Pharaoh fervently. Rulers should know their place. The man had a nice palace, why in the name of Set couldn't he stay in it?

* * * *

And at last Barhket had something to report. "Lord Pahotep, the farthest scouts returned. They have seen the regiment approaching. They found them six days out from Hanish. It took them two days to return to me, and another day to reach Hanish. Thus the Striking Hawk is …"

"I can count. We have three days before Pharaoh and his entourage arrive, if he keeps to his current pace."

Even the slowest snail eventually arrives somewhere new—if it keeps moving in a straight line.

10

The regiment, Khamay, and all other personnel regarded as essential by their ruler *had* arrived. They moved to a flat area beside the Theban Regiment on the late afternoon of the third day.

"Great One, shall I summon the Theban Commander to attend You?" Khamay was dusty, weary, and bad-tempered, but he knew better than to show any of that to his Lord and Master. His Master had no such compunction.

"No, you idiot! Whatever for? I plan to have a long cool bath, a good meal with some of that Kaltic wine, and a long, comfortable night—knowing that I won't have to be on that damned horse or in a jolting chariot in the morning. I'll see the Theban commander once I've risen, eaten, and bathed again. Oh, and Khamay, tell them to keep the noise down around my tent. I'll sleep in and will be really annoyed if I'm woken unnecessarily."

He did sleep in, until the late morning when he rose reluctantly, ate and drank generously, had a leisurely bath in cool, scented water, and decided that now would be an extremely suitable time to thank his God who brought him through so many horrendous perils during two moons travel in lethal territory.

Since Pharaoh worshipped, everyone did so, soldiers standing unsheltered in the blistering sun while their officers crowded under inadequate awnings. The service lasted several hours, while Akhenaten thoroughly enjoyed the undivided attention of two regiments. As the God's favorite son, Lord of the Twin Rivers and Two Lands, Son of the Divine Sun, he was the center of events, made two speeches, and retired only when his voice gave out—to the eternal gratitude of his leg-weary and almost terminally bored regiments.

* * * *

In the city, Pahotep wondered what on earth was happening on the parade grounds. Syamekh, who'd been privileged to know his ruler for twenty years, enlightened him.

"So far as Akhenaten is concerned, that wasn't an easy journey. It was a danger-infested trek through brutal country, probably teeming with bandits, savage beasts, and infested with madmen and regicides who poison waterholes. He arrived last night, and since then he'll have eaten lavishly, slept in, risen late, eaten still more, had two or three baths, and now he'll hold a service to thank the God for seeing that Akhenaten survived a multitude of awful perils."

Syamekh grinned at the open-mouthed Lion Lord. "By the time he's finished talking he'll be hoarse, hungry, and hot. He'll want wine, a long bath, and a six-course dinner, in that order. By which time it'll be dusk again. And if Khamay wants him to see the Theban Commander to find out what's been happening here, Akhenaten will tell him to leave it until tomorrow. If we're waiting in the camp with the merchants in chains along with suitable other gifts, then we may be able to preempt Khamay's efforts to wipe out your domain."

"I can only hope so," Pahotep said soberly. "But I'll keep everyone working on preparations to escape, anyhow."

"I'd advise it. We may yet be able to save your domain, but Akhenaten's stubborn. He gets an idea fixed in his brain and it stays there like an unwelcome mother-in-law in your best bedroom. There may be some good news in another day. I left Remekh working on the final calculations; he thinks he'll have them completed by then. Buy us another three days, Lord Pahotep, and if that child from your sister's temple can dream efficiently for us, we may discover our escape route, if all else fails."

"Our?"

"Yours, I regret to say. Remekh intends to go with you, and I have other duties. If the portal opens, I plan to slip around the army and head back to Thebes as fast as I can."

"Will you perhaps open it another time and ..."

Syamekh shook his head, the look on his face cutting off Pahotep's words. "It's as Remekh told us earlier. If we can do this at all, it can only be done once. If you use the portal, you can never return. Everyone who leaves must make his or her own decision. If they leave, they leave Napata and the Lion Domain forever. In my opinion it is better to be alive somewhere else than dead here, but that is for each of you to choose."

He moved to the doorway. There was no sense in telling Pahotep the other discovery: if, in time, the people of his domain spread out and covered all the lands, they might be able to influence the portal to open again, so that they could either return to Napata or receive others to join them.

However, it would take centuries before that would be possible, and by then who would care? It was likely that all memory of the lands they had left would be forgotten. It was even more probable that the wisdom that had opened the portal would be lost as the centuries passed. He left, saying nothing, and knowing that Remekh was of the same mind. Wherever the people of the Lion Domain went—if that was their final choice—they would make a new life, be the people of their new land now and for always.

* * * *

Akhenaten lolled comfortably on a cushion-piled divan purchased in the marketplace at Hanish and presented by Pahotep, with many prayers for his ruler's comfort. Khamay was talking—when did the man ever stop his orating, come to think of it?

"They remain obdurate, Great One. They have given the traitors into our hands, they have made You gifts, but their High Priestess has not yet agreed to bow before the Sun-Lord on behalf of her miserable Goddess."

"Oh? Yes."

"Divine Son of the Sun, do You accept this flouting of Your royal will and that of the God?"

Did he? He supposed he didn't, but Khamay wanted to start a war, and wars were such a nuisance. If he destroyed Hanish and its people, then, as Syamekh pointed out, he'd get nothing more from them. Better to persuade them into agreement and fine the domain. Maybe take some of the people as slaves. But leave most of the city and people in place. You don't persuade a cow to keep giving milk by killing it; that's what Syamekh said, and it made sense.

Khamay's voice dropped to a softer note. "Great One, You wouldn't want the people here to think You aren't a soldier? If they believe they can get away with rejecting Your orders, then they're like a common soldier who ignores his officer. And the army would lose respect for an officer like that."

His target sat up a little. "What?"

The High Priest of Amen-Ra hid a smirk. Pharaoh still wanted to appear as a solider before his army. Any suggestion that they'd laugh at his pretensions touched a nerve.

"The city and its threadbare Lion Lord expect You to be just another noble, Great One. They assume that if they drag out negotiations, You'll become bored and leave without accomplishing Your intent. They do not understand that in You they face a man the equal of Ahmose, who taught the Hyksos respect for Napata's ruler. They face not some fat and idle noble, but Pharaoh, Divine Lord, soldier and master of men."

Akhenaten straightened. "Yes. They do. As you say, Khamay, they must understand this. But Syamekh rightly points out that a dead cow gives no further milk."

He glanced across the tent to where Syamekh stood talking with a junior priest who bowed and left. Khamay's gaze fastened on Syamekh, curse the High Priest of Thoth, the man had a habit of confusing Pharaoh and encouraging further thought on matters that Khamay would rather his ruler didn't consider.

"Ah, yes, Wise One, in that he is right. But if a farmer has a cow that gives little milk, he would be wise to kill that one for meat and buy another, younger cow that will give more milk."

Akhenaten lost track of the metaphor and gaped in bewilderment. "What?"

"Great One ..." (Make it clear to the idiot. Being clever wasn't useful when you were talking to someone who needed help dressing. And on that thought, he must also rotate the soldiers who played dice with their ruler. They were starting to complain that it was both very hard and extremely boring to constantly lose to the man while praising his ability to game—when he couldn't have tossed effective dice to save his life, and as for thinking that he was a soldier, a man amongst men ...)

"Great One, this domain isn't rich in gold or silver, but were it run more competently, with a harder hand, it could have greater wealth in cattle and men. It could send many more youths to the army, more cattle for leather and meat, more artifacts as tribute to Thebes—and to build Your Amarna. The people are fatter than they should be, lazier, and less inclined to give Pharaoh His due."

He added a very careful measure of sarcasm to the tone he used on that, just enough for it to be felt without his master realizing why. It was having an effect, though.

"Divine Lord, if You reduce much of this city, take the people as slaves and take their wealth—accumulated at Your expense since they pay in taxes less than they can afford—You may then raise someone else to the Rule of the Lion Domain. Someone," he added with a sideways glance, "who would pay well for the privilege and be forever grateful to the wisdom of the one who granted him such glory."

Akhenaten became animated. "Yes, yes. My daughter, Taritaah, is almost of an age to wed. She favors that boy—what's his name?"

"Karowepet, Divine Lord."

"Yes, that's him. Karowepet. Pleasant lad, admires me, asks my advice. Good family."

"Indeed, Great One. Like Yourself, they descend from the great Ahmose through the male line."

Oops, he shouldn't have mentioned the latter. It was the female line that was important. That other, thrice-cursed descendant of Ahmose that the rebellious Domains favored was from the female line—and had the same name, which annoyed Akhenaten. Ah, he could use that.

"He and his House are loyal to You, Wise One. They follow the true male line, not this foolishness of looking back to women."

"The Beautiful One, my wife, was a woman, Khamay. Do not speak slightingly of women."

"Of course not, but she was one apart. Who could be like her?"

"That is true. So you think I should cleanse this city of all traitors and give the domain to Karowepet when he weds my little Taritaah?"

"It would please her, and You would then have a loyal Domain, Wise One. Moreover, You would return to the Royal City laden with slaves and gold, driving cattle before Your army, and with wagons loaded with gear and goods. You would return triumphant and," he added significantly, "other domains that might be thinking of saying 'no' to Your Divine orders would think twice when they saw the might of Pharaoh."

"Ah, that is true. Yes. I would have shown my strength and determination, my invincibility in battle. They would see that I am a man and a soldier."

An idiot and easily manipulated, Khamay thought. If only his juniors could find something incriminating, it would be even easier. But aloud he agreed. "Yes, Great One, all would bow to Your wisdom and might. You would be an example for generations to come."

Adding in his mind, "and that's the only thing you do with any efficiency, *produce* the generations to come. But you sire girls only, who are useful for sealing treaties and ensuring a domain is loyal. But who will rule after you is the important point. If I get Karowepet the Lion Domain, he'll side with my choice."

Akhenaten was still thinking. "So I should attack the domain?"

(Of course you should, what do you think I've been saying for the past hour?) "Yes, Great One, but it would be best to have a reason."

"But we have a reason, you said. They harbor traitors."

"The other domains might not see it so clearly, Divine Lord. They do not have Your wisdom, Your clarity of mind. Better we have a reason that their simplicity will accept."

"What?"

"Leave it to me, Wise One. I'll find something that is acceptable and understandable for all."

Khamay bowed low, departing with relief. Now, all he had to do was manufacture a provocation clear enough that the other Domains would accept it as cause for war. If they didn't, it was too bad. Striking Hawk, River Horse, Ibex, and Baboon Domains sided with the ruler. And unknown to the Domains of the Elephant and the Cheetah, the Leopard

Lord was wavering. If they reduced the Lion Domain and handed it over to Karowepet, they'd have the majority of the domains on Pharaoh's side. He went to seek out his *agent provocateurs* with a lighter heart.

Syamekh watched the High Priest of Aten as he left the tent and suppressed a small grin. He'd heard the conversation. Thoth's Priests, the upper ranks anyhow, had some small abilities of which Aten and *his* priests weren't aware. Listening in to conversations normally out of hearing range, under certain conditions, was one. And knowing Khamay for most of that man's ambitious life, Syamekh could guess some of what he was thinking.

Some of it was inaccurate, or rather, incorrect. Khamay assumed that Striking Hawk, River Horse, Ibex, and Baboon Domains sided with Akhenaten, and that the Leopard Lord was wavering. Khamay assumed that if they reduced the Lion Domain to nothing and handed the land over to Karowepet, they'd have the majority of the domains on Pharaoh's side. Syamekh turned away a little, unable to prevent his flickering smile.

Weteta, Lord of the Leopard Domain, had been quietly playing Khamay for a fool. Far from wavering, he'd throw in everything he had against Akhenaten's plans to reduce all the Gods, save Aten-Ra, to nothing. Weteta's House had prayed to Amun for more generations than they had recorded, as had the House of the Lord of the River Horse. Far from Khamay's belief that he and Akhenaten had the majority, Syamekh's faction had it and planned to keep it.

He sighed softly as he, too, left Pharaoh's tent. None of that mattered. They couldn't afford a civil war, no matter who sided with whom. Such a war would devastate the land, allow outsiders to attack them, give outer provinces the chance to rebel, and chaos would reign long years in Napata.

His Temple had seen this dangerous folly coming for two years, and Syamekh knew Remekh was researching into certain scrolls for far longer. Intellectual curiosity only, but the old man had dug deeper than anyone had before him, found secrets never discovered by the temples—and written extensively to his friend about them. The revelations appeared to be of scientific interest only, but with Pharaoh's determination to raise Aten to be the only God, they had become a possible way to halt that.

Neither man liked what would come from using the discoveries. But if it came down to using them or seeing the whole of Napata ruined and most of the people of the Lion Domain slaughtered, then they would connive together to prevent such events. They wouldn't be thanked for it, Syamekh thought, but then those who might thank them—or not—didn't have to know exactly what had been done, or known about, beforehand.

There came a touch on his arm and he turned. "Tiaahn, what have you heard? Anything useful?"

"Yes, Lord, but before I tell you, something else occurred last night. There was an attempt to steal scrolls from the Temple of Bastet."

Syamekh gaped. "The Temple? Some fool tried to burgle a *Temple*?"

* * * *

Shumere and Atentat crept around the back of the Temple of Bastet. From there they could watch the gatekeeper as he heated a drink within his small gatehouse. The lantern glowed softly, lighting the big man as he lumbered about.

"If we have to make a run for it," Atentat said slowly, "I don't want to fall over that one."

"So we remove him."

"I don't want to be charged with killing, either."

"Idiot! There are robes hanging here, I can tear one into strips. We hit him over the head, blindfold, and tie him. He'll see nothing, know nothing, and be able to tell nothing."

Atentat smiled. "Right. You go over by the doorway, I'll make noises, and when he sticks his head out …"

"I know what to do," Shumere interrupted. "Get on with it."

That part of the program went well, leaving a blindfolded and bound gatekeeper behind them they slipped through the small side door. It hadn't been barred. Who barred the doors in a temple where the wrath of the Goddess waited for intruders?

"The library, that's where they'd keep any letters."

They padded silently along the inner corridor; the library entrance was covered by a thick curtain. Shumere lit the candle he carried and held it up.

"Pull the door curtain and start looking."

Shumere found a bag containing silver scraps; he thrust it hastily into the bosom of his robes: no reason the heretics should have that. They were busily unrolling scrolls, unbinding and reading wax tablets when thundering footsteps sounded, coming their way. Atentat drew a sword.

"I thought you said no killing?" his companion hissed.

"I'd also rather not explain what we're doing—get over by the door!"

Before either could move, a small feline figure dived through the door and shrieked discordantly.

Shumere struck at it. It slipped sideways, and the tip of his sword sent scrolls flying, which only increased the noise. Atentat reached the door just as the maker of footsteps arrived. Isara took one look at the items tumbled across the floor and wailed.

"The scrolls! Blasphemers, destroyers!"

With one powerful sweep of her arm she knocked Atentat aside. His head hit the wall and he slumped. Shumere leaped for her. Isara struggled, swinging him around in a circle as Atentat reeled to his feet—to be knocked down by the pair and stepped on as they staggered. He howled.

The small figure howled louder, the long shrilling shriek of a furious cat. It dug claws into Shumere's ankle and his gyrations with Isara grew more vigorous as his yells vied for attention.

Atentat struggled to his feet, smacked Isara briskly across the side of her head with the flat of his sword, and she tumbled to the floor. He grabbed his companion. "Run!"

A growing hubbub closed in. Women's voices, running feet. The two men dived for the doorway, burst through, and found themselves face to face with four cats and a woman. She stepped back politely to allow them passage. The cats did not. In the next few seconds two tails and a paw were trodden on, and Atentat acquired a fine selection of bites and claw marks to match those of his companion. Hopping and yelling in pain, the men made for the doorway that led outside.

They hurtled through that to find that Shardis, wondering what happened to Shemet, found and freed him. He wasn't a fast mover, and in the excitement he'd seized not his sword but a light practice spear, and by the wrong end. He struck a vicious sweeping movement with the long, whippy shaft that took both men full across the buttocks as they raced past. Their departing velocity was considerably accelerated and screams of pain trailed off into the night as they vanished from view around the nearest bend.

In the library, Isara replaced items on the shelves, still wailing. "What can they want? To enter the Lady's own Temple, to lay impious hands on Her words. They must be madmen."

Khepera stood watching her and thinking deeply. At last she spoke. "No, I think they were very sane. They searched for something. Is anything missing?"

Isara shelved the final items and checked. "No, Shrine's Lady. Nothing."

"Good, then they failed. Let us all return to our pallets and sleep." Her rare grin flickered out. "I wonder how the one who sent them will receive news of their failure?"

Shumere and Atentat also wondered—which was why dawn saw them heading for Thebes.

"If he asks why we didn't return, we can say that we were seen and didn't wish him to be embarrassed if accusations were made against the Temple of Aten-Ra." Shumere patted the pouch of silver bits. "We won't starve. This is enough to get us back to the city and reach the Temple. We can hide there, and our brothers will swear that we never left."

They cantered on—squirming uncomfortably as they rode.

* * * *

Tiaahn recounted the events in Bastet's Temple, and even the dignified High Priest of Thoth found the corners of his mouth twitching upwards. He'd wager that Khamay sent the two intruders in search of some incriminating document he could produce to sway Pharaoh's decision. He'd also wager that with the burglary such a spectacular failure, the pair responsible wouldn't report to their master. Let Khamay wonder and worry. It'd be good for him.

"All right, what other news? Is it something that we can stop before it occurs, if that's possible?"

Tiaahn nodded. "Khamay plans to have certain soldiers start a brawl in the marketplace again, and this time a couple soldiers from the Striking Hawk will be found dead afterwards, stabbed. The soldiers will then riot about these murders. They will attack women, and when their men come to their aid, they can misrepresent this to other domains as an uprising."

Syamekh snorted. "They'd know better, but," he considered, "it could still be provocation enough for Khamay to persuade Akhenaten to throw both regiments against Hanish."

"Yes, Lord, that's why I went to the Lion Compound and told Pahotep and Remekh about it. Then I dropped in on Atepmut."

"Good lad. Yes. That should put a stop to Khamay's plot."

Tiaahn looked at his master, his face sober. "*This* plot, Lord. Maybe …"

"Yes, maybe we should allow it to continue part way." He nodded approvingly. "Yes. Go to Pahotep, Khepera, and Atepmut and say this." He talked for several minutes, as Tiaahn's smile grew wider.

* * * *

The riot began in the food section of the marketplace. Men were watching, and as soon as two soldiers were down, Atepmut's peacekeepers and some of Pahotep's guard surrounded the brawl, efficiently containing everyone fighting. Before the man responsible could discard his knife he was seized, and the bloody blade drawn from the sheath to be held up.

Atepmut's voice was a bellow. "Silence. I am the Judge of Pharaoh. Murder has been done and shall be judged in my court. Bring everyone involved, now!"

Eleven soldiers crowded into the court, flanked by guards. Atepmut was in his element. Witness followed witness in an orderly procession. Before Khamay could arrive to protest events, the judge established that the brawl began for no good reason, and that a comrade—for no apparent reason—murdered the dead soldiers. The man, a known malcontent named Itay of the Striking Hawk, began shouting as soon as he understood what would happen—his fellow soldiers were already snarling ominously.

"Lord! Lord Judge, I was ordered to kill the men. It was an order, I swear. I would have been executed if I hadn't obeyed."

Khamay arrived just in time to hear that revelation. He sagged at the knees, reversed his course, and fled unnoticed. Someone else had given the order to the killer, but if taken, that one would also talk. He had to be spirited away—or disposed of. In the court, Atepmut asked questions, and it wasn't only the people of Hanish who listened to the replies.

"Who gave you this order?"

"Lord, it was a man named Nemeth. He works for Khamay, High Priest of Aten-Ra."

"Did he say if this order was his or from another?"

"Lord, I did not ask."

Atepmut simply looked at him. "I see. A man ordered you to murder two of your comrades. You just nodded and agreed. You asked no questions, you merely bowed and said that that would be no trouble." His tone became more sarcastic by the sentence. "This man who 'ordered' you is not an officer, not even a soldier; he's a junior priest with no authority. You didn't bother to ask his master if it was his order, and you didn't approach an officer of your regiment to check if being told to murder fellow soldiers was acceptable."

Atepmut's tone could now be bottled and used to tan leather.

"You were approached by some man you didn't know and told to kill two people you did know. And you not only found that perfectly reasonable—you actually did it! What are you, a perfect idiot?"

A voice from amongst the soldiers commented, "He isn't perfect, but we can fix that."

There was an involuntary roar of laughter from the crowd. The reference was to an old wives' tale, in which the only perfect man was said to be a dead one.

Atepmut smothered a chuckle and kept his look sternly thoughtful.

"There is little doubt that you committed murder at the behest of another. This man you have named as Nemeth, servant to Khamay, High Priest of Aten. This case therefore does not really fall under my jurisdiction, since all the soldiers involved are from Striking Hawk Domain. The one who suborned murder is servant of a Priest from Thebes.

"Yet the killings happened here in Hanish and witnesses are people of the city. It seems to me that the best solution would be to call on a judge from Striking Hawk to sit with me, and that we agree on the verdict. Let those involved stand to one side. I will hear another case until a regiment judge arrives."

He leaned over and spoke quietly to Kahoret, who was nearby. "Get me a judge from Striking Hawk and do it quickly, quietly, and if possible, get one who may not know what's going on here."

Kahoret nodded and slipped into the crowd. It took nearly two hours, but he found a man who was, in some ways, similar to Atepmut, a man who believed that the law was not to be circumvented, broken, or scorned. He had some idea of what was occurring here, but he disliked Khamay, and he wasn't happy to find some political nonsense was responsible for a soldier of his regiment murdering two other soldiers.

He strode in. "Noble Judge Atepmut, I am Sehotep, Judge of the Striking Hawk Regiment, ready to consult on this case." He turned to stare at Itay. "I may say that this man has come before me on a number of occasions. I know him as a thief, a liar, a brainless incompetent, and a poor soldier. I am surprised to hear, however, that he has become a murderer of his comrades. I suppose the man paid him very well. He'd have had to."

This had the result expected. Itay almost levitated in panicked rage. "Lord Judge, I didn't get anything, not a scrap of silver, not a handful of corn. I was told to pick two men from the group I was with. I had to kill them quickly and quietly, and if I failed I'd be the one who was dead."

"How did you choose?"

Itay was still frantically truthful. "Lord, I didn't like them."

An undercurrent of snickering swept through the crowd while the detained soldiers growled.

"But why?" Sehotep asked.

"They cheat at dice."

"Not why didn't you like them, you halfwit, why did you accept orders to kill them? They were given you by a mere servant."

"Well, Lord Judge, he's given me orders before."

"To do what?"

Itay clammed up. He wasn't a bright man, and he wasn't sure that he could be in worse trouble, but it wouldn't help to add a charge of poisoning a junior priest. The man had asked questions Khamay didn't want asked—and wasn't prepared to answer under any circumstances. But—conveniently—dead men can ask no questions.

"I see." Atepmut did. Whatever the man had been required to do, it clearly included the murder of someone who'd be missed. Only that would seal his lips. He changed tack. "Did he pay you on that occasion, or was it only that he didn't have his threats against you carried out?"

Itay mumbled.

"Speak up."

"Both, Lord Judge. I wasn't harmed and he gave me a lot of silver."

Sehotep looked at his fellow judge. "I think we can be sure that this man murdered two comrades."

"Not comrades. He didn't like them," Atepmut corrected.

"Official comrades. Since Itay is convicted of murder from his own mouth, I see no need for witnesses or a trial, or for Hanish involvement. I'll take him back to the regiment and discuss his punishment with the commander."

"What are they likely to do?"

Sehotep dropped his voice to a level that would not be heard by anyone else. "Oh, I suspect that he'll be executed—one way or another. He knows too much, can talk too much, and he's too much of a fool to keep his mouth shut. He's already shouted a name, and that man will be on the way back to the Temple in Thebes by now. There isn't much I can do, good colleague. I can keep making a noise until someone says I should keep silent. But after that it's my own throat at risk if I continue. I don't like what's planned. But I'm only one man."

"As am I," Atepmut replied softly. "If all the people who object to these plans spoke out, then perhaps they would wither on the vine."

"Grapes all die if the weather is too harsh, good colleague. I'd rather my whole House weren't such grapes."

Atepmut sighed. "Go in the Grace of the Gods. Thank you for your assistance, so far as you can stretch it anyway. I'll pray to Ma'at that your aid weighs against Her feather when the time comes that your soul is judged."

Sehotep gathered his guard, the prisoner, and the Striking Hawk soldiers. He glanced at the shivering Itay before they moved through the waiting, listening crowd. "Pray that your commander does not count the killing of two comrades as treason against Pharaoh, Itay. You know the penalty for that."

Everyone nearby could see Sehotep's comment sink in. Knowing all too well the penalty if his commander *did* call his actions treason, Itay's mouth opened wide and he screamed, a high shriek of pure terror. The idea of being bound as a mummy and sewn in a hide, then being buried alive to die slowly of heat and thirst, possibly being found by ants or scorpions before he managed to die, loosened Itay's tongue as no other threat might have.

"No, no, no! I was ordered. Nemeth said that Khamay wanted it done. That I was to foment a brawl, get some of the soldiers involved, then stab two of them and yell that the citizens here had murdered our comrades. I had to get the soldiers to attack women, and when their men protected them I was to shout that it was an uprising. I should swear I'd heard men curse the Sun-God, and Pharaoh, too, and speak of killing Him."

Atepmut leaned forward and spoke severely, praying that the man's panic would last a little longer.

"Ah, yes, treason, as I said. You conspired against the most noble Pharaoh with this junior priest."

"No! I swear, the priest said that it was Khamay's order, and that Pharaoh knew all about it."

There was a sudden, complete silence. Itay stared around him.

Sehotep took him by the arm, speaking clearly so everyone present could hear. "Your claim is that you had orders to start a brawl, murder two soldiers, attack respectable women, then claim subsequent events to be a uprising—and that you believed this was by the High Priest's and Pharaoh's true wishes and their orders, and not treason for which you should be punished?"

Itay was too confused and too terrified by the thought of what happened to traitors to deny it.

"Yes."

"Very well, then. This must be taken to Pharaoh."

He marched guard, soldiers, and the trembling prisoner away, knowing that the wretched man marched to his death, that everything would be hushed up, but he'd done his best to ensure everyone knew the truth. Some of what was said would travel on the winds to Lords of other domains—who would be warned.

* * * *

Pahotep left quietly through a back door to find his sister, his cousin, and his friends. That judge had done well for the Domain of the Lion. A truth freed was not easily recalled.

Khepera smiled at the tale and then frowned. "It may help, but the truth is, brother, that Khamay will see that the judge is silenced, this Itay is quietly disposed of, and the charges will be dropped. With no prisoner alive, anything he claimed can be discounted as desperate lies to save himself."

"That is so, but what he did say in the court won't be kept quiet; it was heard by too many people. Gossip travels, other domains will hear of Itay's claims, and some will believe. We'll make sure that they hear from us as well."

"Be careful. Letters can be twisted and called treason."

Pahotep nodded. "Syamekh plans to send the news by other methods. Now, sister, stay here this evening and eat with me."

Khepera smiled. "I will. I'm busy, for there is so much to do. Merchants are coming in with their valuables all the time. These must be listed, stored, and guarded. Yet it would be pleasant to share a meal with you and our cousin and our friends."

"It is good to rest now and again," Pahotep agreed, thinking that his sister was looking more than her age of late. Fear for her Temple and priestesses, for Bastet's Children, for her family and her domain, were taking a toll. He sent word quietly to his outland guards that should they feel inclined to make merry that night, it would be looked upon favorably.

They did so, roasting a yearling bull. Later, one of their singers raised his voice in a love song. Khepera moved to listen to the song from the window. The song was sung in her language, a translation, no doubt, but beautiful despite the strange melody.

> *You were my sweet joyous summer,*
> *We wandered the roads of our hearts.*
> *Down all of the tracks through the valleys and vales,*
> *Swearing we never would part.*
>
> *But forever is rarely forever,*
> *With winter your bridges you crossed.*
> *Taking another down paths that were ours,*
> *Breaking your promise, not counting the cost.*
>
> *Now your path in my heart is all broken,*
> *Riven and rent by the frost.*
> *Torn up by betrayal and tears,*
> *And the roads of our summer are lost.*
>
> *Within me is only a snow plain,*
> *Bitter salt-water wave-tossed.*
> *Ruins and desert, and watered with tears,*
> *For the roads of our summer are lost.*

The music cascaded into plaintive chords, resolving into a soft lament. Khepera shivered as it faded away.

Aye, the roads of my summer,
Forever, forever,
Forever, forever—are lost.

She turned away. If Akhenaten stayed with his plans, then the Domain of the Lion, its people, everything she knew and loved, would be forever lost. She would die before that happened. She could survive in a new land. She would not wish to live without all else that she loved.

II

Khamay considered the same problem the next afternoon. If he couldn't persuade Pharaoh that Hanish should be attacked, and if too much of what he'd been arranging came out, then even the loyal domains would turn against them. If that happened, Akhenaten would almost certainly lose the throne and Khamay would probably lose his life. If he did survive, it would be to live as an impoverished priest in a no longer well-regarded temple. He'd made too many enemies for himself and for his God.

He called in two of his priests, gave orders, blessed them in a way that indicated if they failed in their assignment they'd be deeply unfortunate in what was left of their lives, and sent them out. A messenger arriving late that night assured him that they'd succeeded, and he took what felt like the first deep breath since Itay had starting yelling in the court. Itay was dead, an apparent suicide. The commander had agreed that his judge would say nothing, since there was no longer any prisoner making wild claims.

Now all he had to do was persuade Akhenaten to attack Hanish and the Lion Domain. It was essential for Khamay that it be done—and that way around—so that after the attack he could winnow out the people surviving in the city who'd actually heard Itay and silence them permanently, too. If there was only gossip and no one remaining who could provide proof, then the rumors would be denied easily, even if Pharaoh's judge still swore to Itay's words. With no actual proof of a plot against one of them, none of the Lords of the Domains would dare to rebel.

* * * *

In Hanish the mood was lighthearted amongst the people. Most thought that the threat to their city, now revealed to be the work of troublemakers, was over. Pharaoh would listen to their Lord Pahotep, the soldiers would depart, and Hanish could go back to being a small, obscure city in a small, obscure domain. It was a pleasant thought—all but the obscurity. Some would like their city to be better known to the snobs of Thebes.

Others argued that it was better to keep your head down where nobles were concerned—their own Lord exempted, of course. He was a decent man for a noble, esteemed and trusted. They toasted him, The Domain of the Lion, Judge Atepmut, Hanish, the women of the city—most beautiful in Napata—and of course, Napata itself, best of lands. They had sore heads in the morning, but that was usual—all was now well in the city and domain, that was worth a headache any day.

* * * *

Pahotep, Lord of the Lion Domain, did not believe all was well. "Remekh, how long before you can open a portal to some other land where we might flee?"

"Khepera loaned us Shardis, and she's dreamed well for us over past nights. The lands she's seen are strange; some are lands in which we could not survive. Others are inhabited by too many for us to find a place. We have narrowed it down to two lands. Both worship the Goddess's sister-self, and the lands there are wide, fertile, and empty of many people."

But one of the lands is—different, he added to himself. The people there were images of Bastet, were not shaped as Napatans. Their Feline Goddess was more involved with her people, and into this place other portals opened from time to time—usually without warning or assistance—something, however, that might make it easier for them to open a portal to there.

And yes, the glimpses of the Goddess of that land he'd been able to manage through the child showed Her as the mirror image of Bastet. A true sister-self. That made it more likely that they could reach the lands and bring everyone through safely, so long as the Goddess there did not forbid that. He'd discuss the possibilities with Syamekh.

* * * *

Shrine's Lady Khepera was also busy. "Shemet, are you well?"

"Yes, Lady, but I am worried." And the Temple gatekeeper did look upset, Khepera thought. It was probably nothing, as he tended to become distressed over very little, but she could find out what bothered him and give some reassurance.

"What worries you?"

"Lady, Anati is missing."

"What? How?"

"Lady, she left the temple this morning, and she never returned."

Khepera stared. Anati, matriarch of the cats of the Temple of Bastet in Hanish, would have left her territory—and her kits of barely a week old—only if the Goddess Herself had sent her for some major purpose.

"At what time did she leave, Shemet? Can you think of any way you could tell me a time?"

Careful questioning indicated that Anati had gone out perhaps two hours before noon. It was now late afternoon and Shemet hadn't known what to do. The Temple cats weren't prisoners, but they left the Temple rarely, and those who did so were usually the younger ones that went to play just beyond the walls.

Anati had seen more than twelve floods of the great river; she was an elderly lady in cat terms and no playful kitten. Nor was she foolish. If she hadn't returned, either she remained because the Goddess wished—or because she was unable to return. The latter thought distressed the gatekeeper, who adored her above even the other cats to whom he was devoted.

Khepera made up her mind. "Leave it to me, Shemet."

His big body relaxed in trust and belief. "Yes, Lady. Lady? You will bring her back, won't you?"

"I'll do my best."

She would, and first she would go to the inner shrine. Bastet could shed light on this—if She wished. Khepera reached the statue and laid her body down before the Lady in full obeisance to let the Goddess know that this was a serious petition.

"Lady of Light and Dark, of the night and the cats that are Your Children, Your servant Anati is missing. She left the Temple and has not returned. It may be that You have sent her on some important errand, if so then that is Your business, but I fear for her. Set my mind at rest, I beg of You."

The Goddess rarely spoke in words. She showed images, sent emotions, even scents, and Her priestesses understood. There was an art to that translation. This message needed little interpretation, though. Khepera recoiled in horror. She saw Anati trotting briskly through Hanish, out of the main gate and into the army encampment. She saw the cat slip under the edge of a tent, listen to three blurred figures, and leave again.

There was nothing alarming in that, but Anati found trouble only minutes later. A hound saw her and gave chase. Anati wisely fled up a tent pole and perched on the top. Had the dog realized that he was unable to reach her and gone about his business all would have been well, but that was not the way of dogs. He barked, Anati ignored him, but nearby soldiers did not. They came running. A net was tossed over the cat and she was taken to a tent.

Wrapped in the small-meshed net she could not fight or escape, but she could share with her Lady—and she did. Her eyes focused on each man in turn and Khepera could have wept. She did not know most of the faces, but she understood the badges of rank and the robes and pectorals worn. Anati was in the hands of the High Priest of Aten-Ra, one of his subordinates, and officers of the Striking Hawk and Theban regiments. And—unusually—she heard words.

"… spying on us." That was the High Priest.

"What do we do with it?" An officer.

"Kill the beast." The High Priest.

The young officer of the Striking Hawk tensed, his voice hard and clear. "I will not see that happen."

"Take my message to Pharaoh then, Shayohni. Say that we have found a creature of the false Goddess spying on our plans. That we seek enlightenment as to his wishes."

The officer looked at them. "Let one of you take the message. I shall remain here to be sure that the beast does not escape."

Unspoken but clearly understood by all present—including Khepera—was the underlying message. If he left, they would kill the cat as soon as he was out of earshot.

"Very well." The High Priest nodded to one of his juniors. "Go, take that message to the Great One. Wait for his reply and bring it to me with all haste." The young man hurried away and Khamay turned to consider Anati.

"Her mistress can hear through her if she wills it. Wrap a blanket about her and come aside so the beast hears nothing of what we say."

Blackness came over the scene and Khepera held back tears. Shemet wasn't the only one who loved the cat. She loved her too, and was deeply afraid for her. A feeling of warmth and reassurance flowed over her. All would yet be well; turn to the doorway.

She obeyed—to see a weary, grubby, tousle-furred cat walk slowly towards her. Khepera fell to her knees and gathered her into her arms.

"Anati, oh, sister!"

From the cat came communication along with feelings that agreed. She loved Khepera, she was happy to be back, and—just as soon as she'd shared as her Lady wished—could she be cleansed, fed, and allowed to feed her kits, then sleeeeeeep? She was so *tired*. Khepera laughed through tears and opened her mind.

She saw the blackness of the blanket. It lifted cautiously, just an edge, and there came a gust of scent. Male sweat, leather, and wine. A voice, speaking so quietly that none but a sharp-eared cat might hear.

"Lady, my House has ever honored You. I am the last of my line, and I disgrace my ancestors if I do not sire children to hold the House Name. Yet still more do I shame them if I allow one of Your Children to come to harm. I shall release her, and trust to You that I do not go childless into the great dark when that time comes. Yet if it must be so, then it shall be. I, who am Your son, abide Your judgment."

The netting loosened and was plucked aside. Anati was gently lifted and water was offered in a cupped hand. She drank, steadied on her paws as he stood her up. The netting was skillfully bundled again until it seemed as if the cat had oozed from within it, perhaps with Another's aid. The blanket was replaced, and Anati lifted.

"I'll carry you as far towards the edge of the camp as is safe, furred lady. Let you run for your life after that, and I shall pray that no hound follows."

Anati was tucked into the edge of a cloak, casually tossed over a crooked arm. She peered from within the edge so that Khepera saw the camp carrying out its daily business about the cat and the man who carried her. He reached the edge of the camp, wandered a short distance on towards the city gate, and stooped to tie a sandal string, allowing Anati to slip lightly to the ground.

"Go safely, small sister. Tell them if there is a chance to aid, I shall take it."

Anati reached out a paw and patted his hand, licked to get the taste of him and her green gaze met brown eyes. He smiled down. The cat dropped, belly to the ground and slid towards the gate. A questing hound might have seen her, but Shayohni called it to him to be petted. Anati passed through the city gates and her last sight was of the young man turning to walk back to the camp, hound at his heels.

Khepera released the cat and flung herself full-length on the floor. "Lady, bless him, bless one who risked himself and the hope of his House to save Your Child. How is it that a son, an officer of the Striking Hawk regiment worships You?"

There was a sense of amusement, a flicker of emotions. It might have been translated as the suggestion that sometimes worshipers could be found in strange places. And there was the picture of a lioness. A war-beast, harnessed, plumed, trained, and deadly. It pounced on an injured soldier in the uniform of Napata and, at a touch of the great paw, his wounds healed.

Khepera drew in a long breath. So, at some point the young officer's House had worshiped the Lioness Aspect of the goddess, a combination of the ability to fight against enemies and to heal friends. Generations ago more soldiers had worshiped that Aspect. It appeared that the officer was from a family who had done so, and he was yet faithful. Moreover, he'd offered his aid if he had the chance to give it. That could be valuable. She would think on events, but while she did so, she would call Shardis to care for Anati.

The cat was almost too weary to eat, but she managed goat's milk and a portion of finely chopped meat. As she lay down with her kits, Shardis bathed her gently with a dampened cloth, wiping away the dust and grime.

"Where was she, Lady? Shemet said she was gone for hours and that he was worried. He said he'd told you and that she'd come home, so he thinks you asked the Goddess to call her back."

Khepera eyed the girl. In another moon the river would flood, and Shardis would be fifteen. She'd always been mature for her age, she dreamed true, and she had the ability to command, as the informal second-in-command for the Shrine did not. Isara was a good woman and an honest priestess, but in a tight spot she tended to panic—nor did she command people well. She said nothing of that to the girl, but considered her question. Then quietly she told of Anati's adventures as the cat lay sleeping.

"The officer, what was he like?"

Eyes twinkling, Khepera described him. "He is in the Theban Regiment. He must have come from a good House to be an officer, since he has seen no more than twenty floods. He is not tall and his build is slender, but I saw the muscles move beneath the skin, I would expect that he is quick of movement, and stronger than he appears. He keeps himself and his clothing clean and tidy, he worships the Lioness Aspect of the Lady, and he is faithful to that. He freed Anati cleverly. Aten's priests will believe that the Lady aided her, rather than a mere human."

"And he said that he'd help us if he could?" Shardis wanted confirmation.

"Those were his words through Anati."

The girl thought. "Maybe we could find some way to let him know she reached the Temple safely. And once he knows, then he'll know whom to tell if he hears something of use to us."

Khepera nodded. "Yes, that is a good thought. I'll tell my brother, Remekh, and Syamekh about him. The Priest of Aten-Ra called the boy Shayohni, and Syamekh may be able to find out about him. Pahotep can have some of his men who can keep their mouths shut watch to see if the boy comes to the market in the city. If so, we may be able to speak to him without his fellow soldiers or the Aten priests knowing."

"I could speak to him?"

"No one would wonder if a pretty young girl talked to a soldier," Khepera agreed. "Let's see if he can be found and if he offered his aid truly."

* * * *

As Khepera expected, Khamay initially believed that Anati had been helped to escape by her mistress. He turned over the empty net and swore.

"That cat! By Aten, may He burn her, may His rage consume her forever, and all her kin after her! She listened to my words, and her cursed goddess through her. How much do they know? What are they planning against me? I'll have that Temple, that accursed Shrine razed to the ground. I'll see its priestesses slaughtered, and all the people in the House of the Lion enslaved!"

Syamekh had arrived in time to hear the threats, and he struggled to keep a bland face. Entertaining as it was to see Khamay so furious, he'd better give Khamay's thoughts another turn, and in doing so he could add another strand to the twisted rope that could eventually hang Aten's priest—and disempower the upstart God who threatened his own Temple as well.

"Are you certain that the beast escaped on its own?"

Khamay turned to stare. "Why?"

"Well. In this camp, surely your God and mine would have more power?"

"Your God has no power," Khamay said, almost absent-mindedly. "Mine, yes. He would not have permitted the false goddess to use her powers within His territory. So you may be right, priest. Either the beast escaped on its own, or someone helped it. Now, I wonder, who in this camp would do that?"

"Someone who wished to see you look a fool, maybe? Someone who would like to gain power?"

Khamay leaped to the conclusions expected. "Ah, yes, my thanks to you. I have work to do. I bid you farewell."

He left at speed to spend two days grilling his own priests and after them his guards and servants. He started with those who had reason to dislike him and, since this was most of those who worked for him, he had considerable labor on his hands before he was satisfied that they were, if not innocent, then innocent of this particular crime.

Akhenaten heard of the cat's escape by then and, in a mood to be displeased, sent for his high priest.

"Are you certain that the beast was one of Hers?"

"Whose else?" Khamay stared at his ruler.

"For Stars' sake." Akhenaten was irritated. "There are a thousand cats in the city, and not all are Her Children from the temple. What makes you believe that this beast was a daughter of the Goddess and not some hungry stray seeking food?" He snorted. "I have seen cats all over Thebes. They roam through my own palace, keeping down the rats and mice. I don't leap to conclusions that all of them are the Goddess in disguise, listening to everything I say."

Khamay bit back the comment that they could well be spies for Bastet. Why was it that just when you wanted a man to be paranoid, he decided to be rational?

"In Thebes we are a long way from the stronghold of the Goddess, Great and Noble Pharaoh. Here we are right outside Her city. It is more likely that any cat is one of Hers. There is also the way that the beast escaped. It appeared as if it turned into mist and slipped through the netting."

Akhenaten twitched. "You believe this, High Priest? You think that the beast was spying on us—on Me?"

Khamay made his voice portentous. "Whom else, Wise One, great ruler of the Lands of the Two Rivers? You speak and all hear, You give orders and all obey. You are the voice and the Father of the people. You worship Aten, Sun God and Divine One. Who is it that stands against You and wishes You harm?"

His voice dropped to a hissing suggestiveness. "Even Thoth cannot stand against the Sun, but His temple will not support Aten. They too are not for You, and those who do not stand behind You as friends, may stand against You as enemies."

His ruler's eyes widened nervously. "You believe that Thoth too is against me? But Syamekh has given me good advice in the past."

"What would it profit him to give You bad advice—openly—Great One?" Akhenaten fell silent as he considered that, and the corners of Khamay's mouth curled up in a small but very smug smile.

* * * *

Pahotep listened to his sister's account of Anati's capture and release. And also to what Khepera had heard through the cat's ears.

"So, Khamay had Itay murdered, and with him dead and unable to testify, the officers and judge won't ask further questions. But we now may have a source within Akhenaten's very camp. Yes, I'll have those of my guards who know not to talk posted. Shayohni is his name, you say?" His sister nodded. "Good. I'll have a watch at the gates for him, and also in the main market. If he comes into the city, I'll know. What do you want to do then?"

"Let Shardis talk to him."

Pahotep raised his eyebrows. "A child?"

"Not so much a child. She is fifteen in another moon. She is attractive and also very sensible. If she's seen talking to a handsome young officer, no one is likely to be suspicious."

Her brother nodded slowly. "Yes, whereas if they see you or me, or someone in power chatting to an officer of Pharaoh's regiments, they may leap to conclusions."

"In which," Khepera pointed out with some amusement, "they'd be entirely right."

"I know. So, as you say, once we have sight of this officer, you'll send the girl to talk to him. What should we have her say? Best we decide now, as we don't know when he may appear. We should have some way she can be safely alone with him, too, if one of us has news that we don't want overheard."

The discussion went on for some time. Shardis was called, made what she saw as a sensible suggestion, was shouted down by Pahotep, and offered something else.

"We can trust the healers. What if you tell Merem that I'll be her assistant so we can talk freely to this officer? I can speak to him, say he is to have a small accident in the marketplace when he sees me if he needs to tell us something important. Merem will leave it to me to do the work since it will be only a scratch. I can take him to the back of a market stall to bandage it. There are several where the owners would give us privacy. Wound-rot can set in with even a small wound, and he could insist the city provide treatment."

Pahotep considered that. "It should work. Yes." He looked at Khepera. "Sister, tell your healers at once, and I'll have my men set a watch for the boy immediately. Better to have everything ready and not need the plan, than to be unprepared."

Khepera agreed and sent Shardis in search of Merem immediately. She explained everything to the chief healer when she arrived. It was as well that she and Pahotep did so.

* * * *

Khamay spent a little time thinking of his next move between interrogating his people, and decided on a bold stroke to end this irritating peace that had broken out.

"Great One, I have divined with crystals and asked the God. The beast that spied on You was indeed sent by the Goddess. I fear she means harm. Divine Son of the Sun, I would fail in my duty if I did not hasten to stand before You, to shield to the life of the Wise One, Son of the Sun Ascendant."

Akhenaten straightened in his chair. He'd spent a pleasant few hours drinking in the shade, throwing dice with his selected guards, and he was enjoying the feeling of being Lord of All He Surveyed. To be startled out of that complacency with the news that a goddess might be preparing to do him harm met with a mixed reception—initially.

"Nonsense, Khamay. Aten protects me, you said it yourself. I am the Son of the Sun. How shall He permit His own Son to come to harm at the hands of one who is so much less?"

"These are Her lands, Great One. She has great power in Her own place. Because of that power, Her High Priestess must come to Thebes to bow before the Sun-Lord. Once she has done so, then the Cat Goddess shall have no more power and it shall all reside in Aten—and in You, who are His Son." Pharaoh opened his mouth and Khamay swept on.

"Great One, You are defied by this little Goddess in her miserable city. 'City,' they call it? It is no more than a town. If there are more than five thousand people here I should be greatly surprised. Another thousand, perhaps two, in the surrounding villages? And for their wretched minor goddess, a mere seven thousand people far from true civilization dare to defy the Sun God and their own Ruler. Will You allow this?"

"Um—no."

"No! Is that not the decision of a soldier, a wise ruler who cannot afford to have rebellion amongst the domains! 'No,' You say, Great One? 'No,' it shall be, by the will of Pharaoh. Ahmose would be proud of His descendant. What would He do, think You, if He were faced with a rebellious domain?"

This time Akhenaten got his reply in quickly.

"He would say that the city *will* bow to the will of Pharaoh." He slumped in his seat. "But I don't want them all dead, Khamay. Syamekh says that if I kill everyone, the Lords of the other domains will take it badly. I must be merciful. I want to think about how to make things clear to the people here." He propped his chin in his hand and stared at the high priest.

"Syamekh says that I am wise," he continued, "and I should consider before I do anything too hastily; that way is wisdom."

Khamay bit back a very rude comment on what his rival said, and the wisdom—or otherwise—of the ruler.

"Yes, of course, You should think, Great One. Perhaps You could consider doing something that is not too oppressive, as a warning to the Domain?"

"Yes?"

"You could encircle the city. Tell them that no one leaves until they have sent their High Priestess to Aten to bow before Him and submit their Goddess to His rule. With no one permitted to leave they'll come to heel quickly. In a few days, a moon at most, she'll be riding out of the gates."

"That is a—yes—it is a good idea."

"I'll give the order."

His ruler winced. It had been a long tiring day, he'd drunk a lot of wine, and he rather thought that he'd have a headache any moment now. He did not need a lot of soldiers marching about, horns blowing, leather-lunged officers bellowing orders, and every donkey or mule braying protests as it departed.

"No! Let it be done tomorrow and," he added hastily, "not until noon. You can give the orders then. Tell the regiment's commanders that they are to obey you as myself."

Flushed with triumph, Khamay walked briskly away. He'd go to his bed early and in the morning he'd tell the commanders to be ready to act at noon. There'd be no waiting. The moment the time came he'd have them on the march—with silence beforehand, naturally; he was fully aware of his ruler's reasons for waiting. He'd also see to it that none of the priests of Thoth went into the city until then. He didn't trust Syamekh not to make a common cause with the rebels.

Akhenaten returned to his wine beaker. If he was going to have a headache, he might as well make it worthwhile.

No one noticed a young officer who had been leader of the ruler's ceremonial guards—currently drawn from the Striking Hawk Regiment—and who had been listening to royal discussion and the decision, hurry away once his shift changed. It would be useful to have another set of sandal laces from the marketplace, maybe even some fruit, as well—and more useful still if he could find someone to whom he could recount the decision just made.

12

It was fortunate that the tradition of soldiering prevailed still in the Domain of the Lion. When they were young, sons of the House were taught what a soldier's duties were, and once they were old enough, they served under competent officers for three years. It was a tradition outgrown in most of the more "civilized" domains, where it had been five generations since the last war. Pahotep's sire had been a traditionalist, however, and the boy had enjoyed learning the arts and tactics of war.

One thing he'd learned from the very experienced men who taught him, was that you could rarely give an order to make preparations too soon. Once his sister and Shardis had departed, he'd called in his most trusted and intelligent guards and spoke to them before he put them on the city gates.

"Petnake, you are Commander of the Guards of the Gates of Hanish, and you are my loyal men. Watch for a young officer in the Striking Hawk Regiment." He described Shayohni as Khepera had told him. "If he comes into the city, you are to immediately send word to my sister in the Temple! If she asks you to do anything, you obey. Do all of you understand?"

A chorus of rough voices assured him that they did. Which was as well, since Shayohni hurried through the gate only an hour afterward. He stared about him as he walked. This was a city far removed from Thebes and yet, he thought, he liked what he saw. The people looked well fed, happy, and busy. There were no beggars on the streets. These people had self-respect.

He approached an officer of the guard by the gate. "Could you tell me, sir, if you will, where I may find the marketplace?"

"I can." The man gave clear directions and waited until the officer had vanished in that direction before hurrying to the guardhouse.

"He's here, the one we were to watch for. He's heading for the marketplace. Send a runner to Shrine's Lady Khepera and to Lord Pahotep at once. I'm going to follow the man."

Runners sped away. Petnake drifted silently in the wake of the officer. He studied the lad as he followed. Yes, a son of a House of the pure blood, which could go either way. Some of the domains would follow

Pharaoh no matter what he did: they were pure blood, he was of the ancient line, and that was all that counted to them. Others of the domains were not happy with Akhenaten's plans to depose the old Gods. Pure blood or not, they'd rebel if he moved too fast and forced them to go against their beliefs.

Pahotep had always believed—as had his father—that men under command worked better if they knew why they were ordered to fight. The men of the Lion Domain's guard had been gathered together days earlier and had the basic situation explained. They'd listened, and as he concluded, faces had twisted into scowls as one of the soldiers spoke.

"Lord, do you say that Pharaoh and his regiments come to force us to give up the Lady Bastet? Does the crowned one say that we are to pray to Her no more, or to worship in Her Temples?"

"Yes."

Few of his guards were fools, and some had thought past that information already.

"Lord," Petnake had said. "Rumor says that the Great One plans a city where only the Sun-God shall be worshiped. The priests of Amun and Thoth have already hinted that they may be lessened by this raising up of Aten-Ra. Speak to us: you have said what you know, tell us now what you fear."

Pahotep took in a long, slow breath as he looked at his men. They were right to ask. About half the population of the Domain of the Lion were not of the ancient pure blood of Napata. Of the men who had returned with Kahosen five generations ago, some had come with their families. Others had not, but had married into the families already here. In the Hanish of today, at least half the people showed some mixture of bloods. In fact, Pahotep believed, if you made strict inquiry, the number would be greater, since some did not show it.

That being so, and if the city were in trouble, then the people were in still greater trouble. Few from outside the Domain of the Lion would hesitate to kill or enslave the people here, and fewer of the Domain Lords would stand against their ruler to protest what happened to a mongrel domain.

"You ask fairly. I cannot foretell the future, but I can see possibilities, as can my sister and Remekh our learned one. These are the facts: Pharaoh worships Aten-Ra alone and wishes others to do likewise; and he commanded that my sister, Shrine's Lady, attend the great Temple of Aten-Ra in Thebes and there bow before the God." He paused to emphasize his next words.

"She would attend in her person as Shrine's Lady. In that way, her own Lady, Bastet, Lady of Light and Dark, shall also bow to Aten-Ra as Her superior."

There was a sound at that, a soft rumbling growl rising from those assembled. Most worshipped Bastet, and those few who did not worshiped others of the small Gods of the people, and they could see what was coming.

Pahotep clapped his hands for silence. "Yes, I think as you do. That once the Lady Khepera obeys, it will be the turn of the other Gods to bow: the smaller first, those with fewer priests, with few temples and little wealth. The Domain Lords, most of them, will not care, for they worship in the richer, larger temples to Thoth, to Amun, and many already bow to Aten."

He stared out over them. "You have asked what I fear. It is this. That this demand is only the beginning, and that once all the small Gods have made obeisance, then Pharaoh shall demand that the great Gods do so. Then all will be subject to Aten, and once that is so the temples of the small Gods will be razed, their priests converted, driven out, or slain. Then again it shall be the turn of the greater Gods, until all temples, all worship, all people, belong to Aten-Ra."

This time the growl deepened to a snarl. A guard was on his feet. "And how will the Gods react to this? Will they attack Aten, or will they fall on us who have done nothing to prevent it?"

Pahotep shook his head. "I do not know. The Gods do not speak to me, but I cannot believe that She who saved Kahosen, who bid him give refuge to your ancestors, will turn her back. There is hope."

"For what, Lord?"

"It is best that I do not speak too freely. But know this: we may be offered a door to pass through to a place of refuge, as Hanish was for those who founded your Houses. If we could no longer remain here, if the time comes when we must leave our lands or see all we love murdered, all we care about lost, would you follow me down such a path?"

"A place where Pharaoh does not command we turn our backs on the Lady, where we would be free, and you would yet be our Lord?"

"That is our belief."

"Whose belief, Lord?"

"Mine, Shrine's Lady Khepera's, and Remekh's who serves the Lion with his wisdom."

"Then I would follow, Lord; I and all of those who are mine."

Pahotep listened to the calls of agreement and was content. If Pharaoh attacked the Lion Domain as they feared, if Remekh was right and a portal could be opened to another land so that they could flee, then something could be salvaged from the wreck. Some, maybe most, would follow him and live, and that was more hope than they had had before. He dismissed the men with a warning.

"Do not speak of this save within your homes when you can be certain that none from outside can overhear. But carefully, quietly prepare, telling those of your households whom you trust only as much as you have to. Make ready, for if the sword falls it may do so with little warning."

His gaze met that of the Commander of his Gate Guard. "Petnake, some may have to stand rearguard, to hold off our enemies as others escape. Choose men who will stand firm. Consult with Barhket, leader of my scouts, as he, too, will choose men."

Petnake bowed in reply. If that must be, then he would lead those chosen. His grandfather's father's grandfather stood with Kahosen. He would not be less than that man of his line.

Now he slipped through the crowd following another man who, it seemed, also followed his conscience. The young officer turned and paused, looking about him. Yet not as if he looked for anyone, but more as if he made certain that any who looked for him might see him clearly, and have the opportunity to approach. And here came one. The child who followed the Lady Khepera, the one that rumor said true-dreamed, finding a way of escape into strange lands.

* * * *

Khepera received the message, and she called Shardis. "The Gates Commander has sent word that the Striking Hawk Officer is in the city. His name is Shayohni. Find him and find some reason to chat to him. Let it appear as if he flirts with a pretty girl."

"How do I find him?"

Khepera smiled. "You know Petnake, who commands the gate guards?" Shardis nodded. "Good. He followed the man himself. He will show you the one we seek. We must bind this man to us since it may be that the information he can bring will save us all. I want him here at the Temple. Bring him by the spy way and in disguise. Go quickly."

Shardis went, wasting no time in doing more than flicking a quick stripe of water across her face to cleanse away the dust stirred up from her sweeping. She seized a handful of copper scraps from the offering bowl, picked up an old woven-flax basket in the vestibule, and ran.

She trotted down familiar streets. It was probably best that she did not look at all like a junior priestess. Let any other soldiers who saw her assume her to be just another girl shopping in the marketplace, beguiled by an officer's uniform and his sweet talking. And soldiers there were:

she saw two of them considering purchases nearby, close enough to hear louder voices, so she must speak softly.

Plans almost foundered on that. Shayohni had no idea who might be sent to him on behalf of Bastet's Temple. He was certainly not expecting a girl in a shabby tunic, carrying a ratty old basket and bargaining vigorously for fruit as she thrust in beside him. Shardis spoke softly to him between complaints to the shopkeeper—and the man's retorts.

"Have you no fresher fruit? This looks to be over-ripe."

And to Shayohni. "I'm from the Temple."

"Fresh into Hanish today, you won't get better." The shopkeeper's protest came automatically.

"What?" Shayohni was confused. He heard her words, but was *this* the person he should speak to about Pharaoh's plans? And, anyway, he could hardly talk about those here in the open market, for he, too, had seen the other soldiers.

"I'm from the Temple," Shardis whispered again—and to the shopkeeper. "You all say that. I'm no child to be cheated. Show me fresher fruit or do without my custom."

"I can't talk here."

The shopkeeper half-turned to take dates from another basket. While he wasn't looking Shardis leaned closer. "I'm from Bastet's Temple. Flirt with me when I drop the fruit. Offer me something to drink. I'll take you to a place we can talk."

And, as the new dates were offered to her. "Ah, yes, they're better. I'll offer ..." She haggled cheerfully then, as she turned to leave, she stepped sideways, banged into Shayohni, and dropped the basket.

Shayohni caught it before the fruit spilled and smiled as she apologized. "No harm done, girl. The fruit didn't fall, nor did I." He deliberately looked her over in the way a man might while he decided if he should waste his time. "Although such a fierce and powerful attack could have overset me were I not a soldier."

Shardis giggled. "Are you from the Striking Hawk Regiment, the new one that's only just arrived?"

"I am, I am an officer. So, pretty lady, would you care to take wine with me?"

One of the nearby soldiers caught his eye and winked. Shardis squealed. "An officer? Ooh, yes, I know just where we can go. They have good wine and it isn't too dear."

She grabbed his hand, towing him through the crowd. Shayohni looked at the other soldier, smirked, and winked back. Within him he was smiling, too. The girl was no fool, that was certain, but then, if she came from the Temple she was probably a priestess, and the Temples didn't take elevate the stupid.

Shardis towed her catch into a booth that sold wine. It sold other things—and had other trades as well. She glanced behind them as they entered. Good, no other soldier was close. She weaved between tables, across the booth, and out through an unobtrusive exit. A dozen booths later she ducked through another back door and turned to the officer.

"They want you at the Temple. No one has followed you, but from now on a disguise would be best."

"It would. What do you have?"

She grinned and opened a basket by the wall, offering him a wig, a robe heavily but unnoticeably padded inside, gilded sandals, and other items that might be worn by an overweight and middle-aged merchant. Shayohni blinked and revised his first impressions of Hanish. Clearly they had as much intrigue here as anywhere else. As a final touch he was offered a thin leather mask on a light stick, the sort of thing a merchant with pretensions might use. It suggested that he did not wish lesser beings to gaze upon him—and it also served to keep dust from being kicked up into his face.

Shardis switched into clothing appropriate for his daughter, and assumed a timid air. Shayohni swept out into the market again with her clutching his sleeve.

He spoke clearly. "Keep with me, my dear." And under his breath, "Which way?"

"Left at the end of this street, then second right, first left again. Keep going east; the Temple is on the far side of the city, towards the rear gates."

Shayohni knew the way cities tended to be laid out. Usually the front gate was almost precisely opposite the rear one. So, once clear of the marketplace, all he had to do was to travel—as the girl had said—eastwards, since the front gates were to the west. The Temple was on a slight rise, and he could see its roof once he got closer. His swift glance around him revealed no soldiers within sight; nevertheless, he kept his voice down.

"Who are you?"

"Shardis. True-dreamer and Daughter of Bastet."

Shayohni was impressed. If the girl spoke the truth about the second item, she was a full priestess and had a fair amount of status. If the first were also true, then even the younger son of a Lord of a Domain would not find her beneath him as a wife.

"Of what do you true-dream, Lady?"

"Of other lands and strange peoples, and of freedom."

His head whipped around. "Of freedom? Are you then a slave?"

"No, unless to be afraid is to be enslaved. But I fear the purpose of your regiment. I fear what the Great One plans, and I fear the schemes of the Priests of Aten."

Without thinking he laid his arm about her shoulders. "I also fear those last two on your list."

"You offered us aid through Anati."

"Anati?"

"Bastet's Child. You freed her from the netting, carried her from the camp and told her that you would help if you could. Is that why you're here in the city today?"

So, Anati was the name of the cat he'd helped to flee from Khamay. And she had indeed been a Temple cat and not some stray as the priests had suggested. He smiled grimly. He'd done well there. He'd tell the girl something of his reason for coming. If she told the truth about herself—and he believed she did—then it might be useful if she had some idea of events.

"Yes, that's why I'm here. Listen, we seem to be clear of followers, but nothing is certain. If I am seized I'll try to hold them back. You run to the Temple and tell them that Pharaoh has given orders that at noon tomorrow the regiments are to encircle the city."

He shut his mouth. It was sufficient as a warning, and even if the girl were taken she might be able to pass that information off as the boasting of a young man explaining why they must waste none of their time together.

He shivered. If they did take him and wring from him what he'd done, and if he survived their questioning, his death would be one to make the city shudder. Shardis circled the Temple to enter by the small rear door. Shemet saw her and smiled as she passed him. He looked harder at the man with her and came to meet them before they could enter.

"This man, he is with you?"

"He is a friend, Shemet. A man who loves the Lady."

"That is good. Men who love Her are good. He can go in."

"Thank you, Shemet."

"Your gatekeeper, is he injured of mind?" Shayohni asked as they slipped through the door.

"He was a soldier," Shardis said simply. "He was hurt in the head and his family ill-treated him after he returned. Shrine's Lady took him in. He is a gentle and kind man who loves Bastet's Children. He acts as our gatekeeper, but do not be fooled, he can still fight if he must."

"I saw that in the way he moves. Does he train?"

"Sometimes, if guards come to the Temple with an officer or one of the richer merchant and must wait, then they work with him. But everyone likes Shemet and he's a good gatekeeper."

Shayohni nodded. The gatekeeper was a big man, but still young, tall, powerful, and solidly-muscled. Generally a man built like that didn't have to fight, as most men would back away unless they were crazy-drunk. But a man of Shemet's size, trained as a soldier, with addled wits? No sane man would fight him. They might lose and die, and equally as bad, they might win, and as all knew, the mad, simple, or brain injured were under the protection of the Gods. Even Aten would smite a man who harmed such a one with a lifetime of ill fortune. And that was if the man escaped the justice of his Domain Lord, his officers, or the courts.

Shardis ushered her false merchant into a room in the inner Shrine, where Khepera, Pahotep, Remekh, Kahoret, and Neshang waited. Guards stood watch in the corridor outside. Barhket and Petnake bustled in soon after, while Shayohni stripped his disguise and accepted wine. He noticed that Shrine's Lady gestured the girl to remain and sit before her on the floor. Interesting. Yes, Shardis did have status and it wasn't because she was of an ancient House. He'd noted her out-land blood. No, she must be a true-dreamer as she'd claimed.

Pahotep nodded to the young man he hoped would spy for them in Pharaoh's camp and spoke. "Tell us, officer of the Striking Hawk, why you aided Anati, why you offered your aid, what position you hold, who you are, and what aid you can give us."

The man he addressed smiled. "A comprehensive request. Very well, Lord. I am Shayohni, son of the House of Aeferontu. My House is gone now, all but me. Yet in its time it was an old House and a Name to be known. We worship Bastet in Her Lioness Aspect since it was written on an ancient scroll that once She appeared in battle and healed the only son of my House, so that it lived on."

They all understood the significance of that. A woman married into her husband's House, for it took a male to carry the House Name. If the only male in direct line died without issue or was slain, then the House could be declared dead, its possessions divided amongst all living relatives to the second degree, and the name struck from the Temple scrolls.

"The Striking Hawk Domain worship Amun," Remekh said without any hint of disbelief.

"They do, but it is not forbidden to worship another God. I bow before Amun when it is expected, but it is the Lady that I love, and Her I worship. And," he looked around him, letting them see he considered his words, "I fear for Her."

"As do all here," Pahotep confirmed. "Tell us what position you hold?"

"I am the officer of the ceremonial guard that attends the Great One when it is the turn of the Striking Hawk to do such duty." Someone's breath hissed in. "Yes, I hear much of what is said while I stand guard. I have good hearing, the gift of the Lady perhaps, and on my last shift I heard High Priest Khamay speak with the Great One and others."

He leaned forward on his stool and recounted the conversation he'd overheard.

"These were Khamay's words. 'You could encircle the city. Tell them that no one leaves until they have sent their High Priestess to Aten to bow before him and submit their goddess to His rule. With no one permitted to leave they'll come to heel quickly, in a few days, a moon at most, she'll be riding out of the gates.'"

Remekh muttered, "It could be worse. At least he is not planning an attack."

"Not yet," Barhket said significantly. He looked at Shayohni. "When is this to be done?"

"Tomorrow. They are not to move until noon, the Great One said. And he said thus also to Khamay: 'You can give the orders, and tell the regiment's commanders that they are to obey you as myself.' The High Priest left, looking greatly pleased."

Khepera frowned. "As well he might. But encircling us is no easy task. The city backs onto great ravines, wadis that run with deep floods when it rains. It can rain with little warning, even in the dry season."

"And no commander would place his men in danger needlessly." Shayohni nodded to her. "I think the encirclement will be—shall we say—less than total. It gives you a chance to get some of your people in or out of the city. But I have not seen the land hereabouts. Is there safety?"

Pahotep's gaze met the young officer's and he pondered briefly before making up his mind. "There is no escape for us outside the city. We are too many to flee unnoticed, and we have flocks and herds, gear and goods, families, and those too young or too old to survive in the broken lands away from the Domain. Yet there is another way: an escape within the city. I will not detail it, save to say that it is possible a portal can be opened into a world of which our little one has dreamed." He smiled at Shardis.

"What we require is time to prepare the people, a warning when the Great One's intentions towards us changes, and an eye kept on Khamay and those who obey him."

Shayohni spoke carefully. "Part of that I can do, Lion Lord. From what was said, Pharaoh does not plan to attack the city; he gave a moon's grace for the Lady to leave for Thebes. I think even with Khamay's urging he will wait half that—perhaps more—but no less than half. The regiments guard the Great One day and day about, and I am guard commander. But watching the High Priest of Aten is harder. I cannot promise that can be done, though I will try."

"That is sufficient," Remekh said. "A man can do no more than his best. And I may be able to have the man watched part of the time. I have friends he doesn't know." He smiled grimly. "Now, thank you for your information and your offer: we accept. I suggest that over the next ten days or so you make it appear you find Shardis to your liking.

"Tell your comrades that she is the daughter of a minor merchant. Let them know her father's guards watch her, so that if you seem to be evading observation, they will put it down to that. Hint that she has a substantial sum due to her from her grandmother, and that you are considering marriage—and getting her and her goods away from the city before anything happens."

Shayohni grinned. "Yes, that'll account for any urgent desire to know when—or if—we move on the city."

"Exactly. And if I know young men, your fellow soldiers will enter into the spirit. They'll help you stay out of sight of anyone you point out as her family, smuggle you in and out of the camp, and lie blandly to anyone who asks about you."

"One thing I would ask." Shayohni's look fixed on Pahotep. "Lion Lord, if I serve you well and if you find your portal, if it will open to you so that you may escape …"

"Yes?"

"Give me a place with you."

"You would leave everything behind? Rank, name, your House?"

The young man laughed. "I gained rank because an old friend of my grandfather's was Commander, and he died last year. I shall rise in rank no further. I have no goods but my pay, no mount but the one accorded from the regiment's beasts. While I live I have a House and Name, but I cannot afford to wed a woman who is my equal. I stand alone. My parents are dead, I have no siblings, and while I have a number of distant cousins—most are not distant enough to suit me." His face broke into a wide smile as he looked around the circle of faces.

"What, have none of you heard the ancient tales? How men in my position have traveled to far lands, made their Name anew there, and rebuilt their House? If I remain here I may have to prove my loyalty to Aten before Him in His own Temple. And that lie would be found out, since it is not the truth in my heart. Nor do I think that I would like the consequences."

They hesitated and his hope faded.

Outside the room there was a small commotion. Guards hastily opened the door. Anati padded in, graceful, light-pawed, head tilted back, green eyes studying the people there. She walked to Shayohni, gathered herself, jumped into his lap and, as his arms went about her, she licked first one side of his face and then the other before tucking her head under his chin and purring.

Khepera spoke then, a flat command that could not be gainsaid. "He is a true man and comes with us, by Her choice." And none dissented.

13

Shayohni returned to camp and waited. The encirclement of Hanish was carried out the next noonday but, as he'd thought, the regiment commanders weren't overly thorough, and Khamay didn't know enough to demand it be so. The Lion Domain covered a very large amount of land, but it was poor and very sparsely populated outside Hanish. The city and everyone in the Domain totaled less than ten thousand people.

The two standard regiments came to six thousand between them, and almost all were trained soldiers. Even the cooks, riding- and baggage-beast handlers, and servants could fight at need. Of the Domain's people, only half were of fighting age, and those who had received any kind of training and *could* fight were probably less than a tenth of that. The city walls were thick and kept in good condition, while the gates were massive and well-guarded. It was easier for Pharaoh to send a demand before settling down in comfort to outwait the heretics.

Khamay would prefer action. "Great One, they defy You."

"They'll learn better," Akhenaten said smugly. "Once hunger bites, they'll come meekly out of their garbage heap of a city and kiss my feet for bread."

"It does not look well for the Great Lord of Two Lands to sit waiting His people's pleasure."

Syamekh, standing to one side, spoke quietly. "Do you say that the Great One's plans are foolish? That He does not know what He is doing? The plan seems to me to be that of a wise ruler, of a soldier who does not waste his men without cause. The soldiers honor such a man."

Akhenaten's chest swelled. "Do you hear that, Khamay? My people praise my name that I am no fool to toss away their lives. I am a man, a soldier, and Pharaoh. I know what I am doing and my soldiers carry out my will. That is enough."

"But Wise One ..."

"Enough!"

Very wisely Khamay agreed. Five days passed, during which time the city of Hanish, supplied quietly and adequately through the Wadi of Baboons, failed to starve, open the gates, or crawl to their ruler's feet for bread—or anything else.

Khamay resumed his pleas for an attack, and—with Syamekh's subtle assistance—managed to infuriate his ruler sufficiently that Akhenaten decided to send his demand again and wait a further time for reply.

* * * *

The city was busy, just not with answering their Pharaoh's commands. Pahotep was in conference with his scouts and his sister.

"What about the children? If there is an attack we'll need to get them out of the city," he asked.

"That's arranged. I have Isara and another of my priestesses doing the work. They've spoken to the families, and they agree that if Akhenaten attacks us they'll allow the children to be taken away secretly. We have chosen adults too, one each from a number of related families, to care for the little ones. There is food stored in the chambers your men cut into the rock walls of the wadi. The rooms there are above flood level, but below the wadi rim and are well concealed."

"What food do they have available, and can it be retrieved at need?"

Khepera nodded. "Mostly grain. It's stored in hide sacks laced together in pairs. If they need to be shifted in a hurry they have only to be tossed over the back of a beast, or a man could bear them across his shoulders. There are a hundred pounds of grain in each pair. There's dried meat and dates as well, all stored in such a way it can be quickly and easily transported if we must."

"A good job, my sister." He looked at his commander. "Barhket, what of the enemy camp?"

The leader of scouts grinned. "Wide open, Lord. It's generations since Napata fought, and this lot has grown soft. They think that because they encircle the city, none of us can come or go. It's possible to stroll through them any time, so long as one wears the right clothing. I could even get to Pharaoh if I wished."

Khepera jerked her head around to stare at her brother." Not assassination, Pahotep?"

"I considered it," he confessed. "But, no. It would solve the immediate problem but destroy us in the longer term. The other domains would rise to put a new Pharaoh on the throne if Pharaoh died in some acceptable way. But if I sent an assassin—or if they had reason to think I had—they would attack the Lion Lands and slaughter us all. It is blasphemy, and who would not fear the wrath of the Gods falling upon all men if they did not punish the blasphemers?"

Khepera nodded slowly. "Then we are back to our original choices. Either the portal is opened and we get as many of our people and their possessions through as possible or, if the city is attacked, we save some of the children and scatter through the lands. The second may save a few people, but the Domain of the Lion will end. Pharaoh will give the lands to some favorite of his, and to keep favor that one will seek out and slay as many of our blood as he can find. Nor will he be fussy about being sure he has the right people."

"I know. Barhket, I want you and your men to keep a close watch on the soldiers. Scout far out around them and down the road in case reinforcements come. Try to make sure that any game is driven towards the Wadi of Baboons. Our hunters will be killing and smoking all the meat they can lay hands on. Portal or surrounding lands, whatever our final choice, we'll need food." He turned to Khepera. "As for this attempted burglary in the library of your Temple, sister, what do you think was the purpose?"

"Humph. I talked it over with Remekh and Kahoret. We think that Khamay sent a couple of his men to search for letters. Something he could wave at Akhenaten to demonstrate we conspired against our Lord and Ruler. Syamekh agrees, and what's more he says that two of Khamay's junior priests are missing."

Both men looked up sharply. "Do you think he's had them murdered?" Pahotep questioned.

His sister grinned. "No, we think they took the road to Thebes and kept running. They were seen clearly enough to be recognized. They knew that. They also knew their master wouldn't be happy. They probably think that if they get back to their Temple in Thebes and lie low there for a while, Pharaoh and Khamay will have succeeded, and what they did won't be relevant by the time Khamay returns, so they'll be safe."

Pahotep considered that; he exchanged looks with his chief scout and saw Barhket agreed. "Yes. That's likely. Very well, Syamekh and our young officer both think that Akhenaten will send another ultimatum any day now. Remekh thinks they can attempt to open the portal in a week, when the stars are in alignment. We need to stall our divine ruler until then."

"I had an idea."

* * * *

Akhenaten sent his demands into the city the next day. The leather-lunged voice of the messenger bellowed his way through Pharaoh's words in the Courtyard of the Lion Compound.

"Shrine's Lady must set out within the next two days, else shall retribution fall upon this foolish city and its people." He allowed the scroll from which he was reading to close with a slither of rolled paper. "Thus sayeth the Lord of the Two Rivers, Master of the Twin Thrones, Divine Son of the Sun." The titles trailed off as he retired to the camp.

A day passed without any appearance of Shrine's Lady. Khamay struggled to suppress his delight. The silly woman really was prepared to defy Pharaoh, and Akhenaten grew angry—prodded by his loyal and devoted High Priest. Khamay's joy soured abruptly when, at midday on the second day, there was a disturbance at the Hanish gates. A procession exited, headed directly for the camp.

Before them walked a tall muscular man, shouting: "Way! Make way for Shrine's Lady Khepera of the Temple of Bastet, Goddess of healing and dreams, love and fertility, Lady of Night. Way for Shrine's Lady who comes to bespeak her Lord."

Shayohni was about to go on duty. He seized the opportunity, raced to the great tent, and flung himself at Akhenaten's feet.

"Great One, Divine Lord, the priestess of Bastet comes to make obeisance to You."

Khamay opened his mouth and was cut off by his master's yelp of approval. "She comes, I have won! She will crawl to me and all shall see how the great Aten-Ra is honored."

"Lord, Great One, this may be a trick."

Syamekh, who arrived almost as quickly, made certain Pharaoh saw his disapproving stare. "Do you think that the Great One is so easily fooled, High Priest? He is the Son of the Sun, not some ordinary man."

"No, no!" Khamay back-pedaled hastily. "I meant that she may be planning some trick. The Wise One is not to be deluded by a woman; they deceive, they lie, but the Wise One will know the truth."

For that flattery he received a very unpleasant look from his Lord. "All women are *not* deceivers and liars, Khamay. The Beautiful One was above such things, as are my daughters, nor do I like to hear women so miscalled. My mother was an honest and virtuous woman, and the truth was ever in her mouth."

Khamay might have salvaged the situation but for the arrival of Khepera in her litter. Shemet helped her out and she leaned on him briefly, as if she suffered from some infirmity. Then, slowly, she lowered herself to the dusty ground, crawled over carpets in the tent and reached Pharaoh's feet where she lay full length and kissed his sandal strap.

"Great One, Lord of the Two Rivers …"

"Never mind the titles, what is it that you are here to say?"

"I ask Your forgiveness that I have not come earlier. But the second night after Your Glorious Arrival, I was attacked in my own Temple, and I have lain ill ever since."

Even Akhenaten found that startling. "What?"

"Two men broke into the Temple of Bastet, Great One. I came running when I heard the commotion and one of them flung me against the wall and struck me down. I have been ill with fever from the blow and the priestess Isara, my assistant, has been too concerned to send word to You of what had happened. She is a good woman and devout, but she is not one who understands what should come first. As soon as I realized that You knew nothing of this, I came at once to ask Your aid, Divine Son of the Sun."

She watched Khamay discreetly and noticed his slight start, the tensing of his body, and the twitch of his lips. Oh, yes, they were right; the intruders were his men.

She wailed. "Blasphemy! To break into the Temple, to assault Shrine's lady and to steal, to steal from the Goddess!"

Akhenaten was still keeping up—for a wonder. "Steal? Lady, they stole from the Temple?"

"We are a small Temple and poor, and most of what is given to us we spend in caring for the people. We had a pouch of silver bits, a little copper. All was taken before the men struck me down and fled. But I would know them again, Great One."

She reeled off a description: not the vague one of the men she'd seen, but the clear, accurate description of the two young men Syamekh had noticed about Khamay and who were now missing.

Shayohni leaped in. Here was a chance to aid. "Great One," he flung himself down before his ruler's feet. "Wise One, I have seen such men. Often I have seen that they went into the Temple of Aten-Ra here in camp."

Syamekh nodded. "That is true. I have seen such young men. But Great One, this is serious. To enter a Temple, steal from a God, and strike down the ruler of the Temple! If men could do such a thing to one of the smaller Gods, what is to say that they might not dare ..." His voice faded into a threatening silence.

Akhenaten valued his own skin above all and got the point—understanding the possible threat—more quickly than usual. He scowled. "High Priest? I shall be displeased if your men have unlawfully entered the Temple of Bastet, stolen funds used for the poor, and attacked Shrine's Lady. We must respect the other Gods, though they may be lesser. What have you to say of these men? Were they yours?"

"It is possible, Great One."

Khamay had no choice. With descriptions that clear, too many men in camp could identify that pair of half-wits. They were supposed to search the Temple for possible evidence of conspiracy, not march in with horns blowing to announce their presence, waving their connection to him like banners—and allowing themselves to be recognized by everyone and their aunts. If he got his hands on them …

"I fear they may have allowed their zeal for Aten-Ra—Your Divine Father—to outrun their discretion. I knew that they were angered by Shrine's Lady's apparent refusal to bow to Your Divine will. But I had no idea that they could have committed such blasphemy."

"Where are they now?"

"Great One, the night after our arrival they asked my permission to depart for our Temple at Thebes. I granted it. It was never intended that they remain with me, for they merely assisted me on the road. I shall send men after them, and they shall be returned for Your judgment at once. They may be priests and above land law, yet You are the Son of the Sun. It is You they have offended, and into Your hands shall they be given."

Had all that flattery and stressing of his ruler's divinity worked? It had, to some extent. Akhenaten looked less offended, but not completely mollified. Khamay would send men after that precious pair of idiots. And they'd have very precise instructions.

Syamekh spoke quietly. "This is indeed a great offence. If men can behave so in one Temple, what is to say that others will think they can do likewise in other places? It sets a dangerous precedent. But Wise One, if their own Temple becomes involved in the justice to be meted, some may wonder how honest the justice. I suggest that my own Temple be allowed to seek out these evil-doers and return them to Your mercy."

Akhenaten nodded. "That is sense. Do so, Syamekh. Have your people find them and bring them back. I, myself, will question them. My Divine Father is the Great God, but he would not approve of such blasphemous behavior in even a lesser Temple, and nor shall I. Find them and return them to my justice."

Syamekh bowed and left the tent. He kept his face blank but was thinking furiously. Would it be better to really find this duo of fools? He had little doubt that they'd implicate Khamay, but Akhenaten wouldn't let that alter his true plans. He'd make a fuss about trying the pair, he'd have them executed, but in the long run the other Gods would still fall to Aten-Ra. That was the agenda, and neither Khamay nor his puppet would permit it to be changed.

He found his assistant and gave instructions. "Send four men. I want this pair, but don't hurry. Let them get almost to Thebes before taking them. Once they have them, they're to be taken on to our Temple there and held. They are to talk to no one. *No one*, Tiaahn!"

"Yes, Lord."

"Give the men extra mounts, silver, copper, and travel rations. They are to catch up with these two as quickly as possible, but then hang back."

"You want them found fast, but dealt with more slowly."

"Exactly. The Gods and the Temples have their own plans." His smile was dangerous. "As the Great One and his High Priest shall discover. But no plan is perfect; I want these men where I can lay hands on them when they're wanted. I want them away from any place where Khamay can reach them, and I want a good reason why they were not dragged back here in a few days—and not finding them until they almost reach Thebes will cover that."

Tiaahn nodded. "I will see that our people understand everything, master. They can take the pair captive the night before they reach the city. Then they can smuggle them in over the wall to our Temple. Anyone asking will find nothing." He grinned. "And that includes Khamay, that slimy son of a crocodile."

"You malign crocodiles," Syamekh informed him mildly. "Sobek would not approve."

"No, I apologize to the God."

"Good, now go and see to it that my instructions are obeyed. I'm going back to Pharaoh, after that I'll be in Hanish. I want candles—and a long discussion with a friend."

He returned in time to hear the last of Khepera's explanation.

"The blow injured my head, Great One. For many days I lay fevered. As soon as I was able to rise and climb into a litter I came here." She clasped her hands. "Forgive me, Wise One, that I came not earlier. But it would have done no good. Only I may sing the invocations, and there are certain ones that are long and arduous. They must be sung over a day and a night before I can make obeisance to Aten-Ra on behalf of my Lady. I shall be well enough in another eight days, if it please You."

Argument followed. Akhenaten stood at last and cut short the discussion. "I regret your infirmity, Lady, but the time you name is too great. I shall receive you here in five days, no more." His look hardened. "But, Lady, if you do not come, I shall come to you, I and all my soldiers."

Khepera kissed the ground. "At your command, Great One."

He looked gratified. "Very proper. It shall be so then. Go and prepare."

Khepera left the tent, tenderly aided into her litter by Shemet, and she and her group departed the camp. Syamekh followed unnoticed in her wake. He went straight to the Lion Compound, asked for his friend, and was soon after closeted with Remekh.

"Did it work?"

"Well enough. We have the five days we needed, but Akhenaten's becoming anxious. I believe that on the fifth night, if Khepera isn't there, he'll attack."

"A major attack?"

Syamekh saw how frail his friend looked, tired down to the bones, and clearly not eating enough. His voice was gentle as he answered.

"I think I can keep him from that. I'll suggest a sortie: something to scare everyone here into understanding that he's serious. I may be able to convince him to wait a day or two after that, for I can point out that civilians panic. They aren't soldiers like him." Both men roared with laughter.

"Yes, but after that he will attack in strength and in earnest. If you have trouble persuading the people to make up their minds, that first assault will do it. Tell Pahotep all of this. After the minor attack you'll have a night, a day, and a night more at least to get the people and all they own out of Hanish. That's if we have the portal open by then. Will we?"

"I believe so. But you know how difficult it will be. The stars must be in perfect alignment, the invocations must be exact—and only if there is agreement can the portal be opened and held so."

"Has Khepera asked as yet?"

"She intends to do so at midnight. She wanted to speak to Akhenaten first so she could make a full report to Bastet. It may be that she hoped she could say there was no necessity?" He peered at Syamekh, who shook his head.

"No, Pharaoh is adamant, and we know his plans after this. He will not change his mind. Even if we saw to it that something happened to Khamay, his next-to-rule in the Temple is another of Khamay's kind. Our only hope is to strike such a blow that Aten becomes one of the lesser Gods, below Thoth and Amun in power, and that these events convince the other Domain Lords to raise Ahmose to the Twin Thrones, and curb some of the power of the ruler."

"It may be that what we do shall succeed—in that at least."

"And if the plan works in all things, then you shall be safe, old friend. You and the people of the Lion, and those you regard as family."

"Even so. Well, we shall know more after tonight when Khepera speaks to Bastet," Remekh said quietly.

"Aye, but will Bastet answer?"

Khepera, too, wondered that. Bastet rarely spoke to her Daughters, yet she had done so more often of late. Should a Goddess not know of the danger in which they all stood? She went to the inner shrine at midnight, stood before the statue, and bowed.

She raised her voice in the invocation. They were in great peril; let the Lady of Claws, the Ruler of the Night, share wisdom. Hear her Priestess and answer her prayer. Power flowed about her and she knew that the Lady of Claws listened.

Heartened, Khepera recounted everything that had happened that day: the words spoken, the attitudes noted, her fears. And in the quiet of the Shrine she calmed as she opened her mind, so that her Goddess might see and hear as the High Priestess had heard and seen, ending with her summing up in the intimate mode of younger sister to her Elder.

"Lady, we cannot stand against Pharaoh, not if he is utterly determined. We have seen him to be, so long as Aten stands behind him with Khamay whispering in Akhenaten's ear. The Domain of the Lion worships Bastet; we have always done so, and so long as we live it shall be so yet. But the dead do not raise Temples, they do not sing the invocations, they do not care for Your Children. And if the soldiers of Akhenaten enter the city, they will destroy the Shrine and those within. *All* of those within," she added, knowing it for the truth. They would not spare the cats of the Temple any more than they would the priestesses.

"Lady, we believe that there is only one way in which we can survive. Those of the Temple of Thoth think they can open a portal through which we may flee. Should we do this? If a portal is opened, it is to other lands that have their own Lady. Together You must agree on that, You and Your sister-self. Will You consent to that? Will You ask Her if we shall be welcomed? Will You aid us, Lady, that those who are Yours shall survive even if we are no longer under your stars in the lands we have always known?"

There was a long silence. Khepera sat and waited. Her Goddess had the patience of her furred children, and she would consider all aspects before informing Shrine's Lady of her decision.

Dawn was just beginning to lighten the farthest sky when the reply came. A Goddess needed no portal to communicate to another of her kind, and they had agreed. Love washed over Khepera, and the assurance that it was better those who loved and were loved lived on. Far as they might travel, yet they should be in Her heart. A portal could be opened. It would require more than the sons of Thoth understood, but it could be done—if all was done rightly beforehand.

Khepera knelt, arms outstretched before her, her heart wild with joy—and sorrow. They would live: the Daughters, the Children, her family and friends. The people of the Domain of the Lion would continue.

"Yes," came agreement in her mind, the voice pouring through her sweetly, like liquid honey. "But a portal is like the gates to a great city. It requires strength to open them, the more so as we open the portal against the proper time. Thus once the portal is opened, it can be held so for only a certain time, even with aid from the one who is twin to myself. Those who escape swiftly shall live, those who tarry will die. Tell my people this, and see that they understand. The portal shall open here. Tell those who must be told."

Khepera blinked at the place pictured for her, but she could not argue. If that was where it must be, then that was where it would be. She would tell her brother and the priests of Thoth.

"Good. Four shall hold the corners of the portal open: you and my Child Anati, age and youth, two kinds of those who worship. You shall hold the portal within the Temple. The other two shall be the girl Shardis and the man Shayohni. They shall hold the portal within the new lands. Male and female, youth, pure-blood and outland blood."

Khepera felt a sudden chill. When this business first began, Shardis offered blood to the Goddess to give strength to Trah in his battle against the war-leopard. Did the Lady intend to use the blood of Shardis and that of a man who might have offended Her by marching with one who came against the temple of Bastet? Were they to be sacrifices?

She would have asked, but her Lady was now gone. Even if she remained, Khepera thought she would not answer. She rose, staggering from her long vigil, and went to talk to her brother. They must make plans.

Pahotep was uncertain if he should laugh, weep, or cheer at the news. Bastet and her sister-self of the new lands agreed that a portal could be opened. That didn't mean that Remekh and Syamekh would succeed, only that if they did open a portal successfully, those who sought refuge would not be denied. But success meant leaving all that he knew: his lands, his city, the tombs of his ancestors, the Shrine they had built. What would they find on the other side?

"Can you have Shardis dream again, my sister? We need to know more about these new lands."

Khepera smiled and held out a scroll. "Here, brother. By Bastet's grace, she has dreamed for the past three nights, and Isara drew what Shardis saw. This is the map." She unrolled it slowly, laying the center portion on the table.

"Look here. If all goes well, if we escape, these shall be our new lands. Here, past this lake, there is a great area that is flat and fertile. It is bordered on the far edge by the sea, on another by desert, and we go to it by this path." Her finger traced a line slowly down the map.

Pahotep felt his mood lighten as he studied the papyrus. "It looks a good land."

"It does, and it lies empty of people; the nearest occupied lands are ten or twelve days' ride away. The land here is open to us in welcome, if we can gain it."

"If."

"And if we can convince the people to go," Khepera said quietly. "My brother, you know them, they will not leave easily. Nor will they do so quickly or without wishing to talk and talk."

"Syamekh says that if you do not go to Pharaoh in five days, Akhenaten will attack Hanish a day or two after that. Not a great attack, but something intended to scare you and the people. If you still do not bow before him and to his God then he will come in force a day or two later. Remekh says we should use the smaller attack to persuade the people who still waver that they must escape or be slain."

"Some will still refuse to leave, despite that," Khepera said slowly. "Others will choose to escape from the rear gates to go to kinfolk in villages."

Her brother looked at her. "I know, but we can save only those ready to follow us. Those who refuse to go, well, some may manage to survive, but most will not. Akhenaten will kill everyone he finds left in the Lion Domain when he discovers that we have escaped him."

"Does he still hold the merchant, Aashep?"

"Syamekh tells me that Khamay pushes Akhenaten to flog the man for his insults and execute him for treason after that. His family came to me yesterday, asking that I intercede. I said I would do what I can, but Pharaoh is not in a listening mood just now."

Khepera laughed harshly. "That is truth." She gathered her robes about her wearily. "I'm going back to the Temple and my sleeping pallet, for I am weary down to my very bones. Tell Remekh he'd better finish his studies. If that portal can't be opened when we need it, I may have to bow to Aten—and pray that the Goddess accepts that I have no choice but to do so for the lives of the people."

"Do you think that She will?"

"No."

They parted in silence.

14

Khamay was busy. Akhenaten wavered making vital decisions and the ruler must be encouraged, persuaded, propped up to stand firm. The High Priest of Thoth meddled in the affairs of the Temple of Aten: he must be circumvented, spies must be sent out, and inquiries made. Khamay snarled to himself on the subject of incompetent assistance, too. That fool Renzai and his war-leopard had failed, the two sent to spy on Bastet's Daughters had failed—and vanished, and he was running out of time and assistance.

"Khamay, are you sure we should attack this city?"

"Yes, Great One. They have defied You, they have defied Your God, they have rejected all Your kindness and the time You have given them to bow to Your requests. They are hard of heart, heretics, and dangerous to Your empire. If You do not make an example of them, other domains may rebel. Already, some of them mutter against You and Your divine Father."

"They do?"

Khamay produced letters. "And thus sends my fellow priest in the Temple of Aten-Ra in the Domain of the Cheetah.

"'This domain continues to worship Amun, with few worshipers for our Temple. I have recently heard talk also, that since Pharaoh intends to force the worship of Aten on the Lion Domain, now is the time for The Domain of the Cheetah to make it clear that Amun is their God. And to say that while they honor Aten, Lord of the Sun, it is Amun that they worship—and that this shall continue to be so.

"'This talk can be traced directly to the Lord of the Cheetah Domain. I have even heard the suggestion that if the Great One attempts to force the worship of Aten on this domain, it would be resisted with force.'"

Khamay raised his head. "See how they disrespect You, Great One? You have been kind, You have been patient, but Your people are like unruly children. If they continue to disobey lawful commands, they must be spanked. A man does not permit disobedience in his household. A soldier understands grim necessity."

Akhenaten nodded slowly. "Yes, yes, you must be right, Khamay. I am a father to my people, and I must act for their good as a father." He drew himself up straight. "I am a soldier, I understand necessity, also. Prepare for an attack on Hanish. If the High Priestess does not return in four days, then we shall teach the city a lesson."

"A full attack, Wise One?" Khamay's tone was eager.

"No, a father does not slay a foolish child, he spanks it, as you have said." Khamay silently cursed his folly in using that example. Trust Akhenaten to pick up on the wrong aspect of it. "No, I shall spank them lightly as a warning, a reminder from a wise and loving father." He signaled the Theban Commander forward.

"Make ready to attack the city of Hanish in four days. It is to be an assault on the walls, not a taking of the city. I want few or no casualties amongst our soldiers, for I care for the lives of my men. Oh, and the merchant Aashep; I have talked to him. He's an idiot who didn't really mean what he wrote. But he'll make an example so the city sees I am serious. Bind him, set him in front of the attack, and before you pull back, kill him."

Khamay opened his mouth, shut it again, and considered. He'd been given the right to speak as voice of the ruler. Rather than openly arguing with Akhenaten and having his words countermanded, he'd wait until he could get the commander aside. The merchant would die, but in a manner that would encourage the people in Hanish to think how it could happen to them, too, if they did not bow their heads obediently.

* * * *

Within Hanish everyone was busy. Pahotep had his scouts watching the road, the regiments, the lands on the far side of the city, and the herds and flocks pastured there. Khepera was just as busy—and exasperated. One of Anati's kits had escaped the nest box, crawled off, fallen into the fishpond, and nearly drowned. She cradled him on her knees as she dried the wailing baby.

"Foolish small one, barely five weeks old and already you're getting into trouble." The kit purred. He was dry now, warm and reassured, and the hands that held him conveyed love. "Oh, yes, you are happy now. You wouldn't be if I hadn't come in time. I remember another of Anati's kits; you're just like him."

She stopped abruptly, staring at the baby. Yes, he was indeed, *just* like Trah, who fought and died for her. Trah, whom she loved best of all Bastet's Children in the Temple. This one, too, would be a big cat, muscular and powerful. The markings on Trah's forehead were identical with those on the kitten, and now she touched him again wonderingly. She could feel what was within. Khepera shivered; her Goddess had returned the soul of Trah to them, and there must be a reason. Such a thing was uncommonly rare, occurring only when the Goddess willed.

She returned the purring baby to Anati and went to the inner shrine. There she bowed, sang the invocation, and waited. If her Lady wished to tell her why Trah had returned, then her Priestess was open to hear. If not, then—no! There was no word, so she would ask. She raised the sistrum, shook it in time to her words, and chanted softly.

> *Lady of Light and Dark,*
> *Of the Moon, of healing,*
> *Of Love and Light, of Birth,*
> *And of Claws that defend.*
> *To us you have returned one who was gone.*
> *Tell me, I ask, why this is so?*

She waited, repeated the plea, and found only silence. So—there was undoubtedly a purpose, but it was not for her to know, or not yet. She returned to checking the stores, verifying the lists of stored valuables, and ordering in items that might not be found in the lands beyond the portal—if they must flee.

In her corner, curled about her kits, Anati suckled them, licked her largest son now also named Trah, and communed with Bastet, her Mother. She understood what would be, and when the time came, she would act. Within the shrine, Bastet smiled unseen. Even a Goddess could not compel one of Her Children, but the Child had consented. That which was freely given had great power. The strands came twining together, and soon they should be enough to weave a rope that would hold secure the future of Her people.

She mourned already, but within the other domains new worshipers would arise once they had seen what transpired here. These of Her people, if they did not escape, would be dead. And—Her smile showed white fangs as Her claws flexed—no other God should force obeisance or obedience from the Lady of Claws. Her intentions were several-fold. Patience and cunning answered all questions.

* * * *

Four days passed; within Hanish, some of the people wavered—merchant families only—not the ordinary ones, those who had little. Grandparents in poorer parts of the city, remembering the tales of their own grandparents, had spoken.

"We have little, no more than we can carry. If our Lion Lord goes, we go with him to another place, this other land of which he tells us. We may fare better, grow rich in land, and maybe get ourselves a title. He'll honor those who trust him and follow."

"We could all die there?"

Grandparents eyed children. "Aye, we could. But think on this: if we stay and Pharaoh comes against the city, if he breaches the walls, who'll die then? You think he'll spare those without rank or wealth? You think that he'll spare little children because they are only babies? No, his men will ride them down, his soldiers will gut them in the dust. Your women will be dragged away to be raped and enslaved if they survive the soldiers, and your men will be slaughtered or gelded. This family goes with Pahotep."

And in half a thousand households, middle-aged men and women bowed their heads in obedience to aged wisdom. "Yes, grandmother. Yes, grandfather."

"Then get everything ready, check the packs, take this and buy travel food."

And small hordes of copper, of silver scraps were unearthed, some of which had been held since that day five generations ago when the wild men from the south were driven away—here and there, there was small plunder for those who lived. The memory of the peasant is long.

Merchants quibbled, argued, discussed—and panicked.

"I tell you, I don't like it."

A jeer. "Go tell that to Pharaoh; he'll care."

"We could flee south."

"To the barbarians? They'll welcome you with open arms—and cut your throats the minute you sleep."

"North, then. We could leave by the rear gate and circle around the army."

That merchant's wife stared at him. "Oh, yes? With two wagons filled with goods, sixteen servants, nine members of our family, including two babies, with all of our horses, mules, hunting and guard dogs, and the cats? We'll be *so* inconspicuous that we'll be easily overlooked." That last comment in a tone that could have branded hide.

Her husband winced. "But Beloved, we know nothing of this other land."

"We know that Pharaoh isn't there with an army, we know that The Lion is going. Do you think our lord would risk leaving everything behind if the alternative wasn't worse?"

There was a long silence as her husband considered and made up his mind. "No. He wouldn't. But we could give up the Goddess. I've heard that if we bow to Aten-Ra we'll be left alone. We could stay here in the city. Pharaoh will just give the domain to some other lord. We could go on as usual."

His wife, who knew he wasn't likely to bow to Aten no matter what, gave him another reason. "I see, so you assume that another lord taking over the Lion Domain won't have merchants and followers of his own to settle here? You think that he'll come here alone and believe that anyone from the old lord's rule who has stayed will be trustworthy, because he'd already betrayed one lord and the Goddess?"

"Ah. Yes."

"*Yes?*"

"I mean no, dear, of course he won't."

"So do we get ready to leave or don't we?"

In most merchant households a husband drew himself up. "Of course we get ready to follow our lord, woman. Are you a fool? If we stay here we'll be enslaved or murdered. If we bowed to Pharaoh's God he'd still not trust us. Well, don't stand around here, we have to pack—and tell everyone to hurry."

Over four days word trickled in to Pahotep, so that he smiled when he came to the Temple the night before Akhenaten's ultimatum expired.

"Most of the city, my sister. My spies say that most of the households in the city will follow us. Almost every one of the poor people, and the minor merchants. The hunters, the herds-families, even the people of the outer villages say they'll come through the rear gates and flee with us when the time comes. I have promised to send them word."

Khepera hated to speak, but she must. "And Remekh? Is he now certain he can open the portal for us all?"

Her brother hesitated. "He thinks he can. And anyway, did not Bastet say to you that we'd be welcome, that she and her sister-self on the other side would cooperate?"

"I know, but it's the timing that I fear."

Pahotep scowled in thought. "That's my worry, also. As I understand, there is one chance to open the portal. It will remain open for a certain time, then close, and anyone not through when that happens is left in Hanish to Akhenaten's mercy. I do not want to leave the Domain if there is a chance that Pharaoh may reconsider forcing us to bow to his God. Nor do I wish to linger until his men attack and slaughter everyone."

Khepera took his hand and smiled. "Little brother, you are the Lion Lord, you live in ease and comfort with servants, wide lands, and wealth. You have rank and a House. In exchange you make the decisions on which lives depend. If you chose wrongly, then you live or die with that choice; it is all balance. You are the feather of Ma'at's scales. Make the choice and do not waver, for those about you need to see you strong and decided."

His fingers tightened on hers. "Yes, wise sister. I have also decided that if the portal opens our nephew shall go first, together with all those of his household. He is young, but he is sensible and cautious."

Khepera stared. "Ahwere? But he and Kherib and the children were all in Thebes."

"'Were' is the main word in that sentence, sister. He returned through the rear gate to speak to me last night. I asked him why he would run back to a trap, and he said what I expected: that he worships the Goddess, and if Akhenaten destroys the Lion Domain, where would he and his family go? Kherib is deeply devout and she'd die before bowing to Aten. He loves her, and if he turned traitor to the Goddess, how would his own family regard him? And he said I am the head of his House, and my decisions, my fate, are his."

Khepera laughed. "Sensible and cautious, you said?"

"I know."

"Who came with him?"

"Most of his household. He gave them all the choice: to come with him and share our fate, or go to friends in the Domain of the Cheetah. Most decided to follow him. He arrived two days gone to his own place on the far side of Hanish, and his people have spent the time since then readying everything for a run into Hanish if the time comes."

Khepera nodded. The lands of Ahwere were to the southeast, beyond the wadi that led into Hanish from the rear. The regiments had not completely encircled the city and left the wadi unguarded. If the expected attack was merely a warning, then those still outside might reach the city and escape."

"What do the scouts say about the soldiers near the wadi?"

Pahotep grinned. "They say that they gamble, drink, lie about, and that they're terrible sentries. Our people have made very sure not to alarm them. Now and again one of Barhket's men has dressed as an itinerant peddler and sold them fresh fruit, wine, and dates. He gave them the impression firstly that he is harmless himself, and secondly that the city will hold out to the last moment, then agree to bow to Aten. There'll be no major battle, nothing to worry about."

"And your spies in the camp?"

"There has been discussion between the commanders and that Khamay. He wants Akhenaten to make the major attack the day after the minor one if we haven't surrendered, opened the gates, and sworn to Aten by midday."

"I wonder if the regiments have spies in Hanish."

Pahotep smiled at her. "Oh, he's tried, but think, sister. He has six thousand men out there, and the Regiment of the Striking Hawk know almost no one in the Theban Regiment. It has been easy enough for our scouts now and again to enter the camp and listen, and we have young Shayohni who hears almost everything said in the main tent. Yes, Hanish has half as many people again as the soldiers who sit at our gates, but our people have lived here for generations. Any stranger who walks the city streets is seen and known. The commanders have sent spies, but they have seen and heard no more than we wished them to."

"They'll know that."

"They will, but what can they do about it save, perhaps, take some of our people and persuade them to betray us?"

"Khamay wouldn't care how he persuaded them."

"No," her brother agreed soberly. "But the scouts have watched for that. It did happen; some old man named Taphis from a village named Taphere agreed. We saw to it that this Taphis saw and heard what would most please Khamay. He based much of his advice to Akhenaten on Taphis' spying, and he's keeping the man to himself. Barhket's sure that the commanders don't know that Khamay has his own spy. He's giving them the impression that his God is aiding them, and it's making him look good."

"Taphis? How was he persuaded?"

"With silver bits, fine clothing, and rich food. And, so Barhket tells me, with the promise that he'll be of importance to the new Lord of the Lion Domain."

"Taphis, the village of Taphere … The names are familiar, somehow. Will he survive?"

"Not beyond our departure, sister. Before we go we'll deal with the traitor—or Akhenaten will do so later. We've made certain Taphis and his kin know nothing about the portal."

"How large is his village?"

"No size. Barhket says that it used to be larger, but now it is down to one family, perhaps fourteen people living in a third of the twelve houses, no more. And from his description it seems likely that few would back the old man in his treachery if they were not so greatly afraid of him."

He took his leave while Khepera tried to recall the name. Something tugged at her memory. Then a picture slid into her memory of a child wading towards her. The village of Taphere. Ah, that was where she had found Shardis. She went in search of the girl and told her all she heard from Pahotep. She asked a question.

"He's right," Shardis agreed. "Everyone is terrified of my grandfather. I expect the other families fled, for they weren't closely related to him. Now only our immediate family stays. I don't think they support him. Still, they wouldn't go against him even if you told them. They'd probably run if they had the chance, though."

Khepera's expression saddened. "I don't know if we can save them. We can't afford to let him know that we know of his treachery until the last moment. By then the regiments would be between Taphere and Hanish. Would your family be able to avoid them and get to the city if they were warned?"

Shardis smiled. "They know that area as the lines on their hands, and the wadi that was filled with water the day you rescued me actually breaks back to the south. It leads into another that continues south, and that other into the Wadi of Baboons. There is soft sand on the bottom of the wadis, so if you keep close to the walls and make no sound, you can reach the city without being noticed."

Khepera accepted that, then started. "And that could allow your grandfather and others a way into the city. They could enter before they are noticed."

"Why? The armies of Pharaoh can batter down the gates; they have no need to sneak through wadis." Shardis looked puzzled.

"Not for the minor attack they plan, no. But if they attack Hanish with all they have, it would be very useful to have soldiers at our rear. The panic alone could hamper an effective defense. I wonder if your grandfather has told Khamay of this path."

Shardis snorted. "Not until the last moment, he wouldn't. And he'll try for gold as payment."

"When would that last moment be?"

"The morning after the minor attack—if that is what happens. If they decide instead to make only one attack, then the morning of the day before. Once he sees and hears them preparing, he'll go to Khamay and offer him the information. He'll look innocent and say that he isn't a soldier and hadn't realized it could be important to anyone until now."

Khepera's smile widened. "You are certain that he'll wait until the last moment, and he won't talk until Akhenaten's major attack?"

"That's what I think," Shardis cautioned. "But if Khamay asks him about it ..."

"Unlikely, as the man isn't a soldier."

"Or if grandfather tells him earlier in hope of getting paid *and* sneaking into Hanish with—or right after—the soldiers to have the best pickings from what's left."

"But if he does that, Khamay could just send in the soldiers and not pay Taphis or allow him to go with them," Khepera argued. "Wouldn't your grandfather think of that?"

"Yes," Shardis said flatly. "He thinks of anything that might cost him money."

"Then I must go and tell my brother of all this. But Shardis …" She studied the girl's face. "If we can save the others of your family, should we? Are they like Taphis? None of them protected you when he tried to drown you."

The girl stood silent, remembering. It was now more than nine years since Shrine's Lady rescued her. In that time a lot could happen. She turned fifteen, was a valued member of Bastet's Daughters, and was no longer the small, terrified child who her grandfather had regularly thrashed and planned to murder. But she recalled the beatings and the hunger. Others had suffered, and some even died in the same way. She changed once she was free. Perhaps they would also? She said this to Khepera and was hugged.

"Child, you have a good heart. We'll see what we can do, but in the end, know that whatever happens is not your fault. We cannot risk a city for one family, especially when the head of the House is a betrayer."

Shardis nodded; that was reasonable and true. She went to play with Anati's kittens, for their small soft bodies, patting paws and loving purrs, soothed and comforted her.

She cradled Trah and wondered if her cousin, Ritseh, was still in the village. Had grandfather found another man to whom he could sell her cousin in marriage? One who would not kill her as the first man would have, the man Shardis had seen in her dreams? Ritseh was only five years older and Shardis had loved her. They'd been friends. If her cousin knew what Taphis planned, she'd have tried to save Shardis. Wouldn't she? Or was she too afraid of the old man to do anything?

Shardis cuddled Trah closer and tears suddenly slid down her cheeks, dripping off her chin onto his fur. The kitten swore and, suddenly cheered, Shardis held him up.

"Yes, she'd have tried to help me, I know she would. And I'll do the same if she's still alive. I'll ask Remekh if he can help me look at Taphere in a dream." With that settled, she returned to the kittens.

15

Remekh was willing to help. Knowledge was rarely wasted, and knowing what was happening at this village could give insight into Taphis' actions, and perhaps some indication of when he might betray the path through the wadis into Hanish.

"Drink this, lie down, and I'll link with your dream."

"The dream was useless," he reported later to Pahotep and Khepera. "Save to let the child know that her cousin was alive and back in the village. From what we heard, around five years ago this cousin was married to a man who paid for her. He died soon after and his family immediately returned the girl. They claim that she is barren; at least in her half year of marriage she did not become pregnant. Her husband's brother didn't want to take her to wife, so she was dumped back on Taphere without any of her possessions."

"What of Taphis?"

Remekh shuddered delicately. "A disgusting person. His whole family is terrified of him; the child is right about that. They don't seem to be actively evil, just ignorant and very poor—and I think they'd do almost anything to change that." He looked around to make sure Shardis was out of hearing. "Truthfully, getting them all out of the village is too dangerous. Taphis is likely to assume that you conspired against him. He *is* evil and also deeply paranoid; he'd run to Khamay out of spite."

"What about the girl?"

"She's very badly treated. Shardis says they loved each other as children, and Ritseh protected her as best she could." He smiled thoughtfully. "Interestingly, her grandfather promised her another beating in Shardis' dream. Apparently Ritseh didn't perform her day's tasks as he expected, and he half-killed her, with the promise of another thrashing tomorrow night. It would be quite possible to get her away without panicking him. He'd assume that she ran off, afraid of him and his stick. But you can't take the others; that almost certainly *would* alert him."

Khepera nodded. "It really is only Ritseh she wants to see safe. If Shardis can save her, then she won't feel as much guilt about the others. How can we get this woman away?"

Remekh nodded. "Barhket says he'll approach her as a friend of Shardis and say that her cousin offers refuge. She can go right then or the next day. Even if Taphis beats that information out of her, he isn't likely to jump to the conclusion that it's a plot by anyone but Shardis. And considering his actions and plans, he'll find that more amusing than anything."

They agreed to say nothing of their intentions to Shardis. If her cousin could be saved and brought to Hanish it would be time enough to let her know. If not, or their plan failed, then it was better that she wasn't distressed at the failure. They needed her to keep dreaming.

* * * *

Shardis dreamed. The land she saw was green, with an odd lavender overcast. The grass showed veins of purple, and overhead the sun shone, leaving soft, lilac shadows on the land. In the distance she could see people walking upright, if with an odd gait, and clad in black. She moved towards them then slowed, staring, as she got closer. They wore black garments, very formfitting, with an odd furry look. Then one turned in her direction and she stopped with a startled gasp.

The garment wasn't clothing at all, it was the creature's fur! It couldn't know she was there, as she was dreaming, but she could not advance. She'd never seen anything so strange, but as she watched she gradually calmed again. The creatures did nothing evil; they laughed, talked amongst themselves, and the children—cubs?—played, running, teasing, tagging each other. They had many of the aspects of Bastet's Children and, seeing that, she warmed to them.

At the back of her mind she felt Remekh holding her hand, seeing as she saw, as fascinated by the—people?—as she was. And then there was something else: a clear, crystalline presence, studying her with gentle interest, learning her, and the sense that it was coming to a decision. Nothing to fear, for it meant no harm, but on its decision might rest …

She woke in the dawn light to Remekh shaking her carefully.

"Wake, little one, wake."

She clutched at his arm. "What was that?"

"I do not know, not for certain, but I believe that it may have been that land's Goddess."

Something told Shardis he was right. The feeling had been gentle, yet there'd been a deep well of power behind it. It had looked her over, probed her in a touch like a caress, yet she'd felt that if it had wished, that touch could have torn through her like a great storm wind.

"Why did you wake me?"

"I'm not sure that I wanted their Goddess to know too much about us."

"If that's the Goddess of those lands, we have no choice," Shardis said quietly. "Didn't you say that she has to work with Bastet to open the portal? If she doesn't learn enough to be sure of us, then she may refuse. If she refuses, we may all die here." She looked at him, and after a moment's thought he nodded.

"Truth. Yes. Then tonight you dream again and this time if she comes to you, to us, we remain."

Shardis smiled at the old man. "Yes. Now, I must rise and be about my work."

He left her cubicle and she dressed before going in search of breakfast and the cats.

* * * *

In the camp, Akhenaten was being talked at by his High Priest. "It's necessary to do more than slap dust from their walls."

"Why?"

"You need to send them a clear message. Let them see that You are a soldier, a true man, a warrior of the line of warrior Pharaohs."

The look in his ruler's eyes changed abruptly from mildly considering to narrow-eyed danger. "Are you saying that I might appear otherwise? That I am not?"

Khamay backtracked hastily. "Of course not, Great One. All men in Napata know You for the Divine One, Son of the Sun. A great man, a warrior the like of the great Ahmose, and from his bloodline."

"Then why should the people of Hanish think me any the less?" his ruler asked, exhibiting the common sense he could, exasperatingly, sometimes show. "No, I will not waste the lives of my soldiers, Khamay. We shall make an attack on Hanish tomorrow. It shall be a sortie, not a major attack. We do not force the gates, but we make it clear to the people in Hanish that we can, and if we are forced to attack again, we shall do so and take the city."

He looked about his tent, receiving the murmured approval of the regimental commanders. War was expensive; you had to pay death benefits to the families of those who died, support the wounded until they recovered or could be discharged, and those costs came out of the regimental coffers. Of course Pharaoh would reimburse the payments, but somehow the amount returned never equaled that spent.

"At dawn we attack!" Akhenaten said decisively, his expression smug. It felt good to make that decision and to proclaim it. Lately

Khamay was taking too much on himself. Anyone would think that he was Pharaoh and not a mere High Priest.

Khamay moved towards his ruler and spoke, keeping his voice down, angered by the flat refusal before others. "Then will You at least give orders to the commanders that the city should be completely en-circled and that circle locked down. Some—perhaps even Pahotep and his kin—might try to escape." Despite himself his tone was edged, and he winced at his stupidity when he saw that register.

"No, my dear High Priest, I won't. I think it unnecessary." He looked at Khamay and his tone was sweetly unpleasant. "I realize that you do not come from a Great House, but even so, you should understand that a Domain Lord does not flee and leave his people to die. Nor could many escape unnoticed from Hanish."

His tone became that of a teacher who instructs a rather dim student who has missed the point. "If the Lion Lord did escape, then his own people would turn against the man who left them to be slaughtered, with none to speak for them. The other Domains would at once discount the Lion Lord; they would turn their backs on him, and no matter what I did to this Domain they would stand back and allow it. I wish Pahotep *would* run; it would mean I had to do nothing but bring in a new Lord. And the people here, abandoned, would accept him."

His gaze sharpened on Khamay. "Do you understand? It would suit me for Pahotep to lose his courage and flee. I would have all that I wish from that alone. The city would open its gates to me and make obeisance to Aten-Ra. I could hand over this domain to a whole new bloodline without protest from other domains. We could all go home—and that, you idiot—is something I would much appreciate."

Despite himself, Khamay opened his mouth again. "But shouldn't a watch be kept to see if Pahotep does flee?"

"Why? If he runs, then half the fat merchants in Hanish will be in front of my tent begging for mercy the moment his departure is known. And no, I do not want the scouts, the army, the priests, or even a stray mule to turn him back if that's what he intends. Stay away from possible escape routes and let him cut his own throat, if he wishes."

Khamay saw that the commanders, neither of whom liked him, weren't going to step into this. Both voices had risen as they argued and the commanders looked quietly pleased at the rebuke the High Priest had just received. So he wasn't from a noble family, so he wasn't a soldier, but he was still sure that none of this was a good idea. He made one last attempt to prevent the approach of the unspecified trouble he felt in his bones.

"Great One, couldn't the Thebans make the attack?" They were the royal regiment, and he trusted them to press an attack more thoroughly.

Akhenaten stood. "No, the Striking Hawk shall have that honor. If we must make a major assault later then that shall fall to the Thebans. Now, I'll go to my bath and have my servants bring breakfast. Who shall eat with me?"

He considered those present. It was an honor to share a meal with Pharaoh, and just now he didn't feel inclined to give such an honor to Khamay. Let the man take his whining and his gloomy face elsewhere. He noticed the young man who led the ceremonial guard. It could be entertaining to hear the views of a common soldier, one who'd be over-awed by the privilege of being close to the Divine Son of the Son and hearing his words.

"You," he beckoned. "What is your name?"

The officer flung himself on the ground, making the obeisance due a God in His own Temple. Akhenaten was subtly flattered; this boy knew who held power in Pharaoh's tent.

"May it please the Great One, I am named Shayohni."

"Very well, Shayohni, you shall eat with me. I would hear what a true soldier thinks, and not the wailing of a fat priest."

Shayohni put on a stare of wide-eyed awe. "Divine Lord, is it fitting that a mere man of very minor nobility eats with Pharaoh?" From the corner of one eye he saw his commander nod approvingly.

"It is if I say so," Akhenaten said flatly. "Leave your command to another and follow me."

"To hear is to obey, Divine One."

"Yes, it is. How pleasant to hear from one of my subjects who knows his duty."

Shayohni noted the smirk that his ruler gave the High Priest—and the look the priest passed on to Shayohni in return. How fortunate he didn't plan to remain here, as Khamay would have him murdered if given a chance. But this was an opportunity to hear Akhenaten's possible plans, to get some idea of the timing, and maybe—if he was very careful—to plant a thought or two of his own into what passed for his ruler's brain. (Shayohni had no opinion at all of Pharaoh's commonsense or military ability, an opinion shared by most who knew him—although they had the self-preservation not to say so to anyone who might pass it on.)

He handed over the small command to his junior officer and followed in Pharaoh's wake. He found that he was expected to stand to attention inside the tent while his ruler bathed, then to join him at breakfast.

"Sit." Akhenaten pointed to a clear space. "On that cushion there and talk to me. Here, have a date."

Shayohni averted his eyes and kissed the ground. "Divine One, You should not sully the Sun of Your Divinity with me. I am the least of Your subjects, a man of no great House."

Akhenaten's chest expanded. "You are of the pure-blood, are you not?"

"Great One, I am."

"Then that is sufficient. You are a true son of Napata, in many ways almost my equal."

Shayohni drew in a loud, shocked breath. "No, Wise One. You are the Divine Son of the Sun. Were I a Lord of a Domain, senior son of a Great House, still I would never be Your equal. I am a candle to Your Radiance."

He couldn't lay it on much thicker, he thought, but from what he'd seen and heard at his guard post, you couldn't lay it on thickly enough for Pharaoh. He managed a glance and saw Pharaoh's approving, condescending smile. Yes, he'd said the right thing.

"Truth, indeed truth, yet I am also a man and I weary of being Divine. It is an order from your Pharaoh. Sit with me, my young soldier, and talk to me of your small concerns. Tell me of your impression of the commands I have given, of your own beliefs."

Ouch, Shayohni thought. He'd avoid the latter, as he preferred not to lie outright, as the Gods had a habit of punishing the man who did that, especially if the lie concerned them. But he could talk honestly about his own concerns—and a few other things—and maybe drop a beetle in Khamay's beer while he was about it. He took the proffered dates from the platter, and spoke quietly.

"Great One, the regiment knows that You, too, are a solider." He saw the reaction to that and hid a smile. So, it was true; this over-bred, soft-handed weakling wanted to believe he was a warrior. "If I speak as a soldier, you will understand."

Akhenaten nodded. "I will, yes, of course. Speak freely."

Shayohni made small talk, of his own House and its decline, the kindness of his grandfather's friend who had got him into the Striking Hawk as a junior officer. As he spoke he deferred to his Pharaoh, hinting that any true soldier would comprehend such a life, no matter how high he was in rank.

Akhenaten listened. It was all so different from his affairs. Still, he could have been a warrior if he'd not been the ruler. He liked this lad, he thought, warming to the boy who spoke gravely and trusted his ruler to understand.

"And what do you think of my commands? You know, the High Priest would have me attack Hanish outright, make forced conversion and dispose of the temple there, its priestesses and the beasts."

Shayohni spoke carefully, watching Akhenaten's expression closely, ready to shift tack at need. "A soldier goes to a city in search of amusement, Great One. But while he amuses himself he hears the people talk. In Hanish they are unhappy with their Lord, for he has brought the rebuke of Pharaoh down upon them, even as a father admonishes a foolish child. They have worshiped as their Lord does, but now they feel that Aten must be a greater God. Does his own son who is also divine not worship him? I am a mere soldier, yet I think that more flies are drawn to honey than to vinegar."

Akhenaten threw back his head and laughed. "Ah, wisdom is not only the province of the old. Yes, that is well said, and so I shall say to Khamay. You are right: the people will come willingly to Aten if they are given time."

"Nay, Wise One, it is Your own decision to do this. You understand the temper of Your subjects, how they trust You. A small smack instructs a child, but a dead child learns nothing. You are a solider, and a warrior is a patient man."

Akhenaten drew himself up on his seat, "Yes. You are right. I understand this as Khamay does not. And it shall be so. I am a soldier and patient." He grimaced. "If I must stay a little longer in this boring place I shall do so. Thank you for your company. You may leave me now, for I must consider other matters." He sighed. "A ruler has many heavy burdens."

Shayohni made his obeisance and departed, hiding a broad grin. If that worked, then Pahotep would have more time to get his people away. If it didn't, well, they were no worse off. But he really would have to stay away from Khamay, for when he heard the new decision the High Priest would be fit to be tied.

* * * *

Khamay was, but he could do nothing. Akhenaten quoted Shayohni's words to him—without attribution of course—and was obdurate.

"No, a wise father corrects a foolish child, then allows it time to understand the mistake it makes. I shall give these foolish children of mine time to do so once they have been smacked." He nodded to the Striking Horse Commander.

"You know what you are to do. Smash down the postern gate, enter the square, kill a few of the people and then withdraw and attack the main gates. Do not completely break down the gates; stop once it is clear that they will fall at one or two more blows. You will then retire most of your men to the camp, while one of your men reads a proclamation to the city."

"A proclamation, Great One?"

"Yes, I shall go and write it myself now. Find a suitable man to read it and have him waiting."

The commander bowed, and went to find his most leather-lunged officer. Not an easy task, finding a man who could both shout very loudly and read what he was to bellow.

Akhenaten retired to compose his speech. He'd use that metaphor he'd thought up, about a good father correcting a child. That would impress them. Yes, it'd do nicely.

With the dawn came the army, while the citizens of Hanish watched. Most had the sense to stay well back from the gates, but there were always a few who want to see what's happening. They died when the postern gate was smashed in one rush of a carried log and stamping footsteps, that only briefly faltered before speeding on. The army stayed long enough to kill the foolishly inquisitive—fewer than ten of them—overturn a stall at the edge of the square, and gather up two straying donkeys, then they withdrew to assault the main gates.

Syamekh stayed in his tent. He knew what was happening and had no desire to watch—nor to listen to his ruler's pompous platitudes shouted afterwards.

Akhenaten was delighted with his efforts.

"Did they flee you, Commander?"

The commander knew his duty. "Yes, Great One, they ran, screaming in terror."

"And the proclamation? Did they listen to it?"

"Yes, indeed, Great One. I saw them returning to listen, and their expressions were of awe."

"And interest? They appeared to be interested in my words, in my offer that they should be unharmed?"

"Deeply interested, Great One. They talked amongst themselves and I would say that their attention was passionate."

"There, Khamay. What do you say now?"

"That time will tell, Divine Son of the Sun."

The Divine One glared. "I am tired; it's been an exhausting morning. Everyone go away."

They obeyed, all but the guard, and Akhenaten beckoned to their officer. "What did you think?"

Shayohni bowed. "You spoke to the city as a father and a soldier, and Your words were clear and plain. They understood you, Great One. Let them now think over what they must do, for no wise man makes up his mind hastily."

He received an approving nod for that platitude. "Truth. Well then I must wait, and you shall go into the city again when you are off-duty. I want you to listen to what the people say. Report to me if they appear to be making a decision."

"Yes, Great One. To hear is to obey—and it is my delight to serve You."

Akhenaten smiled approvingly.

* * * *

Shayohni went to the city as soon as he was dismissed and trotted through the streets to the Lion Compound. Remekh arrived with Kahoret, Neshang at his heels. Shayohni was greeted, swept inside, and offered wine. He took it, sat, and explained.

"I think I convinced him not to be hasty. If I'm wrong, you haven't lost any time. If I'm right, then I may have gained you a few more days. Khamay has been trying to persuade Akhenaten to attack the city in all-out war."

"So Syamekh told us."

"Yes, but Khamay over-reached himself. He treated Pharaoh as if he were a child needing instruction. It wasn't well received." He grinned. "Then he kept arguing, so Pharaoh went against him just to be contrary. You'll be delighted to know—if Syamekh didn't tell you—that the regiments are pulling back from the far side of the city at Akhenaten's orders."

Pahotep, who'd just entered, stared at him. "He's what? Why would he order such a stupid thing? What were his commanders thinking to agree to it?"

"I may have had something to do with it," Shayohni said modestly. "He demanded that I have breakfast yesterday and talk to him. Somehow he got the idea that the city was turning against you. With Khamay annoying him so much, he decided to make his smack less harsh, and to wait more patiently for you to flee the city and the people to throw open the gates, swear to Aten, and kiss ground before him."

Pahotep blinked. "He thinks I may be about to desert my people, my city, and the honor of my House?"

"He would," Kahoret said. "So that's why the army's withdrawing from the rear of the city. That fool on the throne thinks that you're about to abandon everyone, and he wants you to be able do it without hindrance." He looked at his cousin. "It's isn't that foolish, you know. If you actually did flee, the other domains would turn against you. The people would give up and bow to Aten."

"And what does he think Khepera would have to say about it?"

"He probably thinks that, as your sister, she'd escape with you, taking cats, priestesses, and healers."

Khepera, who'd been sent for, arrived with Shardis in time to hear that, and snorted savagely. "My people would not desert the city. No," as Kahoret would have interrupted, "if we go through the portal to other lands with almost everyone, that isn't the same."

She turned to her brother. "We have the last of the merchants' valuables in temple storage, with everything listed and checked. We have food, drink, beasts standing by ready for pack and riding, and the herds and flocks on the far side of the city are gathered with their herd folk waiting for our word. Remekh, when does Syamekh join us?"

"Tomorrow night. He plans to announce that he goes into seclusion for two days to commune with Thoth. He will be represented by Tiaahn should anyone need him. Then he'll come here and we'll try to open the portal. I want Shardis to dream these next two nights."

"Good." She checked with the girl, received assent, and added, "She's yours."

Kahoret picked up a scroll and studied the map they had made. "This is the land where we go? It looks to be good land, with a large lake—there should be fish—and wide flat areas for a city, a long seacoast, and streams from the lake. I think that we should also discuss the order we allow people to go through the portal. We should mix them. What if Akhenaten is convinced not to wait and attacks early? If we break people into groups we have a chance that some of the Lion Domain would survive."

Pahotep nodded. "Yes. Your priestesses and the Children of Bastet go within the first group, sister. Ahead of them go one half of my gate guards and scouts, with you, Kahoret to lead." He chopped with one hand as his cousin would have objected. "No, it is for me to stand rearguard. You are the only one of my House here whom I can trust to do this. If my sister and I fall, you lead the House of the Lion. You are to find a wife and breed children so that our line does not die."

He returned to the original subject. "Behind those guards shall go the merchant Houses of—" He listed them. "And the people of the southern city quarter. Behind them shall go their flocks and herds, their baggage, and then your women and Bastet's Children, my sister.

"We shall send the remainder of my people in that order. There shall be four main groups, each being a quarter of the city, but each self-contained save for the guards. The second half of the guards shall remain with me to hold the city and temple gates at need. If we are attacked, it is for us to hold the soldiers long enough for as many to escape as possible."

Kahoret shook his head. "No, cousin. I know that this is what you wish, but I say it is wrong. Your people know and love you; they trust you, and in a new and strange land you are the leader they need.

"Any good warrior can hold a gate, can fight and die, if that is the will of the Gods. Ride before the people and send scouts ahead to search for danger. Lead your people, Pahotep; the gates are mine to hold."

Argument followed—but in the end—Kahoret won.

16

The people of Hanish were terrified by the attack. Those who had wavered began to come around to their neighbors' way of thinking—and, as one old grandmother pointed out: "If we stay we must bow to Aten-Ra. I have nothing against him but I have worshiped Her all my life, and how will the Lady of Claws take it that I turn away? The Gods tend to be jealous. Yet if we stay and refuse to bow before the Pharaoh's Divine Father then he has said it himself, we shall bow or suffer his wrath. I think that the wrath of the Pharaoh isn't likely to be much less than that of the Lady. We are between a river and a river horse, and either will slay us."

Her old crony nodded. "So I think, and the best way to escape both is to run away. The Lord of the Lion offers us a road, one he takes, and with him go the Lady's Daughters and Her Children. Better that we flee and live, than we stay to face the anger of a ruler and his God, or the wrath of our Lady deserted."

In their small mud-brick houses, other people said much the same thing. Here and there were holdouts, those who would risk remaining and bowing to Aten, but they were few. Headmen and women of local villages slipped through the rear gates, listened, agreed, and gathered all they could carry. In small groups they returned and were given shelter in the Lion Compound.

Only the village of Taphere had no one come to it—or not officially. Ritseh was scrubbing platters in sand in the corner of the wadi where the sand was fine and white. A voice spoke very softly to her and she listened. No one could be afraid of someone who spoke that gently and quietly.

"I come from your cousin, Shardis. She fears for your safety at the hands of the one who would have slain her."

Ritseh was told, a day after, of that attack on her little cousin. She'd been sent to buy cloth in the city and afterwards guessed it was a plan to get her away, to foil any attempt she might make to prevent Shardis' death—as she would have.

She smiled secretly for weeks at the outcome. Taphis lost his granddaughter—and not in the way intended. He lost considerable face in the process, and the beating he was given for his insult to the High Priestess kept him from handing out beatings of his own for those weeks. Ritseh subtly encouraged rebellion amongst her family while Taphis was laid up.

Now she listened to the one who was sent. "What does my cousin say to me?"

"That times are changing, and those who do not change with them may die. There is a place for you beside her."

Ritseh considered. "I am no priestess."

"Not all who serve in the Temple of Bastet are Daughters; some are Her servants in other ways. Shardis discussed this with the High Priestess. It is said that you weave well, that you spin fine thread and have a deft hand with dyes. The woman in the Lion Lord's compound who does such dye work is old and has no successor. The Temple, too, could use such a one."

She made up her mind abruptly. She did good and skilled work. If the Lion Lord or the Temple would give her a home, she would be a fool to turn that down. They would not beat her for the fun of it, not abuse her because she was said to be barren.

"I will come. Give me until this evening."

"Will you be able to escape safely?"

Ritseh chuckled. "I shall return with the platters. Pack what I wish to take. Then I shall refuse the evening meal and go early to my bed, saying I am unwell. That I do not eat will convince my grandfather I am indeed unwell. Once I am alone, I shall leave unnoticed and join you here."

"I shall wait," the voice promised. "Can you ride?"

"A donkey, not a horse."

"I have a mule, quiet and sensible. He will bear you well," the voice offered.

"Then I can ride. Anything, to be away from this place and safe."

"That you will be, lady, my oath on it. Go now and prepare."

She went quickly, the crude platters stacked in her arms. Once back in her own hut she packed her meager belongings, looking down at them. So little for a lifetime. She had seen the great river flood twenty times, and all she had to show for it was this bundle. She counted the contents: a spare robe and loincloth, a breast-band, a pair of sandals with a broken ankle strap, a carved wooden food bowl and spoon, a knife with the blade worn to a sliver, and a string of worthless beads.

She kept the beads not for their value, but because they were the first gift given by her young husband. She had him for so short a time, half a year, but he was kind. She hadn't loved him, but she'd been grateful for his kindness and, if he'd lived, she'd have had an almost decent life. She sighed softly. Ah well, the Gods gave and took away, it was Their will. Maybe now the scales shifted again and Shardis' summons would turn her dark life to brighter hope.

She went to the evening meal, held her stomach, moaned and complained and ended by refusing the food.

"My belly hurts, I feel faint."

"Worthless bitch! Go without food then, and let others enjoy the feast," her grandfather snarled. "I am generous. I won't beat you tonight, but if you are not up and working by first light in the morning, I'll teach you with my stick how to work."

She nodded weakly, cowering, holding her stomach. Let him believe her broken by his stick and threats. Feast? A thin stew of scraps; only the starving would ever call it a feast. Her gaze slid around those others who sat in the circle about the cooking pot. Her own mother, like that of Shardis, was long gone, beaten to death by Taphis. Her cousin's father was unknown, hers fled, and his fate was a mystery.

Those males who remained were cousins or uncles following in Taphis' footsteps, brutal and uncaring. Their women too cowed to stand up for themselves, let alone another. The children were feral, savage little animals who would bite any hand held out to them. She'd be well out of here; there was no one she loved, no one she even cared for. Only her little cousin had ever touched her heart, and now she would go to her.

She left the room, left those of her blood, left the village where she had been born. And, pausing only to gather up the small parcel of belongings, she threw herself on the mercy of someone she had not seen for nine years, and on the mercy of a man whose face she had never seen. In all of which she gambled, but the gamble succeeded.

"Well done, lady. Here, this is your beast." He helped her mount. "Now, I am Barhket, master of Pahotep's scouts. I am to take you directly to his house where the High Priestess will meet you in the morning."

"Will Shardis be there?"

"I believe so, lady."

Ritseh looked at him. "There is no need to name me 'lady,' commander of men. I am a peasant. I cannot read or write, I am a rejected widow named barren and returned as worthless. I am no one and nothing."

"You are the beloved cousin of Shardis who dreams a road for us. You alone of your village are offered a home in the compound or Temple, and a place on our road. The Lady Khepera herself bid me find and save you if you so willed. How are you so little if the High Priestess of Bastet says you are not?"

"The High Priestess does not know me."

"Shardis does."

Ritseh looked at him and tears brimmed slowly, slipping down her cheeks. "I was not there for her. I did not know what Taphis planned. But when she needed me, I was gone. I heard what happened on my return and I wept for her fear and pain."

"She escaped the fate he would have given her, lady," Barhket offered, having heard the story. "She has been well and happy and," he grinned, "your grandfather limped for weeks. I'll warrant none of your village mourned his bruises."

Ritseh's lips peeled back in a savage smile. "They did not."

And, she thought to herself, I have given them a chance. They would have fled Taphere—as the other families had done—if the old man had not forced his kin to remain. The village had been dying for a generation or more. The land it owned was less fertile with every season. Taphis was wealthy by village standards, but he hoarded his wealth in his own hut, hidden in small caches wrapped in cloth and buried in the earthen floor.

Her smile, unseen by Barhket in the growing dusk, widened. She would not have dared had she not been leaving, and assured a place of refuge. But she was, she had, and before she left she sneaked into Taphis' hut and left him a memento of her affection. She also took something that should have been hers and had long been withheld. She rode into Hanish as full dark fell, and her heart lifted as she passed the gates. Safe! Soon she would see her little cousin, she would have a place and status, and— she considered the possibilities—she might even learn to write her name.

* * * *

In the temple Shardis dreamed. The fertile lands, the great lake, the wild seacoast. All that should be theirs once they passed the portal. A crystalline voice reached her, spoke like the soft tinkle of tiny crystal bells that sang the words.

"That is so, but a price must be paid."

Shardis drew on her courage. "Great One, I offered blood once to Your Sister, I offer it again to You."

"Maybe." The voice was faint. "Maybe—maybe not. We shall see."

Shardis was swept away over the land, towards the distant mountains, northwest to a pass. Halfway down there was an entrance, and through that she was hurled. To stand in a great enclosed valley. It was wild land—she knew somehow—never owned, never taken or tamed.

"Here," said the crystal singing. "Here you will arrive when the portal opens, and from this place you shall leave at once, the moment first light shows again, for the lands you will own. Understand this warning, Daughter of my Sister: you must leave at once. Even as your people pass free into this place, you shall not pause nor hesitate beyond the dark hours. You shall continue in the next day and no longer, following the path I have shown you. Only thus shall you survive and come into your own place."

Shardis woke in the half-light of an early dawn, clutching Khepera's hand. "Did you see? Did you hear?"

"I saw and heard." Khepera affirmed. "I do not know the reason we must do this, but be sure that I shall tell my brother and we will obey."

* * * *

In that half-light Remekh and Syamekh stood, weary and sweat-stained. Before them on the stone pavement the dawn breeze blurred magical figures laid down in colored and powdered grain. The men's gaze locked and Remekh nodded.

"We have succeeded, brother in faith. In two days' time at dawn, the stars are in the proper configuration. The people will be ready. We can call in the herds and flocks, have the baggage packed. Let the word go forth. Those who wish to leave will have a portal opened and the Lord of the Lion Domain will lead them to new and richer lands, where Pharaoh does not rule."

Syamekh studied him. "And you go with them?"

"I do. Yes, I am an old man. Yes, I may not live to see the end of this work, but there is a greater purpose in what we do here. I have written, and that scroll goes with me. If I do not live past the portal, Pahotep and Khepera will read what I have written. They will know and understand what we have done and why. If I live, then I shall tell them myself once we are free."

Syamekh bowed, a low bow of respect and farewell. "Then as you wish, so shall it be, Wise One. I must return to the camp now. I shall not see you again." They embraced. Old friends, each knowing that their destines lay apart.

"Be cautious, Syamekh. Leave Khamay alone. Be ready when the time comes."

Syamekh grinned wryly. "Oh, I shall be. I have spoken to my people quietly, and our baggage will be packed the night before you depart. As soon as Akhenaten advances we shall retreat—to Thebes where my Temple will also be ready. Shayohni has arranged that word will go to Khamay too, as soon as you have most of your people safely away. If Thoth favors our plans, Akhenaten and his regiments will rush into the city to prevent your escape."

"And all will be accomplished as we hope."

Syamekh made the sign invoking Thoth's favor. "Let it be so, brother in faith and cunning. Let it be so."

They hugged again and parted reluctantly, Syamekh looking back at the gates of the Lion Compound for a final glimpse of the man he loved and respected. Remekh found him, a bright but ignorant child, taught him, cared for him, and been happy when his protégé rose to be High Priest in the Temple where Remekh had begun. But the old man was a learner of strange lore and, despite having been so long in the Lion Domain, at heart he was still a wanderer.

The High Priest of Thoth sighed as he strode past the city gates and into the camp. Now, he must begin, very carefully, to start the rumors needed to excite Khamay—and Akhenaten—into action.

* * * *

Ritseh arrived dirty, sweating, and aching. But her smile as she passed the rear gate of the city was so wide that Barhket smiled in response.

"Follow me, lady. The compound isn't far now. There you shall have a room for what remains of the night, and in the morning, those who await you shall be there."

She and her shabby bundle were ushered from the stables into the main building. She was given into the hands of two servants who smiled, took her to a small, clean room, provided—oh miracle—a large tub of clean, hot water, towels and soap, and left her. She soaped herself, wallowed, loving the feeling of being completely clean. Washed herself again, scrubbing at her hair, and whimpered as the comb they left tore at the knots.

She smoothed the long black strands, rose to dry herself, and walked to her bundle. Her other robe was threadbare and much mended, but it was clean. Something lay across the end of the pallet and she halted, then with a soft cry of delight she bent to scoop it to her. A robe: clean, white, embroidered about hem and neck, and of good quality. Secondhand perhaps, but better than anything she ever dreamed of owning. She donned it and waited for her hosts. In an hour they returned with food and wine. With them was a man of middle age, clearly of the pure blood.

"Be welcome, Ritseh of Taphere, kin to Shardis, dreamer of the Temple of Bastet."

She bowed, wondering who he was. A steward perhaps, a man appointed by his lord to oversee the House of the Lion and those accepted as guests. She looked at him as she straightened. She was used to men who were prematurely aged, bowed by long, hard, and heavy work, but she was still a good judge of age.

She would think this man to be in his late forties. He was heavy in the shoulders and upper arms—the muscle development of a warrior—and his features were a little blunter than the usual aquiline, framed in black hair that fell, cut square across the brow, to just above his shoulders. In the style of the older families he wore no wig, but his robe was of good quality. *Very* good quality, and the small pectoral he wore contained genuine gems on the electrum wire. She stared, realized who he must be, and flung herself down to kiss the ground.

"Lord, forgive me that this humble one did not recognize you at once."

Pahotep grinned cheerfully, stooping to gently lift her to her feet.

"No matter, Ritseh of Taphere, you are forgiven. We have better things to do in the Lion Compound than to kiss ground every time I pass. Sit, eat and drink, and listen to what I shall tell you."

He watched her as she ate, clearly starving but polite. The wine made her blink. They'd sent her a good vintage and that un-watered; it was probably too strong for her. A surreptitious signal and one of his servants left to return with thin beer and a pitcher of clean water.

"You may prefer to water the wine, or to drink beer."

He left it at that, since to say more would rub in that she was unused to good wine. But she watered the wine, sipped, and watered again, until it was about half and half. Then she drank with clear appreciation. Not a fool or crude of taste then. He considered her as she ate. According to Shardis, her cousin would be about twenty now. The woman appeared older, probably the hard life a peasant led. But there was a delicacy to her movements and appearance that made him wonder if somewhere in her line there was noble blood.

At that moment she lifted her eyes to smile at him and his breath hissed in silently. Her eyes were a warm gold, like those of her cousin; they had depths that drew him in. He felt briefly as if he could drown in them, and that if he did, it would prove worthwhile to do so.

Ritseh met his eyes and felt a shiver slip down her spine. There was a warmth in his gaze that enfolded her, a feeling of safety that drew her in. A small, faint blush reddened her cheeks, and without thinking Pahotep reached out to take her hand.

She snatched it back. "Lord, do not look so upon me; it is not fitting." She repeated her words to Barhket. "I am an unlettered peasant, a widow, returned to my kin as barren and worthless."

"And a guest in my House, lady. Let us address your other concerns. One who is untaught may learn, and I wonder, who was your mother, or perhaps your mother's mother?"

Ritseh nodded, understanding the implied question. "My mother's mother was sister to Taphis, when a Lord visiting the Lion Domain saw her and lay with her. He gave her gold, which her brother took. Before I departed Taphere I took back that which should have come to me."

"Let me see it?"

She went to her bundle and took from it the gold amulet. It was of Taueret, named as the hippopotamus to those of another land, Goddess and River Horse to those of Napata. Pahotep examined it carefully after she placed it in his hands. Yes, he recalled hearing from Remekh of that visit. It was recorded on the domain's day-to-day scrolls. The younger brother of the Lord of the Domain of the River Horse was a friend of Remekh and of Pahotep's grandfather, and he had stayed many weeks in the Lands of the Lion. He hunted, explored, and—apparently enjoyed other pursuits.

He smiled at Ritseh. "So you aren't entirely of peasant blood, either. As for your being a widow, there is little that can be done about that, but barren? How long were you wed?"

"Half a year."

He snorted. "And on that they named you barren? They were fools. My gate commander was wed almost two years before his wife bore their first child. Now Petnake and his lady have five sons." His gaze seemed to hold her motionless, scarcely breathing as she listened, but his tone was gentle, almost diffident. "Lady, I never wed. I saw no woman with whom I wished to share my life and my burdens, nor do I say so now. But we go to a strange land where our customs will change. I ask only that you remain and let us learn if there is truly something between us—and if it dies quickly, or survives to grow into that which binds us both."

She raised her gaze, meeting his, evaluating the offer before nodding slowly. She could lose little by agreement. This was not a man to ill-treat her, she thought, and if she were cast off he would see that she went in honor and with goods. If she bore a child while unwed to him the child would still be cared for, as this was not a man to deny his blood. And—she wanted him more each time she looked into his eyes. For the first time ever, she truly desired a man. Her hand reached out, to be taken gently in strong fingers.

Pahotep smiled down at her. He could guess some of the reasons why she would agree, but he sensed that she did desire him as a man, and it delighted him. He and Stephos were the only children of his father. The old man wed twice, each time producing only one child. Pahotep believed the line was wearing thin from inbreeding and Khepera agreed. She spoke of it only a day earlier.

"If we do make this journey, brother, you should take a woman."

"I know."

"You say that, but you have no wife, not even a woman to live with you. Brother, this is important—who rules after you, if you have no heir? What if you die before you have one? The Domain we build may be fragmented, and there are no other nobles here, no one the people would follow, save Kahoret, perhaps. He would do well as regent, but you must have an heir. Look about you for a suitable lady. There are those about the domain with noble blood, even if it be of generations gone."

Pahotep sighed. "Yes, I know, sister. But unless one such comes to my door and falls at my feet I won't have time to look for her, I am too busy."

And one had come, he reflected. She'd fallen at his feet, proved to have some noble blood in her line, enough to make her acceptable to his sister, while not as inbred as their own line. She was not pretty, but with her good bones she would be elegant in her old age—and before that, once she was better fed and cared for.

She was sensible, kin to one who would in time and in turn—or so he believed—be High Priestess to the Temple and Shrine of Bastet. Then, too, Ritseh was disposed to desire him as a man; that he had seen— seen, too, her surprise at her own desire. It said much about her previous husband, he thought, and little of it good—clumsy puppy that he must have been. And perhaps, if he moved carefully, she might also come to trust and like him. She could be barren, and if so he would have to find another woman. In that his sister was right, he must have an heir for the new Domain, but until that was proved he'd give Ritseh the chance.

* * * *

In the camp Khamay woke, looked at the half-light, turned over and slept again. Syamekh came quietly back and summoned Tiaahn.

"The portal opens—if nothing goes wrong with Remekh's plans— two mornings from now."

"When should I start the rumor, master?"

"This evening. Go into the city to shop for me. Return, appearing to be drunk, pause to gossip with the guards, and let slip some of what you saw in the city. You have in mind what you should say?"

"Yes, master. Shall I also move the horses and mules, and warn your servants?"

Syamekh nodded. "Say no more than that I believe the city is about to be surrendered to Pharaoh's will. That as soon as that is done we will leave at once for Thebes and our Temple there, since I will not be required here any further."

Tiaahn, in his master's confidence to a considerable degree, smiled. "Truth enough. If one considers that the word 'surrendered' may have more than one meaning."

"Exactly, and I wish to be far away when that happens."

Something in his tone alerted Tiaahn. "Do you think they plan to fight instead?"

Syamekh shook his head. "No, they will not make a stand of the sort you mean. But other things can happen. There are other dangers. Do as I have told you."

Tiaahn informed those making preparations for their coming journey, changed into an older robe, and left for the city. There he noticed things happening he could honestly mention to the guards. But as he sat in the square eating dates and watching the people, he wondered. Dangers, Syamekh had said. There were other dangers. The Temple of Thoth had ancient knowledge, power from the God of Wisdom, and their priests knew many strange things. What was it that Syamekh knew?

In Hanish the people were packing; he saw several already scuttling from house to house with baggage. Pack beasts traveled to the rear of the city, laden with packs that did not look like ordinary merchandise. And there were very few children. There were still women about, but fewer than usual.

He glimpsed possibilities and made up his mind. He'd go back to the camp now—and he'd be very careful what he said to the camp guards. He'd make sure that Syamekh's people were prepared, the beasts shifted away from the main camp, packs readied. If he was right, they might have to leave in a hurry.

The guards listened. "Not many children, an' the women are fewer, too?"

"Aye, that's so. I wondered if they are getting ready to flee or fight. Didn't look much like a city preparing to open the gates to the Great One and surrender."

The guards looked at each other and their officer nodded to Tiaahn. "Well noticed, young priest. Our thanks for your information. I'll pass a report up the chain of command and see what my superiors say."

* * * *

Noble Judge Atepmut was talking to his old friend. "Yes, I see no choice; almost all in the city will follow Pahotep and his sister."

"And you? You are appointed by the Great One."

"I notice you don't call him 'wise.'" Atepmut's tone was tart. "And yes, he appointed me, but I am a judge for justice. Where is the justice in forcing an entire Domain to bow to a God they do not worship? It is wrong, Asosi, and I will have no part in it. Yet if I stand aside, I will be removed from office."

"Whereas if you go with the Lion Lord, you will be the sole official judge in his new lands—wherever they may be."

"I will, so he has confirmed. Moreover, I shall be able to appoint assistants, and it shall be pure justice that rules, not the whims of a weakling who believes he's a soldier."

Asosi sighed. "I'll say nothing of this to anyone who might prevent it."

Atepmut looked down, then pursed his lips, thinking. Asosi observed the signs. There was something Atepmut didn't know, and his friend considered whether to confide in him. He spoke gently.

"We have been friends for many years, Atepmut, so you know my word is good. I swear to you that whatever you tell me I shall not reveal and endanger you."

Atepmut nodded. "Your word has always been good, but this is more than a minor secret. In Hanish there are only two Temples—that of Bastet, and the small one to Amun that you rule. You have only one junior priest, your servant. So I will risk half the secret. I believe Amun will preserve you, so do as I say, my friend. Do exactly as I tell you—for your life."

He met Asosi's wondering gaze with a steady, serious stare. "When Akhenaten enters the city retire, you and your servant, to the Temple of Amun. Remain within the inner shrine. Do not on any account leave it, even if men call you to Pharaoh. Say you are praying both to your own God and to the Sun God for victory, and it would displease the Gods for your petition to be interrupted. But whatever happens, whoever calls for you, whatever they may threaten or beg: *do not leave the temple!*"

"For how long?" Asosi's voice dropped to a whisper.

"You will know the time. There will be no doubt in your mind when it comes. But until then, remember what I have said. Do not leave the temple, and remain within the inner shrine. Pray also, Asosi; pray hard for all the Empire and the people of Napata."

The sole priest of Amun in the city of Hanish returned to his tiny Temple very thoughtfully. He had the feeling that great events were about to occur, and when the Gods contend, men may end up trampled under their feet. After a night of thought, he went out and bought a large supply of food and drink before announcing to his junior that they were going into seclusion.

"We will pray to Amun for the Glory of Pharaoh. I declare five days of prayer in the Shrine, and that may be extended, according to the God's Will."

That should be long enough, and if needs be he'd declare a longer time apart. He honored the Gods, but he was a prudent man.

* * * *

In the camp, the rumors set about by Tiaahn reached Khamay's ears by the next day and he acted at once.

"Great One, the people of the city plan to escape or hold the gates against You."

"How do you know this?" Akhenaten was doubtful.

"I received reports from the city. The children have been taken into hiding. Many of the women, too, have gone. Goods and gear are moving about." He elaborated on the theme and added in charges of disobedience, distrust in the honor of Pharaoh, and the general lack of cooperation of Domain Lords.

"Very well. We shall make it clear to the city and the Lord of the Lion that I will tolerate no dissent."

Pahotep received the scroll bidding him open the gates to his ruler in the morning, ordering him to wait before the opened gates together with his sister, both ready to bow to Aten in the persons of His Son and the High Priest—or else.

Remekh read the demand aloud to those assembled, before turning to look over them and speak again. "I will open the gate as the sky pales tomorrow. Warn everyone today to make ready. Kahoret, you must hold the gates, stall Pharaoh, do whatever you can to keep the soldiers out of Hanish while we get our people away."

"I shall."

Pahotep gave the remainder of the orders, and went to his rooms. There almost all of his belongings had already been packed. Only the pallet and its bedding remained. He could eat his final meals seated on the floor. When next would he be seated at a table?

The city buzzed. The gates were closed early, hours yet before dark, enough time for the occupants to prepare. They'd known for weeks that this time would come. Some made final decisions, fleeing silently from the rear gate, unwilling to leave their own lands, gambling on survival. Others decided that, after all, they would go, and scrambled possessions together.

Darkness fell. Pahotep ate alone by candlelight, standing in surprise as a slender figure joined him.

"Ritseh?"

"There is no time to move slowly. We may die in the morning: let me be loved tonight."

He took her in his arms, carried her to the pallet, and lay down with her. By morning she was content in one thing. If the day brought death, she had at least been well loved that night.

17

The morning was fair, the sky—paling at first light in clear shades of blue—indicated that it would be a light, bright day. Unusually, a brief but heavy shower occurred during the early morning hours and the air was clear, almost crisp, with an invigorating feel. Ritseh rolled up the pallet, bundling her possessions remaining into a cotton bag. Pahotep stepped out into the courtyard and smiled at the small streaks of light sky.

"Hail to Aten. Thank you, Sun-Lord, for this day." He grinned, adding in a softer voice, "And to Bastet. Lady, I thank you for a most wonderful night."

Remekh arrived hastily, settling his robe into place, with Barhket behind him, carrying a large bag filled with the essential items for opening the portal.

"Follow me." He set out, Pahotep and his scout commander in his wake. They trotted through the silent streets, Remekh explaining.

"I've made arrangements with your sister. Khepera will have everything ready at the Temple." He slowed and glanced at the man he loved as a son. "Have you spoken to Petnake?"

"Yes. The gate guards slept at the gates last night, along with half of Barhket's scouts under my cousin's leadership. Half of each group will join us shortly, the other halves remain to hold the gates if needed. Messages went out to the herdsmen in the wadi. As soon as the rear gate opens they will bring the herds and flocks into Hanish. My people in the compound are packing the last items and will follow us to the Temple once that is done."

He looked at the old man. "How long will it take to open the portal?"

"Syamekh and I did much of the work yesterday. We raised the power, called the balance of the stars, and laid out the cornerstones. If our Lady and her sister-self do not fail us, I should have the portal open by the time the invocation is finished."

Pahotep sucked in his breath. So little time before he saw a new land? He wanted Ritseh with him, he wanted to see his sister and lean on her strength. He stared about him as he reached the Temple. He wanted, oh, he wanted not to have to do this. To be able to stay in the lands he'd been born to and loved, knowing every rock. He wanted to keep his home, and everything that was familiar.

His shoulders went back. He couldn't—and that was all there was to it. If they stayed they would be faced with an untenable choice: forswear their Goddess, or be killed or enslaved. Kahoret was right. It was for him to lead, to make a new home for his people, who trusted and followed him. His sister approached, Shardis at her heels.

"Welcome, my brother." She hugged Remekh. "And you, my old teacher."

Remekh scowled. "Not so much of the old, woman. You're no spring chicken yourself."

Khepera smiled at him. "No. I'm not." She rubbed her back. "And I'm reminded of that any time I have to work half the night. But we are ready here. I'll send all my women and Bastet's Children through as soon as you open the portal. Word's gone to the herdsmen already; they have the beasts divided into four groups to bring up in turn. The first will be here in another hour."

"Good." Remekh beckoned Barhket to follow him and moved into the Temple courtyard. "Open the gates here, and have them back against the walls. Shemet, I trust you to watch the street. Go up into the niche above the gates and tell us as each group approaches. Watch also for strangers, soldiers." The big gatekeeper nodded obediently.

"I watch and tell you as everyone comes to the gates."

"Good man. We rely on you. Bad men may come to harm Bastet's Children. Your warning is important."

Shemet glared down the street as it began to fill with people. "I watch so no one hurts the Children. I am Shemet, I am gatekeeper."

He swung nimbly into the niche above the gates and settled there, sword in hand, stabbing spear standing beside him. His normally smiling face was set in a brooding look. Anati spoke to him of this, and he felt the touch of the Lady last night. Above anything that the old wise one said, Shemet knew that this was his day, his hour.

Remekh moved into position, linking with the cornerstones that were built into the four corners of the large courtyard within the walls of the temple. He allowed his power to build slowly. As he did so, Khepera touched Shardis' arm and whispered softly to Shayohni, who had joined them in the half-light.

"As soon as he opens the portal you two are to enter. Halt at the end of it; you will see a clear line. Link back with Anati and me." She smiled at Shayohni. "I know you don't understand linking, but you will. Just take Shardis' hand and her power will draw on yours. That's all that's required, save one thing."

Her gaze seemed to pierce him. "You must hold, the two of you. The portal requires a number of us to open it and keep it so. Remekh will anchor it in this courtyard and sing the invocation that calls the portal here. The Goddess and her sister-self lend their power to shape it and make it strong enough to be the bridge from one land to the other. Once that is done, Remekh's part is over and he goes with my brother. It is then work for us four. I hold the portal open at this end, you and Shardis at the other. If we fail, if we flinch or our strength and courage are not enough and the portal closes, then many of the people will be trapped here to die at the hands of Akhenaten's soldiers."

Shardis placed her hand atop that of the woman she loved: rescuer, craft-mother, High Priestess, and friend. "We shall hold. I shall hold, until death or the Lady comes for me. To the last of all that I am or have, I shall hold. I swear to Bastet, let Her hear my oath."

Shayohni took her other hand. "I too shall hold thus, and my oath on it to the Lady also."

There was a flicker about them and both jumped. A claw scratched the linked hands, and three drops of blood oozed from each to mingle together. Khepera nodded to them.

"Heard and accepted. It appears that Bastet approves. So shall it be then. If you die keeping your oath, She will take you to Herself."

In the courtyard Remekh cleared his throat.

"Be ready," Khepera said quietly. "Wait until you see the other side of the portal, then go through at once." She hugged Shardis. "Whatever happens, be well, my daughter, and know you have my love always." She patted Shayohni's arm. "And you take care of yourself and this child. I entrust her to you."

He drew himself up self-consciously. "I shall not fail you."

"I know. No more time now to talk; let you be ready."

She moved to stand by Remekh, Anati joining them, sitting neatly, tail tucked about her, the kitten Trah racing up to enjoy a final meal before an older sister grabbed him, hauling him over to be with the other cats.

Remekh hummed, the sound modulating into something sung in a clear sweet voice. It was unintelligible to those who listened, more sounds than words as he strove to fit them into the spaces between the stars. Power rose up about the courtyard, lifting the hair on people's arms, the fur on cats' necks and backs.

Then, as a slow cresting wave rises over the sand, other power joined that of the man who sang. It poured like molten honey, the sound of a great cat purring, and threaded through it: a high, sweet singing like crystal. A patch in the courtyard darkened into a circle that flattened at the bottom, the inner portion of it receding, stretching out into some unfathomable distance.

None of them could look at it. The darkness was that of a starless night, utter blackness without light or hope. It snapped abruptly into both sound and motion, forming a circle, golden at the far end, misting clearer as that broke in turn into a true sunlight that beckoned them to itself.

Shardis felt a drawing seize her, and she grabbed her companion's hand. Together they raced for the circle, running endlessly down the blackness, finding it solid beneath their drumming sandals. They broke into golden light at the other end and the girl halted.

"Here, stand on the other side and hold out your hand to me."

He obeyed as her own hand lifted. There was a wide gap between them as they pressed backwards, one against each side of the portal wall. It had drawn inwards to allow them a deep, safe hollow in which to stand. But he felt the link form and gasped. It drew on him. As yet it was nothing, merely a light touch, but he guessed that if they must hold for long, then it might not remain so gentle. Nonetheless he had sworn, and he would keep that oath.

He smiled reassuringly across at Shardis. He'd been a solider and was not afraid to die, for all soldiers knew that death waited for them on every road. And there were worse ways to die than in keeping a vow to his Goddess. But it was hard on the girl; she looked so brave as she stood there, her face set in determined lines. She had barely lived as yet, no more than sixteen. A girl-child. He was years older and a man.

Shardis smiled reassuringly back at her companion. Poor man, he was not a Daughter of Bastet, and he could not know with her own deep certainty that the Goddess would take him to Her so long as he kept his oath. He had never stood in the inner shrine, looking up at the statue, feeling the power of the Lady as it blessed Her Daughters and Her Children. He had never sung to Bastet, the words echoing in her heart, knowing they were heard. A young man, Shayohni, he could have lived little as yet. Poor man, she hoped they would survive this, and he would have a long life where they went.

In the courtyard, Anati walked to stand on the far side of the portal. Power caressed her and she purred. She was a Child of the Goddess; they fought until death came, and then they fought death. It was good to die fighting, and to know that the Mother would gather her into warm arms.

Khepera felt that and smiled. Yes, if it must be, then they would return home to She who sent them here. Link power grew between them. Remekh nodded to the Lion Lord, who signaled his guards and with a slow, steady step they marched forward, Remekh in the lead, Barhket at his shoulder. They passed the end of the portal, nodding to Shardis and

Shayohni, and continued into the true sunlight. The land about them was empty, the light an odd shade. Remekh gave them no time to wonder.

"Guards, form a circle and move out. We hold this end of the portal. Turn outwards, ready weapons. Your Lord trusts you."

Pride glowed. They were the chosen. For all of their lives they would remember that they stepped first into the new lands. They would recount this moment to their children and their children's children. They loosened their swords in scabbards, grounded throwing spears, checked belt-knives, and stood looking over the land that would be theirs.

It looked strange. The plants weren't the usual green or yellow. They were greenish, but with purple veining, or a soft lavender overcast. Above them the sky, too, was more lavender than blue. Yet there was the scent of growing things, and better yet, the clear, wet scent of flowing water. They saw nothing living save, far above them, birds circling. They relaxed a little—only to jump at Barhket's howl of disapproval.

"Don't stand there gawping! You're Pahotep's guards, not girl-children seeing a man for the first time. You don't know what might come out of the grass to bite you. Stay alert! If something attacks and you aren't ready, I'll kill you myself. Our Lord trusts you—the Gods alone know why—and your people depend on you—poor fools! Stay alert or I'll alert you with a sword flat to the backside."

His men hid grins and, while staying outwardly alert, also relaxed further inside. If old Barhket yelled like that, things were still normal. Their commander chuckled to himself, reading postures around the guard circle. Soldiers liked to know where they stood and he'd just told them. New land or not, their job was the same. He ordered the circle to open out into curved lines, like claws that guarded a vulnerable belly. The first of the merchants would come through in a moment. He could hear the thump of hoof-beats.

He was wrong. Isara led the Daughters of Bastet. Mounted on a donkey and holding Anati's kits in a basket in her arms, she passed him at a slow, steady walk. The Daughters walked behind her carrying packs, leading laden mules, and around and about them trotted the Children of Bastet. Large, sleek cats, with green and gold eyes, watchful as they entered a new land. The guards cheered quietly at the sight. It was comforting to know that new place or not, the Lady had not forsaken them and the Children would draw down the favor of the Goddess.

Isara moved clear of the guards, drew the women back to one side of the portal, and nodded to Remekh. "Where do you think we should make camp?"

He'd considered that. So far as he understood, the land here was empty of people. All they had to worry about was wild beasts—but who knew what those might be or do and whatever had been said about moving on at once, he interpreted that as meaning 'once everyone had assembled', not that the first to come through the portal should leave immediately. He believed that if he were wrong he would be told.

"Make camp there," he pointed to a large clump of young trees. "Cut down two sets of four saplings towards the center, weave branches through the others to make two enclosures, one for you and the Children, and one for the beasts. Set up camp and find water. No one is to go far, and never alone; always travel in twos or threes. Find dry wood and start a small fire, keeping it as safe as possible."

Isara nodded and set off for the trees. Barhket pointed to the two outermost guards. "You. Go with them. Do not leave them, even if there's trouble, unless you hear me call." They trotted away after the priestess and the sniffing, pouncing cats.

And into Barhket's mind slid a soft, sweet voice, like rubbed crystal. "Do not fear, commander of the guards. In this place there is no danger, nothing to fear. It is when you depart My sanctuary that you must be wary."

Without thinking, he replied. "Your pardon, Lady, but a guard must be alert at all times. It would be bad for my men to relax here, and then be alert again as soon as we leave."

Crystal laughter chimed. "You are a warrior. Let it be as you have said. But you must depart in the morning. Tonight let you allow them some sleep."

He inclined his head. "Thank you, Lady." The presence was gone and Barhket took a deep breath. Interesting. In Napata, Bastet seldom spoke directly to her people, aside from her priestesses. It seemed that in this new land things were different. He smiled, a slow, deep, warm smile. He approved.

* * * *

In Akhenaten's camp, Khamay's warning started the ruler thinking. He'd sat here long enough. It was time the rebellious domain learned it was bad manners to keep their Pharaoh waiting. He summoned the Commander of the Theban Regiment.

"I do not want you to attack just yet, but advance to the city gates. Ask for admittance."

That was done and the commander reported that there was no reply. He reported the truth. Kahoret decided that saying nothing was the best policy: it should make things no worse, and at best it might give the people more time to escape.

Akhenaten sent messages. They went unanswered. He made threats. They were ignored. He tried bribery, soft words, promises he had no intention of keeping, and threats again. By mid-morning he was annoyed: by noon he was furious.

"Attack the main gates. Force them open. I shall ride into this city in my chariot, and all people shall bow before me. I will declare the Glory of the God, my Divine Father, and the people of Hanish will accept the power and majesty of Aten-Ra—or they will die."

* * * *

Within the city the people, marshaled by guards, and hearing no sounds of battle, remained calm. The portal had been open six hours thus far, and half were safe. Another quarter were entering the portal even as the Theban regiment began to beat on the gates.

Kahoret sent Neshang with a message.

"Lion Lord, Pharaoh is attacking the gates. Kahoret has begun dismantling some of the houses near the walls to reinforce the gates. He suggests you hurry the people and you join them now, in case the soldiers break through."

Pahotep nodded. "Say to my cousin that he is to hold as long as he can, but I do not command him or his men to die. Say it to him privately," he added significantly.

Neshang bowed and trotted back towards the gate. He would obey the Lord's word. It would not do for the guards run as soon as the battle raged.

Pahotep walked with a steady stride into the portal, leading his best stallion, and with his grooms following him, leading the other beasts. The finest jack donkeys, the best mares and foals, and the great horned bulls of his stud walked in his wake. He bowed slightly to his sister and the cat as he passed, then to Shardis and Shayohni at the other end.

"Remekh, how far are we on this journey?"

The old man sighed. "Your commander is a good man. He has everyone spread down the land in the direction we are to go. They are in order, so at first light tomorrow they can head out on your word. How many more people are still to come though the portal?"

"Possibly too many, I fear. Kahoret sent word that Akhenaten has attacked the gates."

As they talked, the vanguard of the third quarter of the city flowed past, were directed to their camp and, with much marveling and conversation, started to settle in.

"It's taking about three hours per quarter. Now we don't have that much time."

Barhket stepped forward. "Let me return, Lord. The people aren't hurrying and I can see that they do. You take charge here and move the guard away from the gate, for once I get back, everyone will come through on the run."

Pahotep's gaze met his and he nodded slowly. "You have my leave to do whatever you feel is required to save as many of the people as possible. And Barhket, if you can, get my sister out."

The scout Commander's movement was halfway between a shallow bow and an approving nod, but it conveyed his affection and deep respect. Silently he turned and thrust and wriggled his way back towards the city. He was swiftly out of sight as Pahotep turned back to look over the land.

* * * *

At the gates, the Theban Regiment brought up three logs and wound them together with looped cords for handholds. They swung this in unison as the officers chanted the strikes. The gates boomed protest. Kahoret worked with his men, and had no time to do anything but nod breathlessly as Neshang hurried up. They dragged material from abandoned houses, barricading the gates, while a second group on a similar mission placed partial barricades across the streets that led into the city.

At last Kahoret straightened and wiped sweat from his face. "Neshang, take ten men and go back to the Temple. I want barricades on all the streets leading into the square before it. Once you've done that, barricade other streets; not at the end closest to the gates, but at the far end, nearest the Temple." He grinned.

"If we can trick them into those streets, they have less room to maneuver or fight, while we can move about freely. Oh, and the city wells! Break in the walls about them, fill the wells."

Neshang stared. "Fill the wells?"

Kahoret looked at him, and his voice was gentle. "I know, it's against all laws and customs. Water is precious, but Pharaoh attacks Hanish against all of the land's laws and customs, and I'll do anything I must to save our people. If the soldiers find no water here, it must be carried with them and they'll advance more slowly."

"A compromise, master? If I smash the buckets and the gear that raises them, will you accept that?"

"They'll expect that, and will bring poles and water containers. They could use the wells as fast as they advance. No, Neshang. Smash the walls surrounding the wells and toss the bricks into them. I want them filled above water level."

"At your order, Lord."

He trotted off, calling men to follow, and Kahoret smiled after them. He'd done a good day's work when he freed his servant, and he'd see to it that the man escaped, if possible. In a new land, people would forget that Neshang had been a slave once and that he was of outland blood. He'd find a place for himself and be happy.

He turned to check the gates as they boomed again. How long would they withstand that treatment? A lot longer, he hoped, for there were many more still in danger.

There were fewer than he thought. Barhket reached the Temple and consulted the guards. Or rather, he discussed the matter—then gave abrupt and definite orders.

"I don't care if some merchant worries about hurrying his cattle. I don't care if he thinks it isn't dignified to trot. I don't care with what fate he threatens you. Explain to any idiot who refuses to move faster that the soldiers of Akhenaten may be right behind him, and does he want their swords through his fat stomach? Get them all *moving!*"

They moved. Lyre-horned cattle first at a loping run, then the sheep: baaing, shoving, woolly bodies staggering as they bounced off each other. Goats emitting shrill, high-pitched bleats of protest followed. Pack beasts bumped packs but kept moving, and after them mounted riders at a slow, rocking canter. Those who could not afford to ride were walking, trotting, and a few of the younger ones running. All of them carrying packs or the smaller children, toddlers and babies, many crying from excitement or over the fear they sensed.

Between the first two halves of the population there had been a comfortable gap. There wasn't between this group and those ahead. The third group hit the rear of the second one just departing the portal and people were trampled, fell, yelled in pain, fear, or merely angry protest, and were hauled out of the way by Pahotep and his guards. One merchant halted directly in the opening to object.

"Get out of the way!"

The merchant opened his mouth to answer that snarl with measured dignity, saw that the Lion Lord faced him sword in hand, and was still more deeply affronted.

"Lord Pahotep. I protest"

"Don't stand there in everyone's way, you fool! If you want to protest you can always go back and protest to Akhenaten. I haven't time to listen." He faced the suddenly scared merchant. "If people die because you're blocking their exit, you'll be buried with them."

The merchant turned white, bolted past the Lion Lord, and vanished into the heart of his group and family—where he stayed silent for far longer than usual.

* * * *

Akhenaten listened to Khamay. "The gates will be breached very shortly, Great One. The rebels barricaded them, I am told."

"How? With what?"

"They have torn down houses and used the materials."

His ruler thought about that. "But the people won't like having their homes destroyed."

"No, Wise One, which suggests that the reports are true. Somehow the people have fled. Not through the rear gates, because the Striking Hawk Commander sent spies around to check. The herds and flocks were brought into the city and have not left. Yet our scouts have seen no sign of the beasts."

"The nobles may be sacrificing them to my Father in the hope he'll spare them," the Son of the Sun said brightly. "If that's so I may spare some myself."

Khamay wasn't touching that one. "There's no sign of most of the people either, Great One." The unspoken corollary being that even if they were sacrificing animals by the thousands, it was unlikely they were doing the same with the citizens. The outland blood in Hanish rendered the people recalcitrant to that sort of suggestion.

"Ah, yes. Well, get someone over the walls. I want to know what's going on."

Khamay passed on the order and waited. Unfortunately for Pharaoh, Pahotep, Barhket, Petnake and a number of others anticipated that idea. Groups of men were hidden, with orders to kill any strangers who came over the walls. One spy managed to elude them and saw something of events in the Temple, but he had to dodge his hunters across half the city before he could rejoin his commander.

Khamay received that report and gaped. "They're *what*?"

"All going into the courtyard of the Temple of Bastet, High One. Thousands of animals, people, baggage, and everything."

"You're either an idiot or a liar!" the High Priest snarled. "How could the courtyard hold that many? It wouldn't hold a hundred people."

"I know, High One, but they are. They line up in the streets outside and walk in, over and over again. Like water pouring into a bucket that never fills."

Khamay opened his mouth to yell again, and shut it. Whether the man was an idiot or not was beside the point. If he was so sure of what he'd seen, it was possible he really had seen it. And if he had, then it *was* possible. And faintly, dimly, he recalled reading a scroll written by some mad theorist named Amatsunake, a priest of Thoth, the God of Wisdom.

"Take this man to Pharaoh to make his report. And say to the Great One that all things are possible; I go to make further inquiries on his behalf."

That is, he thought, others will make the inquiries, and I'll make the report. If somehow the whole city is escaping, then they have harnessed more power than I have—or have ever seen. It would be better not get too closely involved.

More spies were sent, and this time more than one returned to agree with the first man's claim.

"They're walking or riding into the Temple, High One. They don't return. I watched as more than two hundred went in and there were more behind. I know it isn't possible—but that's what's happening."

His comrade agreed, and Khamay nodded. "Very well, come with me." He listened as they reported to the stunned ruler, and spoke quietly once the men were dismissed. Akhenaten stared.

"There may be a way? They are going to some new land and escaping me?" He stood. "They shall not! Commanders!" The Commanders of his two regiments leapt to their feet. "Follow! We attack the city. We shall pass the gates, strike down the heretics, and the Glory of Aten shall be made manifest."

He swept regally out of his tent. Men brought his horse-drawn chariot and he mounted, seizing the reins before a driver could arrive. The horses, standing too long in the sun, fretted, sidling and snorting. Akhenaten raised his hand.

"Men of the Regiments of Pharaoh: follow me. We attack the city. We shall burst open the gates, and all shall flee before the might of my soldiers. We shall prevail. *Follow*!"

The horses, startled at his high-pitched shriek, charged with unexpected speed and enthusiasm. Akhenaten fell back against the rim of the chariot and the regiments cheered, racing behind him. The chariot-horses reached the gates, kicked their way through the men already there, and fetched up against the barrier. Akhenaten regained his balance and his dignity.

"Open the gates, do you hear me? Guards, nobles, anyone in the city, open your gates to Pharaoh and live. Refuse, and I'll kill everyone when I get in!"

From the other side of the gates an anonymous voice said in a neutral tone, "When."

"Yes, when, and that'll be very soon. I am Pharaoh, I will not be denied." He waved at the barrier. "Tear down those gates. I will have free passage."

The hammering began again, but with Akhenaten fuming, the attempt gained force. Slowly, so slowly at first that he wasn't sure it was happening, the impatient ruler saw the gates parting. He cheered his men on, and behind the gates, Kahoret knew the days of his life in Hanish were numbered—one way or the other. He sent Neshang to Barhket with another urgent message.

18

"Barhket, the gates are weakening." Neshang panted from his run through the empty streets.

The commander of the Lion Domain's scouts cursed inventively. "How long before they fall?"

"Very soon, but we have barricades up in other streets. They'll have to tear those down, and they'll find more barricades when they get this far." He indicated the barred entrances to the square, before the Temple's outer gate.

"That won't keep them out forever, or even that long, if their officers are smart."

Neshang grinned. "Akhenaten is leading."

"That'll help our side." Barhket said dryly. "Go back. Tell Kahoret to fall back once the gates are breached. He can't hold in the open and his men will be more use in the narrower streets, where the soldiers won't be able to attack them so easily."

"Barhket?"

The commander turned back. "Yes?"

"Can we get everyone out before the soldiers march in?" Neshang's face was sober.

"I don't know." Barhket met the outlander's questioning gaze. "We may not get everyone out, no matter what we do or how well you hold, but I swear this. I'm going to have a damned good try."

Neshang nodded and loped away towards the gates. If he died, he'd die with good men—and his master not the least of them.

* * * *

In his tent on the outskirts of the camp, Syamekh heard the triumphant shout that heralded the first breach of the gates. He walked to his mount, Tiaahn and the servants following. Their group drifted unnoticed past the remount herds, past the milk cattle and the sheep held as army supplies.

Tiaahn listened to what Syamekh said about the possible dangers to come. He paid out almost all they had in copper and silver to one of the Theban quartermasters. The spare riding beasts wore saddles and bridles with the reins looped up, so it would be easy to change mounts. He'd also purchased several extra baggage mules, and all were now lightly loaded. They could keep up with the riders.

Syamekh looked at the sun. It was perhaps two hours after noon, and they could travel a fair way before dark. They'd make a cold camp then—if they survived—and travel on at first light. He led his small group past a rise that blocked their view of the city walls, but he heard a long, harsh scream from many throats and knew that the regiments were almost into the city. He looked back at his people.

"Thoth warned me in a dream last night. The Gods are angry at Akhenaten and what he demands. They have set their faces against him and all those who follow. Death shall rain upon them, the earth shall open and swallow them, the sky shall rain thunderbolts to consume them, and few shall be spared. Let us ride now for our lives, lest we be too near when the wrath of the Gods descends."

He loosed rein and his mount sprang into a slow, steady gallop. Tiaahn gave a small whoop and followed. Behind him thundered the servants, the spare mounts, and baggage beasts. Together they left a rising cloud of dust on the road towards Thebes, but none in the city behind them noticed. They were all facing the other way, watching the shuddering gates, knowing that a glorious victory—much loot and many slaves—would be theirs in just moments.

The gates groaned and broke from the great hinges. They burst open, and the soldiers entered the city of Hanish, screaming battle cries as Akhenaten posed in his chariot—while on the road Syamekh, his junior priest, and the servants rode for their lives.

* * * *

Kahoret saw that the last assault would open the gates. "Back to the barricades. Break into your groups. Call in the men still waiting. They are to hold the barriers by the Temple. When we fall back to them they may flee through the portal. Petnake, send a man to the Temple to tell them that Pharaoh is in the city and we can buy them only so much more time."

Men ran, calling to each other. The soldiers stormed in and halted. There was no enemy opposing them, but—ah—there ahead of them, running men, and they raced after them. Men ran down narrow twisting streets, yelling, howling in blood-crazed delight as others fled before them. The joyful shouts stopped as their prey turned to face them, throwing spears flicked into the air, finding homes in cringing flesh.

Kahoret had requisitioned as many spears as he could find, both stabbing and throwing. Once the gates were breached they'd have to fall back, so he ordered the inner barricades supplied with weapons. His men were veterans, not of major battles, but of the endless nagging cattle raids, the pinprick attacks from the wild southern lands. They were experts at the game of tag as played with merciless killers.

They vaulted the barricades at the end of the streets, seized throwing spears and flung them as their pursuers closed. Most managed to get away two flights before taking up the stabbing spears and standing ready. They were about two-thirds of the way back to the Temple, and in the square Barhket dimly heard cries. He grabbed his trumpeter by the arm.

"Sound the recall for the city men. No use watching for spies now, we need them to reinforce the Temple barricades."

Even as he spoke, his trumpeter hoisted the long curl of cow horn and blew the recall. It echoed in the square, the sound drifting out over the city. The long low moaning, like that of a beast protesting, rang out in the series of long and short blasts that told the listening men they could return.

Barhket went back to hurrying the refugees. The last stragglers of the third quarter trotted into the portal. He waited briefly and was about to signal the final group to follow, as breathless men raced into the square.

He faced them. "Man the barricades here, and hold Akhenaten's soldiers from entering the Temple square."

"They're still held back there," he was told, a man pointing behind him.

"I know, but they can't hold for long and there are ways around them—if the soldiers can find those. Here we have all streets into the square blocked off. Are any of you archers?"

A lean man showing a strong streak of outland blood nodded.

"Go to that barrier and you'll find a good bow and a large stack of arrows. Stand on the edge of the podium here and sight over the heads of the others. Shoot any officer you see, and any man who seems keener on the attack."

The man grinned, ran over to take the bow and the bundle of arrows and took up his position. Barhket looked at the men waiting behind the barriers.

"On your courage," he told them quietly. "On your willingness to fight for your city, your kin and friends. You must hold until I give the word you may retreat—and that word may not come, if the soldiers arrive first."

He knew many of them, good men all—at least as fighters. Several were brawlers, some had been suspected of other crimes, but nothing in the scrolls of wisdom said that a man might not be a criminal while loving his kin and his city. The last group to flee was pouring into the portal.

A man on a powerful, short-legged horse halted the beast beside him. From a basket a large, sand-colored cat glared through the wickerwork and commented bitterly on events.

Noble Judge Atepmut nodded to the archer, and then to those behind him at the barricades. "I know you, Nehuche. You've escaped punishment for many crimes where I had insufficient evidence." The lean man tossed back a ponytail of light hair, and grinned up at his nemesis. "Yes," Atepmut added, "we both know that." He leaned forward over his mount's withers, allowing his gaze to rest in turn on all of the men silently watching him.

"But we go to new lands, and in new places old crimes may be forgiven. Fight as warriors today, and when you join us on the other side of this portal, all previous sins are forgiven. We have need of brave men, and some of you have kin you love who will wait for you." He smiled suddenly, a rare thing for Atepmut. "To give you heart, I give a gift and trust that you'll live to spend it."

He rode forward, taking solid silver chain links from his saddlebag and placing one in the outstretched hand of each man. "Drink the health of comrades when you rejoin us. If you fall, this token shall weigh heavy on the scales of Ma'at in your favor." He touched his heart as he gathered up the reins. "Show Pharaoh how the men of Hanish fight."

He walked his horse into the portal mouth and was gone as they cheered. No one saw a tear trickle down one of the judge's cheeks. They would die, all of them, but he'd offered them pride in that. They would fall knowing that Bastet would take them to Herself, cleansed of evil, bearing silver to show that they had made an honorable ending. Their souls would not fall to the crocodile, and believing that, they would fight like demons until the very end.

* * * *

At the barricades deep in the city, the regiments pressed forward. A man hauled towards Pharaoh's chariot by Khamay wasn't happy to be here, but had obeyed a direct demand. Akhenaten smiled at the cowering man, flung before the horses' restless hooves.

"Merchant, your city falls! You wrote that I was unable to rule my men. Now you die, seeing my triumph. My men obey my lead, for I am a soldier and they follow me."

He gestured. Khamay slit Aashep's throat and stepped back. Two soldiers tossed the quivering body to one side.

"Khamay, stay here. Find a mount to keep up, but I will have you ready to proclaim the Glory of Aten once we have Bastet's Temple in our grasp."

Khamay hid a scowl of fear. Now was not the time to argue, as his ruler was wild with battle and he would do something unfortunate to any who defied him. He followed as Akhenaten led the way in his chariot, the horses dancing about the gate square as Pharaoh turned, pointing men down the streets, attacking only where men resisted.

An officer protested. "Great One, some streets may not be barricaded."

"Attack! There, yes, there. What?" He turned to the man.

"Great One, some streets may not be barricaded. We should seek out those."

His ruler snorted. "Nonsense. Why would they fight at barricades if some streets are open? We could just run down those and be behind them. No, if they're fighting it's because there's something they want to protect. Attack!" He pointed at the streets thick with fighting, dying men and urged his soldiers on.

* * * *

In the portal, Khepera and Anati held. Another hour and a little more before all were safe. Their strength drained as the long parade moved by. They watched as the people of Hanish passed, old men looking back at the city they'd lived in all their lives. Young women clutched the hands of their husbands, husbands carried small, weeping children, people led laden donkeys and burdened mules, dogs and family cats trotting at their heels.

Sheep came jumping, running, and baaing in anxiety, for this was far outside the normal way of things and they didn't approve. Goats yelled like small, spoiled children, leaping and bucking as they were urged along. Wide-eyed cattle passed, tossed horns clashing as they pushed and shoved each other, anxious calves running beside worried cows. Herdsmen called their names, tapping rumps with the long, light cattle sticks to encourage them or break up disagreements.

Small groups of loose donkeys and ponies came by, eyes rolling to show white rims. At the far end of the portal they ran, spreading out across the rich grass, content to graze until their owners reclaimed them. Many of the people, as they passed into the portal, saluted with fingers to heart and dipped head as they met the High Priestess' gaze, and to them Khepera nodded.

And still the power drained from her. Anati showed no open sign of weariness, but as Atepmut rode past them and Khepera knew that most of the Domain must now have escaped, she felt a touch.

"Anati?"

She received a wordless exhaustion, and a flickering of fear. A question: what would they do if this one could not hold much longer?

"We die, sister in fur, beloved. We die together, and there is no one else who, if I must die, I would rather have as company to walk beside me to the seat of the Gods."

Pride, love, and grim determination.

"Yes, sister, yes. We hold."

Someone spoke and she flinched. "Lady, forgive me for startling you. I wished only to ask, what I should do about this?"

He held a bundle and she stared, almost too weary to focus. It was the mummified body of a cat. She recognized the symbols on the wrapping and found a brief, loving smile. Trah, brave warrior, heart-friend, honored as such, and now at the last come to her again.

"You are Shahmere?"

"I am, High One. I have worked until he is ready, but where now shall he lie? We leave the Temple, and the Compound of the Lion is deserted. Even the great caves in the wadi stand empty. Where shall this one be placed?"

Khepera touched Anati with her mind, since she was his dam and—she had loved him equally, so she should have an equal say.

Pictures came at once in reply. Let this man bear the body of Trah, Child of Her, to the Temple. Let him lay it upon the altar of the inner shrine before the statue there, and the Goddess would care for Her own, whatever befell them.

Khepera nodded, passing that to Shahmere. "And hasten to do so. There is little time left."

He gestured respect and ran, holding Trah carefully. Woman and cat exchanged glances, Khepera's puzzled. There'd been something in Anati's mind, some knowledge she withheld. There was some reason why Trah should lie in the inner shrine. She asked, and received the enigmatic look of a cat that knows something it doesn't plan to share.

She laughed. "Very well, Child of Bastet, keep your secrets. I should know better than to ask."

She jumped again as a second voice spoke. "High One, Lady, you should go now."

"Shemet?" The big man stood flatfooted in front of her, his stare disapproving.

"Yes, Shemet keeps the gate. You should go now."

"I may not. I must hold the portal open. It needs power," Khepera explained gently. "It needs Anati and me to do this, to balance powers."

His look was obstinate. "Shemet's job. I hold."

"This is different. I am the High One, Shrine's Lady, and it is my work to do this. You should leave the city now, Shemet, before the soldiers come."

He snorted and strode away as she smiled after him. People could be evil, incredibly so sometimes, yet for all that, most were good, kind and loving and decent. Shemet, hurt in the head, rejected by his family, huge of size, was great of heart to match his body. In the midst of all, he worried about her. She hoped he would leave before the soldiers came.

She thought then of Shardis. Would the child be well and happy in the new lands? She hoped so, and hoped too that holding open the portal would not damage her. The girl could be obstinate; she would hold until she was drained.

And at the other end of the portal, Shardis watched as the flood continued. She worried about Khepera and Anati—and Shemet who might remain too long. But surely someone would see that he left the city? Her strength ran from her like water when a wadi dam is breached. Shayohni, too, was almost drained. Yet this was for the lives of everyone in the Domain of the Lion. She must hold until they were safe. She set her teeth and held the link, praying to Bastet to allow her to live long enough that everyone might escape. Then she could let go.

* * * *

On the barricades Kahoret whistled, the clear sharp sound slashing through the cries and sounds of battle. Every second man turned and ran down the street behind him, a second whistle and he was running with the remainder. Behind them the soldiers poured over the barricades yelling triumph. Kahoret smiled savagely as he ran. They wouldn't sound so happy when they found that the battle still wasn't finished.

They didn't. Surviving Hanish guards and scouts—less than half of them now—tumbled and vaulted over the Temple Square barricades and spun to face the enemy again. But above their heads came the whistle of shafts, and the enemy faltered. A bray of sound ordered shields, but in the closeness of the narrow streets to the square, they were more hindrance than protection.

Nehuche was one of the best archers Hanish had ever bred. He lacked discipline all his life in everything but this. His father had taught him as a child and to that training he brought raw and tremendous talent. It had been one of his secrets as a thief: that he could place an arrow through the narrowest or most deeply recessed or angled aperture. Now his gift stood between his love and death, and he would die before he fled.

He shot until the last shaft left his bow, before taking up the sword of a fallen guard and joining Kahoret and Neshang where they had stepped back to briefly rest. On the far side of the barricades the bodies of those slain by his arrows lay thick. Neshang grinned at him.

"Never thought I'd be fighting with you at my back."

"The same here, Kahoret's man. But people suggest, the Gods decide."

"I didn't know that you were devout."

Nehuche laughed. "Not me. But, well, there's someone I care about. Never knew she existed until a few years back. I've seen her often enough since; she doesn't know me, but I know her. Funny, before I knew about her I wouldn't believe I'd care, but I do."

"Her?" Kahoret knew the value of talk at such times.

"Aye, my daughter."

Both men stared. "I never knew you were wed or that you had kin living." Neshang said at last.

Nehuche laughed, blue eyes glinting. "Married? No, but when I was younger I courted a girl. She lived in a small village out in the rough lands. I loved her and might have married her, and in any case I lay with her once when we had the chance. When her father found out his men beat me almost to death. He sent me a message that if he ever saw me around the village, even anywhere in the area, he'd have me killed." He shrugged.

"I liked her a lot but not enough to die. So I stayed away. I got word a year later that she'd died so I had no reason to go back anyhow."

"Aaaahhh," Kahoret said. "But you didn't know she was pregnant. So you have a daughter."

"Yes, I met one of the girl's uncles in a tavern about four floodings ago; he was drunk, too drunk to attack me, but he remembered my face. Told me his sister died bearing my daughter, that the girl was taken by the Temple years back and was a Daughter there." He chuckled. "I was proud about that. They take only the clever or talented ones. I managed to get a look at her and ..." He hesitated, remembering. "She smiled at me. It was like sun on my face. Warming all through."

"And you've kept an eye on her ever since?"

Nehuche nodded. "When I was tapped to go and watch the walls I thought, well, it's something for her. A way to help."

Kahoret looked at his men. The fighting was growing more intense again and others needed to rest. He nodded to Nehuche. "If you fall here, should we tell her?"

"Aye. Tell her that I was a young fool, but that I'd not have left her mother if I knew about the child. Tell her," he paused, making up his mind. "Tell her I love her and she's to have a good life. But only if I die, mind you; if I get out of this she's not to know about me. A father who dies heroically is one thing, but a man like me isn't any great thing to boast of when he's still around. Swear she'll not know unless I fall here!"

Kahoret whistled an order, men fell back obediently to rest again as he and his companions moved up to take their places.

"I swear," he said quietly.

Neshang echoed the promise as their swords swung.

* * * *

At the portal Barhket shouted. Less than an hour more and all should be safe—if the portal could be held that long, if Pharaoh's soldiers could be held off. People thrust forward anxiously, cows bawled, horses whinnied, and slowly, agonizingly slowly, the last people crowded into the Temple square, lining up to enter the courtyard.

Within the Temple, a Goddess waited patiently as events flowed about her. Before Her, in the wrapping that proclaimed to all that he had been a great warrior and much loved, lay the body of Her Child. Shahmere fled and was even now hurrying through the portal. Her people had done well, a sacrifice that She might continue, and that the balance might tilt back to equilibrium. She trusted that her other Self would hold them safe, and that no more would die here than must for the balance to be met.

In the portal entrance Khepera staggered; her hand and her back against the portal wall now all that held her upright. Anati swayed where she sat, even her fur seeming to pale as she weakened.

Barhket shouted a warning, and the speed of those entering the portal became faster still: people running, shoving, as the barricades behind them gave way. Most of those that held them were dead, and fresh soldiers fought exhausted men.

Kahoret's whistle carved the air, calling a final retreat to the gate of the Temple. Men fell back, a mere two hands of them, most wounded. Neshang limped, his master had a bloody slash across one shoulder, and Nehuche's side welled blood from a sword point, although he still fought. They gained the gate and turned at bay. Behind them, people screamed and fought to gain the portal as soldiers raced across the square. The clash of swords sounded almost on top of them.

Beside the Temple gate, Shemet waited unnoticed. For years he had honored the Lady of Claws and the High One. They had given him a home and a place, status and affection. How many nights had he gone silently into the inner shrine and talked to Her? She spoke to him, to Shemet who was nothing since he returned, rejected by the army, brokenminded and cast out. He loved the Lady's Children who did not judge him, and the Daughters who always had kind words. She promised—it would be his time soon.

Near the far end of the portal Pahotep talked to Remekh. "We'll move out in the morning."

"Yes, but now you must also move."

"What? Why?"

Remekh looked at the portal. "That will not remain open for much longer, and when it closes there may be—ah—some disruption. It is well if we and all the livestock are away from it."

Pahotep eyed him thoughtfully. "And I shouldn't ask questions about this?"

"Truth. Now, listen. The portal is nothing but power: power to force it to open, power to hold it open, power to make it solid enough for thousands of people and beasts to walk upon. Huge amounts of power poured into it from a Child of Bastet, three people, and the Lady and her sister-self. And the use of all this power is contrary to the balance of the Gods. Tell me, if an earth fall dams a deep wadi so that much water is held back behind it, and then the dam gives way all at once—what happens, Pahotep?"

The Lion Lord looked at him, remembering the times he had seen that happen. "The water runs mad. It scours out the earth, great pieces of the banks topple into the water, it rises and takes with it anything nearby; it kills all whom it finds in its mouth."

"So with the power. It was not meant for this portal to open. Yes, they open sometimes into this world, but only when a balance requires it. This time the Great Ones forced that balance. They have their own purposes, as we have ours. But when the portal fails the power must go somewhere: it must be used. For that, too, Syamekh and I planned." He smiled wryly. "And the Lady too had a hand in the planning. We shall be safe enough here if you move the people and the beasts back down the valley. For those who come through at the last, have riders and spare mounts waiting, for they must move away as swiftly as possible."

Pahotep looked at him. "My sister?"

"She may live, but she will be too drained to walk. The time when the portal must shut grows close, and as that time nears, the passage shortens. By the time it closes, it will be only steps from one end to the other, and this may save her—and perhaps others."

Pahotep nodded and went to give the orders, thinking of those who were dying to hold Akhenaten back. Barhket was his Scout Commander for more than ten years, Kahoret was kin, a second or a third cousin—he could never remember. Not that it mattered, for they had always been friends, he and Pahotep, and Khepera. Petnake commanded the guards at the Hanish gates for almost six years now. He was a good man, solid, sensible, and always to be relied upon. Who of them would die, and who would live?

He oversaw the move away from the portal, wasting no time in politeness. Most had moved away already, and for those who hadn't he had little patience. He called in riders. "Each of you choose a saddled mount as a spare. We may have to get the last people away quickly."

* * * *

In the Temple square, having driven up proudly in his chariot, Akhenaten could see over the heads of the men still fighting at the barricades. His jaw dropped in disbelief; a great circle of darkness took up most of the courtyard. Into that people ran, animals driven ahead, dogs and cats followed. He stared; it was impossible—yet—he saw with his own eyes.

He reached down blindly, dragging at the shoulder of the man by his wheels. "Khamay, get up, see this. How is it *possible*?"

Khamay clambered up and gaped in turn. "Amatsunake!" he gasped. "Who?"

"The priest Amatsunake. He wrote of other lands, very far away, and said that if conditions were right and sufficient power was raised, it would be possible to reach them through a portal." Something nagged at the back of his mind, some warning, but what?

Akhenaten's expression changed to one of awed delight. "Other lands? I would be the greatest ruler ever known. I would bring them to the worship of Aten: more people to bow to Him, and to me, the Son of the Sun. I must have that portal, the power, the new lands!"

He leaned over the chariot rim, screeching to his soldiers. "Attack! Take the Temple, kill everyone in your path. On for the Glory of Aten!"

The soldiers howled and pressed forward. The last people in the square screamed, dropping their possessions, running through the portal. In seconds the courtyard was empty save for the handful of guards.

Neshang smiled at Kahoret. "I could die in worse company."

"Yes." He looked at Petnake. "Fall back and get away. You too, Neshang, Nehuche."

Nehuche laughed. "I'm bled almost white; I couldn't run that far. If only I had arrows."

Neshang laughed. "If that's what you want, archer, I see some, dropped by those last to run through the portal. Look." He dodged a sword, leaped back several paces and returned with a full double quiver, handing it to Nehuche. "Don't say that you ended this battle unarmed."

Nehuche laughed, dropped his sword and reached for the bow still slung across his back. "I'll tell the Gods that. Now, you three run. I'll hold them off with an arrow storm that will darken their sky." They looked at him and hesitated. "Go, I say! I cannot run; I have my token from old Atepmut. The Goddess will take my soul and the crocodile will be empty of belly. *Go!*"

They ran. Behind them the promised arrows flew. One took Akhenaten through the skin of his upper arm and when he squealed the soldiers faltered, holding back to see if there would be new orders.

Within the portal entrance, as the final three ran towards him, Shemet acted. Khepera had slipped to her knees, and now, as she fell slowly sideways, exhausted almost beyond breathing, he scooped her up, pushing her limp body into Kahoret's arms.

"Take her with you. I am Shemet Gatekeeper. I keep the gate now."

Kahoret glanced at the man. "Honor to Shemet," he said, touching the robe over his heart in salute. "Honor, gatekeeper for the Goddess."

Shemet smiled at him, seeming in that moment an intelligent and trained soldier, a true man, and one who knew what he had always loved.

Kahoret lifted Khepera and ran on. With him ran Petnake and Neshang, both helping take the weight of the High Priestess. In the mouth of the portal Shemet reached down to stroke Anati.

"Child of Hers, hold the portal with me now, and walk with me thereafter."

He straightened, sword in hand, as at the gates Nehuche fired his final shaft and fell. The soldiers of Akhenaten paused only long enough to thrust a sword through his heart before running towards the big man and the old cat. They hesitated briefly, then attacked. Aten-Ra was with them; He would protect them against the beast—and the other was only a man.

Shemet fought; he had been a good solider, and he was still a very powerful man, despite his years. A soldier cast a spear and Anati fell. With her last strength she crawled two paces to lay a paw on Shemet's foot. He glanced down and a sword took him through the ribs and into the heart. Dying, he fell, cradling the old cat in his arms. A promise was made, a promise would be kept. He saw Her coming and smiled as they were taken into warm-furred and loving arms.

At the end of the portal two still held, Shardis sagging on her feet, holding grimly with everything she had, the golden light pouring from her, arching overhead, touching the boy who held the line with her. For those who waited, watching, they became growing legends: the two who held open the gate to save the people of the Lion. Whispers passed, speaking their names, telling what was known of them.

Kahoret burst from the portal, yelling a warning, Khepera limp in his arms. As they passed, Neshang scooped up the sagging Shardis. Shayohni gathered his strength and staggered beside them as they reeled across the grass. Riders came galloping; the five on foot were flung onto mounts and the loose reins gathered as horses and riders raced from danger.

* * * *

Within the Temple courtyard Akhenaten screamed orders. Few made sense, but then, as his commanders quickly realized, he was mad with excitement at his victory and had no idea what he was saying. Khamay, standing behind his ruler in the chariot, could not shake the unpleasant feeling. What *had* that accursed scroll of Amatsunake said?

He saw the big man and the cat slain, saw their bodies fade into golden light and—remembered. He screamed, "The portal, run!"

He scrambled from the chariot and hurtled, howling in terror, through the startled soldiers. Akhenaten stared after the High Priest of the Temple of Aten in the city of Thebes. Khamay was not suitable; he panicked so easily. Oh well, once back in Thebes he could appoint another High Priest. He could also explore the marvelous idea of new lands—accessible through this portal.

Before the astounded gaze of the soldiers, their officers, two Regiment Commanders, and their ruler, the portal moved, engulfing the Temple. From the clear sky above, a shattering crash of thunder sounded. In the distance Khamay howled again. He burst into a group of soldiers, seized a horse and mounted, flogging it towards the Hanish gates.

Beneath him the ground heaved. The sky blackened, then lighting ripped across the darkness, arcing down to the city. The portal closed. Akhenaten, convinced he'd lost his new lands, screamed in rage, a sound drowned out by an ear-shattering roar of thunder. Within the blackness, the Temple was instantly transported to the other end of the portal. Several thousand tons of stone moved abruptly. And—nature abhors a vacuum.

"Do something," Akhenaten howled at his commanders. "I'm losing it."

They were his last coherent words—or thoughts. The city of Hanish imploded with a noise so far beyond sound it became only vibration. With it went everyone within the city walls and those outside in the regiment's camp, save the tiny Temple of Amun and the two within. The village of Taphere became dust, along with all of the inhabitants; the main road disintegrated in a long line, reaching towards Thebes, and well down that road Syamekh slowed his mount as the land shuddered. He halted the sweating, exhausted animal, looking back towards Hanish.

Tiaahn halted beside him. "That was the city?"

"It was." He slid from his mount. "We'll camp here. We survived."

"And Akhenaten?"

"Is gone, along with everyone in his regiments, and any people of the Domain who didn't escape in time." He slumped to the ground gracelessly as servants began to prepare a meal. "We can rest tonight, but we must get to Thebes quickly."

"Why?"

"The land needs a ruler and the Domain Lords won't accept the Beautiful One's daughters, not after this mess. We need to tell Ahmose that Akhenaten is dead, two complete—and loyal—regiments have vanished with him, the Domain of the Lion is empty of all the population, and he's now Pharaoh—who must set right all the problems Akhenaten left behind."

"Do you think he'll want everyone to worship whatever God he follows?"

Syamekh smiled grimly. "Ahmose isn't unduly devout, and he's a sensible man. He'll heed the warning from recent events." He stretched, rubbing his back. "I wonder how Pahotep and his people are getting on."

19

The portal closed in Aradia. In the far Homelands many Aradians glanced about them, for thunder on a clear day was unusual. The black clouds gathered far to the west were dissipating, however, so the feline people of the land shrugged, turning back to their own affairs again.

In the valley where the portal had been there was a shuddering through the ground, followed by a powerful gust of air that knocked over old people, small children, and a number of tents. Pahotep staggered, caught his balance, and looked about. Dust rose in the distance. He blinked, straining to see to the far end of the valley. Then he shrugged. He had no time to worry about whatever that was. He had people to organize, new lands to claim, and—what of his sister, what of the woman of his heart?

"Khepera? Ritseh?" His voice rose in a clarion call.

Ritseh ran towards him, laughing, from the trees where Bastet's Daughters and the cats had taken refuge. "You live, we escaped!"

He caught her to him, swinging her in circles as they hugged. "Yes, I did and we did. Have you seen the High Priestess?"

"Your cousin brought her into their camp just before that wind hit. She's exhausted, as is my cousin and the soldier, but the healers think they'll be all right."

Pahotep nodded, hugging her again. "The healers, yes, of course. I need to talk to them. Ritseh, please bring them to me as soon as you can. We can't stay here."

"Why not?"

"I don't know the reason. I only know that Bastet made some sort of bargain with her sister-self, the Lady of Claws who rules here. We must leave as soon as it's morning and head to the lands granted us, which are far from here."

Ritseh looked about. "Probably well that we do," she said practically. "There isn't room in this pair of valleys for all of us. We fit in while we're camped—just—but we couldn't farm, even if this land is the most fertile I've ever seen. It would create bad feeling if some stayed here while others had to leave."

Pahotep nodded. "Yes, and that's no way to start a new life in new lands. Go and find the healers for me, sweet one."

Ritseh tossed him a saucy smile as she headed back towards the clump of trees. He grinned after her, feeling an odd combination of younger and older than his years. She made him feel young again, yet he couldn't risk wedding her until or unless she proved with child. Then he could marry her safely, acknowledge the child—whichever sex it was—as heir, and settle down. Even if this promising thing between them failed, they'd stay friends, and he'd have the heir who was vital to continuity in leadership for his people.

He groaned as he stretched, massaging the small of his back. He felt older, too. He had a lot to organize and suspected he wouldn't see his bed before they began the trek to their promised lands in the morning.

Khepera walked up slowly, while the healers Merem and Temmah, together with four apprentices in their trade followed, all of them carrying small traveling satchels.

"Khepera, are you well enough to be walking about?"

"I can if I don't hurry, but a good night's sleep is all I need. I have some training in healing myself and you need healers now, even an old, tired one."

Merem stepped past her. "You know your sister, Lord of the Lion, she won't rest until the injured are cared for. It's fortunate that we had warning of Akhenaten's plans. Our supplies were packed, and we purchased extra ponies and packsaddles to carry everything. We were some of the first to come through the portal and we unpacked medical supplies at once."

She grinned cheerfully. "We already had clients, and the other two apprentices are out looking at plants. Nothing I've seen so far is familiar. We'll have to build a whole new knowledge."

"And you don't mind?"

"Mind? Of course I mind, Lord; I've studied healing all my life and my mother before me. But look about you." She swept an arm out. "Look at this place! Richer, more fertile than Napata, what wonders it may hold. What new and more potent medicines we may brew here. How many cures may we discover?"

Pahotep stared.

Beside him his sister laughed softly and quoted: "'For behold, I am come up from the lands I knew into a new land, and the wonders I have seen shall live with me always.'"

Her brother recognized the passage from the scroll of Atashke and nodded slowly. "Indeed. A new land. There will be wonders, dangers, deaths, but in the end this land shall be ours and our children's forever.

Come now and prepare the people. In the morning we must move on, so any injuries must be dealt with tonight."

He was right about getting no sleep, Pahotep thought as he waited to lead his people the next day. He was weary to his bones, but at least he was only tired and not injured, and he had a good horse to ride. Of the guards and scouts who held the final barricades against Akhenaten, only Petnake, Kahoret, and Neshang survived—and all carried wounds that, while not life-threatening—unless they took the wound-rot or wound-fever—were still serious.

Many people had bruises and skin scrapes, testimony to the last mad scramble to reach the portal. There were broken bones, some internal injuries, and a number of people kicked or gored by frantic beasts, leaving them with open gashes. It didn't matter. The injuries had been tended, friends and family helped, and mounts—or donkey-litters—provided for the wealthy. Pahotep commandeered beasts for the injured poor.

"Bring the maps you made." Remekh nodded, unrolling one and holding it open. Shardis laid a hand on the scroll rod to keep it flat.

"We go down the valley here, then up the pass, down the line of the hills and this way," Remekh indicated the way they should go. "The lands we seek are here, past the big lake."

"Do you think the river floods?" Pahotep's finger traced the stream from lake to sea.

Shardis shook her head. "No, in dreams I saw no sign of flooding, at least, nothing beyond water over-spilling the banks now and again when the weather was very wet. There are drifts of wood here and there along the banks. They will show where the water rises."

"Remekh?"

"I saw the same, but the land is good, rich and fertile. The people of this place live far from where we pass. They are a strange people, not like us, but the Lady would not give us passage if she believed we would die here under their spears."

Khepera looked at the old man. "The Lady, you say? Which Lady, Remekh? The Lady of Claws in Napata, or the other Lady who rules here?"

"They are one: Sister-selves. I think we shall find them little different. And in another thing too you should rejoice, High One." She raised a brow in question and he responded. "In this land, She rules alone."

Khepera's breath hissed. "You mean—there are no other Gods in this land?"

He nodded. "There are no others. Here Bastet—or however She is named— rules. While the child dreamed I looked at the customs of the peoples here. They fight, but they seldom go to war, they live in clans, like our Domains. They are very different from us in appearance, High One, but at heart they are very similar. We come as guests to the table, so let us remember our manners with our hosts."

Pahotep spoke, raising his voice so that those gathered nearby could hear him. "It shall and must be so, and this is the word of the Lion. No hand shall be raised first against the people of this new land. They have opened their home to us, their Lady has given us safe passage and freedom from all that Akhenaten would have done. To behave discourteously here is to shame Bastet and her sister-self who gave us life. Hear me: the man who lifts his hand first against one of the people of this land, will I slay with my own hand."

A murmuring arose, half agreement, half question, as he swung onto his horse and looked out over them. "I swear, we have come in peace; the man who wars does so against me. I am the Lord of the Lion, hear my words and obey."

Khepera's voice rang out. "I obey. I, High Priestess of Bastet, swear in the name of Her whom I worship, and I and mine shall follow this oath."

Pahotep's gaze was intent. He waited, and slowly, family-by-family, group-by-group, his people acknowledged the command. It would not always hold, but it would keep all-out war from them in the days and years to come—or so he prayed. He signaled his mount to walk on, leading the people of the Domain of the Lion on a trek that would take many days before they settled on the wide plain between the lake and the sea.

Not far behind him, Shardis' pony walked beside Shayohni's mount, the girl talking of what she had seen in her dreams. "The people here are the true Children of the Goddess. They look like her, like the statue in the inner shrine. But they are black, and they are no taller than we are."

"Black? Not the color of sand, like Bastet's Children?"

"Black. And they have claws too that are strange." She held up a hand, touching the back of it between the knuckles. "They have small claws on their fingertips as we have nails. They use them for grooming their fur. But here," her finger tapped. "Here they have claws, fighting weapons that hide between the bones and appear only when needed."

"Strange indeed. What of their customs? Did you see anything evil?"

Shardis shook her head. "No. They have Temples where they worship the Lady of Claws, they have their givers of Law, their Domain leaders, the parents who love their children, and beasts that give them wool and meat. Beyond their cleared lands there are fierce animals that prey on others. Of those, some may be good eating."

She smiled at Shayohni. "I think, as Pahotep said, they are not so different, and we are guests here. It would be foolish to escape one war only to leap into another. I have no wish to die because of some silly argument built on misunderstanding."

He eyed her soberly. "Nor do I."

Her breath caught then as she looked to one side. "Shayohni!" She called forward. "Lady Khepera, *look*!"

Pahotep and his group halted and turned, following her gesture.

Khepera gasped. "The Temple! The Shrine, it's here. It can't be ours?"

Remekh nodded. "It is. Go to it, Lady, you and Shardis."

Khepera beckoned the girl and together they approached the Temple. It now stood tucked towards the back of the small valley they were traversing on their way to the pass.

They dismounted, leaving Shayohni to hold their mounts as they ascended the shallow steps. They entered the building silently; the light was gold about them, the air sweet. In the inner shrine Trah's mummified body lay in honor on the altar, yet there was an echoing in the building, a feeling of absence. Shardis waited as the High Priestess advanced to stand before the statue of Bastet.

Khepera bowed and softly, with an aching in her heart, she sang the invocation, then she waited.

> *You of the Sunrise who wake and sleep.*
> *You who lie sprawled in dreams.*
> *To you appears Bastet the Great,*
> *Whose eyes see all, whose claws are death.*
> *Bright Lady who sees and strides this world by night and*
> *   day.*
> *Vanquish those enemies who would assail us,*
> *Guide us forward and bring us safely home.*

The statue moved, the eyes opened, showing green-gold. The sandstone darkened to black, the stone hardening, the jewels that adorned it falling in a hail of single beads that vanished as they struck the floor. And into the minds of the old woman and young girl came words, not in the honey-sweet familiar voice, but in a ringing crystal.

"She who is my sister-self is gone from you."

Khepera dropped to kiss the ground. "Lady, will you stand in Her place for us?"

The statue was warm fur then, a lithe, living, breathing power as She stepped down from the plinth, crystalline rainbows playing about her head. She took Khepera gently by the shoulders to raise her to her feet again.

"I am Pasht, and you are my Daughters beloved, for now and always. Do not kneel to me. My people stand, facing me with pride. To me have you been given, be sure that my hands shall not let you fall. Now, you have ahead of you a long journey to far lands, and you shall not return. The valley closes behind you and it shall be long and very long before another enters. Go with my blessing and confirmed in your place, I think I could do no better than my sister-self's choice."

Shardis came forward, looking up in awe.

Pasht looked at her. "And you, Daughter, you too are blessed. Live in joy, and power shall you hold in your time." Light surrounded them and they found themselves standing on the outer steps. Khepera looked back.

"Let us go. We have a long road ahead."

She walked to her horse, mounted, and went to join her brother. Shardis mounted and fell in behind her, Shayohni at her side.

"What happened in there?" he asked.

"The Goddess here came and said we were hers now, that we were her Daughters, and there's a new custom. We don't kiss the ground or even kneel to Her. She likes her people to have pride."

Shayohni approved of that and said so. "Anything else?"

"Yes. The temple here is closed to us now. But we go with Her blessing. Oh, and Khepera is confirmed as our High One here, too. Pasht said she couldn't do better than her sister-self's choice."

He changed the subject abruptly. "Tell me, Shardis, how old are you?"

She counted on her fingers, shrugged, and considered. "In Napata, I had just seen my fifteenth flood. But if there is no great flood here each year, I wonder how we will count?"

"The same as always," Shayohni assured her. "By the sun and moon, by the seasons and the changes." He leaned across and took her hand. "And remember, we held the portal together, neither of us failed our Lord or the people. We are friends, Shardis. And with friends one may face whatever comes."

She laughed. "Truth. And see, behind us come many friends."

He turned where she indicated and smiled. Behind them rode the healers and the other Daughters, leading a line of pack-saddled donkeys. Atop the packs rode the Children of Bastet, large sand-colored cats, claws comfortably hooked into pack covers, kits tucked into baskets lashed on top of the loads.

"Yes, many friends, and that's good. There'll surely be mice and rats where we settle."

"There are. I saw them in my dreaming. They aren't exactly the same as the ones in Napata, but I imagine that they are as much a nuisance."

He nodded and they rode on in a comfortable silence. About them the new lands spread out, the sun shed a warm lavender light, the purple-veined grass leaned away from the breeze, and the darker trees that they would come to know as Miro showed the purple puffs of their seed pods.

Talking, laughing, arguing, and wondering at each new thing they saw, the people of the Lion moved on to make another history for themselves in the land that its own people called Aradia.

EPILOGUE

It took a long time to reach their new lands. They settled the area between sea and lake, building a city and a Domain that would eventually be named Shallahah. The initial settlement was quite close to the
lake, later that settlement spread towards the sea. The Mersa Lake Shrine
became a day's ride from the city edge.

The human population in Aradia bred slowly. A woman would com-
monly bear two children in her lifetime, three children quite often, four
children rarely, and five children only very occasionally, while multiple
births would occur perhaps only once anywhere in any generation. That
lower fertility was part of the bargain between the sister-selves.

In three human generations the goats died out. Horses throve, and
the native people of Aradia saw them as a useful and valuable asset.
Cows and sheep also died out, although more gradually. By the time
they were gone, trade between the peoples brought in the two varieties
of native animal used for the same purpose.

No record exists of the first meeting between humans and Aradians.
It was probably relatively peaceful since legends say nothing of major
wars between the two folk. The imported worship of Bastet in her Three
Aspects shifted easily and quite comfortably to the worship of the Four
Aspects of Pasht, but the Temples remained almost exclusively the domain of women as priestesses, the more so as that was already Aradian
custom.

Certain cats altered over the centuries that followed their arrival. The
common cats that had fled with their owners bred less often and were
even more highly valued in consequence. The Temple cats, larger and
more intelligent to begin with, gradually moved into the hills beyond
Shallahah, growing larger still, more intelligent yet, and becoming the
true Children of Pasht. In time they would form what was another intelligent race—the Dravencats.

And the people? Ritseh bore twins, a boy and a girl. Pahotep wed her
ten days after their birth, and five years later confirmed her as his queen.
He was old by the standards of his time when he died, and Ritseh lived
even longer. In her last years she became a song-maker. Khepera ruled

the shrine built to Pasht by the Mersa Lake. She lived another eleven years and Shardis took the rank after her.

Kahoret remained a bachelor, loved by his kin, and when he died the Domain of the Lion mourned deeply. Neshang did marry, and he and his wife cared for Kahoret's home, served him all their days, and their children after them served the Throne of Shallahah.

The Noble Judge Atepmut wed late, and he and his wife produced sons to raise his House Name after him. His greatest legacy, however, was the purpose for which he'd accepted exile—the rule of law codified and written down. Scrolls of law would be held in every shrine, greater temple and major city in time to come.

In his courts, Atepmut demanded justice tempered with mercy, without bowing to rank or wealth. For the most part that system, once established with Pahotep's blessing, continued in varying rewritten forms, within the realm of Shallahah for more than two thousand years—long after his House was dust and his name forgotten as the author of the laws the people followed.

* * * *

In the lands of Napata, his friend Asosi survived the destruction. He and his junior priest walked out of the ruins five days later and followed the road to Thebes. They met Syamekh and many of those who obeyed him as they returned to the Lion Domain with Ahmose. The path of Napata and its Gods was forever changed, but that, for them, is another story.

* * * *

Petnake's family had come through the portal, as had Barhket's. They did well in the new lands and the families were raised to noble rank two generations later. Shayohni wed a merchant's daughter after five years, once he saw that Shardis would be High Priestess and would have shrine and Goddess as her first and greatest love always.

The new shrine to Pasht was raised over the fourth, fifth, sixth, and seventh years of arrival. It still stands, greatly enlarged after so many generations, but the inner core remains as it was originally built. No one knows now exactly why the four figures are carved into the statue plinth—although probably they had some significance at the time—and their names remain as they were first engraved there.

* * * *

Pahotep surveyed the shrine as the last stone was hoisted into place and a party of panting men placed the great bronze gate on its hinges, checking that it swung easily.

"A good job."

His sister tucked her arm through his and smiled. "It is, the more so considering we've done it while breaking in new land, dealing with wild beasts unfamiliar to us, and coping with families who always think that someone has received better from the Lion Lord than they have."

He moaned. "Do not remind me. But it's done. Will you keep the healers here?"

"No, it's half a day's walk to the edge of the settlement. We agreed to have two places. Within the shrine the healers will have rooms, both bedrooms in which to sleep and storerooms for supplies. They will also have a house within the busiest part of the domain. Healers who wish to study in peace or are ill or injured can come to the shrine. Those who have duties amongst the people will remain with them."

"That should be useful. What about the inner shrine? Do you plan to borrow carvers?"

Khepera smiled. "No, my brother. The Lady has her own will in this. I have been told to do nothing but provide a plinth, five steps up and no more, carved of that hard black stone found near the desert coast. Far wider than it is deep, it's been quicker and easier to carve out since we found a slab of it that was near the right size."

"What do you think she plans to do?"

His sister shrugged. "I have no idea. Something to indicate her Four Aspects perhaps? She will probably act tonight. I am bid to have everyone out of the shrine before the sun sets."

That order was obeyed. They returned in the morning light: Pahotep and his sister Khepera, Kahoret, Remekh, and Shardis. They walked slowly and cautiously into the shrine to see what had changed—or been added. Something had.

A statue was there, a little taller than humanity, of the same black stone as the plinth on which it now stood: an image of Pasht with eyes that shone from inset jewels, the same green-gold as the eyes of the Goddess Khepera and Shardis once faced. It was a marvel, the fur appearing soft to the touch, the eyes looking at everyone, the upturned, outstretched hands showing the grooming claws and, between the knuckles, the razor-sharp tips of fighting claws, while the tail curled down around one ankle.

Shardis's gaze dropped to the plinth and her eyes widened. "Shemet?"

They looked down. Along the base of the waist-high plinth were four figures, two on either side of the steps. All four would be recognized by any who had ever known them in life; they were half-sized, but perfect in their depiction. And for those who did not know them, their names were inscribed beneath each figure. On one side stood Shemet Gate-Keeper, with Anati beside him, a front paw touching his foot. On the other side stood a man with—

"Trah!" Khepera recognized the heart-friend she had lost.

"Who is this Nehuche, the man with Trah?" Shardis asked. "I can see why Anati and Shemet are there, for she held the portal and Kahoret said that Shemet held it too, after Khepera had no more strength. And Trah fought and died to save the High Priestess earlier. But who is this Nehuche?"

Kahoret stepped forward. "Nehuche was a great bow-man. He was the man who held off the soldiers before the Temple gate so we could escape. He was wounded and near death, but he fought to his final breath to give us the chance to flee. He did it to save his daughter, and he asked me to tell her of him."

"Who is she?"

Kahoret ignored the question, falling into the cadence of a storyteller in the market place. "He said that years ago he loved a woman he would have married. But her father drove him from their door, had Nehuche beaten so badly he almost died, and when he could stand again her father sent word that if he came back he would be killed.

"He said to me that he would have gone to her, but he feared what her father would do to the woman if he disobeyed. The man was hard and ruthless, brutal and cruel. So Nehuche left and heard later that the woman had died. He grieved for her and took no wife.

"But the woman's brothers came sometimes to Hanish. Years afterwards one brother was drunk and told him the woman he loved died, not from illness or accident as he believed, but in childbirth, bearing a daughter who was surely Nehuche's child. He heard the child was accepted into the Temple of Bastet, and he went there from that time on, Finding comfort in seeing his daughter, finding her beautiful, and her smiles at him—even though she did not know who he was—were warming as the sun.

"So, when the soldiers of Akhenaten came, Nehuche guarded the walls in the name of his daughter. At the last when he might have escaped, he chose to fight and die with the guards. As he fell, he asked that I tell his daughter of him. I was to say to you, Shardis, that he loved you, that his last thoughts would be of you as he prayed you would be safe and happy beyond the portal."

She stared at the face of the man on the plinth, the bow in his hand, the sheaf of arrows thrust into his belt. "My grandfather Taphis said that my mother was a wanton." Her lips drew into a thin line. "He lied—as ever. This Nehuche was my father? He loved me?"

"He was your father, and he loved you enough to die fighting to see you free and safe."

With a low cry Shardis dropped beside the figure, her hands touching it. "My father! I remember seeing him at the Temple. He always smiled so kindly at me. Why didn't he tell me then? My grandfather let me think that my mother didn't even know who my father was. Instead, he loved her, and he'd have married her."

"He felt unworthy. He wasn't always a very good man, Shardis; he lied and, well, other things. He said that you wouldn't want his sort around. But he loved you. He really did."

Shardis flung herself into his arms and wept while he patted her shoulder. Finally she straightened and wiped the tears from her face.

"I'll remember him."

"As we shall remember them all," Pahotep agreed softly. "In this land the laws shall run so that no man can again force his beliefs on others." He turned to look at Remekh. "What of Akhenaten? Will the Temples in Thebes stand against him?"

Remekh's smile was dangerously satisfied. "No one stands against a dead man." They gaped at his words. "What Syamekh and I did had a twofold purpose. If we had not opened the portal the people of the Lion would have died, all of them, at the hands of Akhenaten and his soldiers. But in opening it, we drew Pharaoh into Hanish, and when the portal closed power rained upon the city. Everyone within it and in the camp nearby, within the villages close enough, all of them died. Akhenaten is gone, his regiments are dust in the wind, his daughters will hold no rule, and Aten-Ra is only another amongst the Gods."

"Who will rule?" Pahotep took in a deep breath before asking.

"Ahmose, of the line of that Ahmose who defied and conquered the Hyksos in a single great battle. Do not think that I endangered and exiled you all to accomplish this." Remekh said earnestly, watching their expressions. "You would all have died if we had not opened the portal. But by opening it we also gave life to those of Napata who would have died at his hands in the years to come. They too have set their feet upon a new path. Let us rejoice for life and love and joy are still ours."

* * * *

They did so. In the centuries to come much of the history of how they had come to Aradia would be forgotten. The names would live on as names tend to, children would be called Nehuche and Shemet, cats would be named Anati and Trah—and other forms of those as the language altered. Legends would form about two who'd been young when they saved their people by holding a golden shield of power about them. Heart-friends, corrupting the original names, would name themselves various forms of Shar and Shao, asking that Pasht bless them as She had blessed the friends of legend.

And in her final years, Ritseh made a song as she had made other, earlier songs. It had a strong rhythmic beat. For some generations the humans of Aradia understood it, after that the words changed to become a children's song for counting, skipping rope, and sometimes for fishermen as they hauled in their nets. But like the names on the plinth, the song too would never be quite forgotten, even if the truth of the events it celebrated was lost to memory:

> *Pharaoh came to kill us all,*
> *So we answered to Pasht's call.*
> *Walk into gold, pass through black,*
> *Through the portal without turning back.*
> *At any time there's those who'll die to save you.*
>
> *Some are good and some are bad,*
> *Some are sane and some are mad,*
> *Power rises and the city falls*
> *All our enemies lie under the walls*
> *At any time there's those who'll die to save you.*
>
> *Honor the names, of those who came,*
> *Those who fought and those who died,*
> *Giving us land to live in pride,*
> *From sacrifice our new land grew,*
> *At any time there's those who'll die to save you.*

www.ingramcontent.com/pod-product-compliance
Lightning Source LLC
Chambersburg PA
CBHW020319260626
47156CB00004B/1297